M000170091

THE

LIGHTHOUSE
BABY

Laura Thomas

THE LIGHTHOUSE BABY by Laura Thomas

ANAIAH Romance
An imprint of ANAIAH PRESS, LLC.
7780 49th ST N. #129
Pinellas Park, FL 33781

This book is a work of fiction. All characters, places, names, and events are either a product of the author's imagination or are used fictitiously. Any likeness to any events, locations, or persons, alive or otherwise, is entirely coincidental.

The Lighthouse Baby copyright © 2019 by Laura Thomas

All rights reserved, including the right to reproduce this book or portions thereof in any form. For inquiries and information, address Anaiah Press, LLC., 7780 49th ST N. #129 Pinellas Park, Florida, 33781

First Anaiah Romance eBook edition May 2019
First Anaiah Romance Print edition May 2019

Edited by Candee Fick
Book Design by Eden Plantz
Cover Design by Laura Heritage

ISBN 978-1-947327-52-8

Anaiah
+Press
Books that Inspire

For Lyndon: Truly, I can only write about love because of you.

ACKNOWLEDGEMENTS

This book was a joy to write, but I have several individuals to thank for keeping me sane, and for making *The Lighthouse Baby* the best that it could be:

My publisher, Anaiah Press—thanks to the Anaiah "family" once again for giving me the opportunity to share my heart in the form of a book. It means the world to me.

My fabulous editor, Candee Fick—you have a knack for extracting the very best, and for that I am ever grateful. Thanks for your patience with me!

My children: Charlotte, Jameson, and Jacob—much of this book touches on motherhood, and being your mom is by far my greatest achievement in life. Thank you for all the joy you continue to bring me.

My husband, Lyndon—thank you for literally driving me back to the Oregon Coast, finding "my beach," visiting numerous lighthouses with me, and for always believing I have a story worth sharing. I love you.

My Heavenly Father—for giving me life and light and words.

CHAPTER ONE

RUN.

Bella King's heart clenched. *What was I thinking?* Overcome with panic, all logic fragmented like the grains of sand beneath her pounding feet, as she surrendered to her familiar motion of survival. *Faster.* A quick over-the-shoulder check confirmed a decent head start, and not a solitary soul to witness the chase. Maybe he would choose not to follow.

He'll come after me. Of course, he will.

The ocean breeze lashed long strands of blonde hair across her face, her vision obscured through a blur of tears. Escape, run—it was the only thing she knew. Bella stifled sobs and pressed on. She couldn't stop now, even as the evening sun blinded her and the sounds of crashing surf thrummed in her skull. Both feet sank, hopeless, with each step in the silky sand, until she discarded her sandals and sprinted freely across the wide stretch of desolate beach.

Sand flicked, wind whipped. Salty air filled her nostrils as she sucked in each breath. Seagulls screamed overhead— a savage cry, as if they sensed despair. She found a decent stride and with the cadence of each footfall, she chanted,

"No, no, no." But deep down, her soul longed to stop running, just this once, and cry, "Yes!"

Beach left in the dust, Bella continued her grueling sprint uphill to the only place she felt safe. She dared not glance behind again, that would be far too dangerous—looking back spelled disaster. Besides, even if she spotted his form outlined against the spectacular vista of great boulders rising like ancient tombstones from beneath the ocean, it would only slow her down. And derail her courage.

Must keep moving.

Her bare feet stung as they pounded a mix of gravel and dirt on the familiar path up from Cape Cove. Why hadn't she thought this through? How far could she get without shoes? Far enough. Sea air mingled with whiffs of earthy, lush vegetation as coastal rainforest melded with beach.

Blackberry bushes and brambles claimed their pound of flesh as she brushed against them. She bit her lip in an attempt to ignore the trickling sensation on her ankles. Her long, flowing skirt caught on a branch and Bella winced as the fabric tore. If only the skirt was the only thing ripped apart tonight. Why had he ruined everything?

At this elevation, biting wind dried the wetness from her cheeks while perspiration trickled down her back. Feverishly hot and deathly cold. Her chest heaved as she mustered every ounce of strength for the final stretch up the steep hill. The familiar rhythmic crash of wave against rock—so like the constant barrage of fears preventing her life from ever changing—started to fade. She was close.

Rounding a corner, the Cape Cove Bed and Breakfast caught her eye. The old lightkeeper's cottage stood like a statement of all that was good and true back in the days of simple living on the Pacific Coast. The gleaming white siding and red roof welcomed visitors from far and near, its white picket fence and striped flag blustering in the wind screamed The American Dream. How many times had she sat on the bench and dreamed of a simple life? How naive. How foolish.

Just a little farther.

Taking the path used by lightkeepers of old, Bella ran on, the ocean slamming against rocks on her left, the sprawling woods silent on her right.

Through watery eyes, her gaze fell upon her ultimate refuge, and she slowed her steps. Breath caught in her throat, as it always did when she reached this pinnacle and looked out upon a horizon that stretched to forever.

Frantic found familiar.

The lighthouse—her haven. Solid, stoic, still.

Always bold as a saving bright symbol amidst monstrous darkness.

On quivering legs, Bella continued to the far side of the structure, where she collapsed on a patch of prickly, dry grass.

Will I ever stop running?

She leaned back against the coolness of textured concrete and attempted to slow her hammering heart and laboring lungs. With desperate hands, she stretched out to either side and touched the lighthouse behind her. She was grounded. It was there. It was real. Not some outlandish nightmare. Her sanctuary of light.

Breathe. Exhale. Pray.

With only the old lighthouse to absorb her apology, she sighed. "I'm sorry."

Her whispered words caught in great gusts of wind. Nausea rose from the pit of her stomach and without warning, sobs took over. Great, uncontrollable cries that racked her petite frame without mercy. *I'm going to break his heart.* Hurt so deeply by others, now it was she, the lost soul with a tragic story, who inflicted anguish.

She glanced around. At least there were no spectators to observe her mammoth meltdown. With the lighthouse tours done for the day, tourists would be enjoying a seafood dinner somewhere pleasant. Experiencing a regular life. A normal life.

This charade she was forced to play was like a sick Ferris wheel—a sham. Get on, ride it for a while, enjoy the view, and pretend everything was peachy and prosaic, until it reached the bottom again only to be dragged through a tunnel of heartache and loneliness and fear...

"Bella?"

She swiped at her drenched cheeks and blew out a steady stream of air. This had been the hardest run yet. She cringed at the crunch of his footsteps as he rounded the lighthouse. Why did he have to follow? Bella bit her lip and buried her head in trembling hands. This could not be happening. She had always been so careful, protected herself all these years. How had she not seen this coming?

"Bella?"

She inhaled and gazed up at him—a blur of handsome and hurt. His eyes, those windows of love now misted with tears, pinned her to the lighthouse. There were no words. What could she say to take away his pain when he stood before her as a crushed man—his fingers clasped around a diamond ring?

4

CHAPTER TWO

BELLA FROZE IN PLACE WHILE Adam Lexington crouched before her, his fist clenching a promise he apparently longed to secure. How had she not seen the signs? When did she get so caught up in love?

"Adam, I'm sorry." Her whisper sounded pathetic to her ears. What could she say without breaking his heart into even more shards? The wind wound around the base of the lighthouse as shame washed over her in great waves.

He reached out a hand—the one not clutching an engagement ring. She stared at his upturned palm. How could he want her after she had run from his offer of a future together? Didn't the bitter sting of rejection course through him the way it had flowed through her time and again her whole life?

"You must hate me." She shuddered. "You *should* hate me."

A romantic proposal on a beautifully rugged beach should not result in heartbreak and grief. Adam deserved more. He deserved more than her. An expert in the realm of rejection, now she was on the administering end. Unworthy of a diamond.

"Bella, I could never hate you. I'm worried about you. Whatever it was that made you run back there, let's talk about it." His short, black hair fluttered in the wind and she longed to run her fingers through it.

How could she begin to explain? What was she supposed to do? Melt into his embrace, become his cherished wife, and forget the fact that she lived a lie and had been running from ghosts for years? He at least deserved a sliver of an explanation.

She put her hand into his, their fingers intermingled. His warmth and tenderness threatened to melt the protective wall around her heart. "Sit with me a while? You're right. We need to talk."

She took a cleansing breath. Why was opening up so difficult? Although, she didn't have to tell him everything, maybe just enough to explain the rejection of his proposal. A mere chink in the wall of granite.

"We should have had this conversation a long time ago. I don't know what I was thinking, leading you on. Pretending we could have a future together. I've been unfair to you and I'm sorry." She looked away from his face. "I can't marry you."

He swiveled around and planted himself on the patch of grass next to her, both their backs now braced by the sturdy lighthouse. He ran his thumb across her hand and sighed.

"Please tell me. I can fix it. I hate to see you upset. I guess I miscalculated where I thought we were heading. But there's nothing in this world that's ever going to stop me from loving you and wanting to be your husband one day. You know that, right?"

Bella bit her lip and closed her eyes. She couldn't look into his—the flecks of caramel would be glistening against the blue-green depths, so like the ocean. He looked even more handsome than usual in his black dress pants and black collared shirt this evening. She should have clued in something special was happening. The proposal. How many times had she dreamed of spending forever with this man? She should have run sooner. Now, for the sake of her battered heart, she had to give him the barest of facts as clinically as possible.

"You've known me for exactly twelve months. But what do you know about my childhood? My teens? Where I've spent the past few years?" She risked a glance and watched him frown.

"I don't care about your past. I really don't." He squeezed her hand. And melted her heart.

"But my past is a huge part of this." A shiver shot up her spine, and it had nothing to do with the ocean breeze. "It's not that simple. Tell me what you've pieced together up to now. Please? I need to know."

He shrugged. "Okay, but it's not much. It's not like there was anyone I could ask for permission to propose or anything. I know you were adopted and you originally lived somewhere here on the Oregon Coast. I'm guessing you didn't have the best relationship with your adoptive parents because you never speak about them—you only said they were killed in a car crash a few years ago."

Bella gulped. He needed to know the truth.

"And you're rather a brick wall when it comes to sharing about your childhood, but I've respected that. You grew up fast. You're independent. I know you found God when you were seventeen and your faith has helped you through some tough times. You shared that with me when we first met at church."

She nodded. "Yeah, I dread to think of my life without God."

"When it comes to family, I thought you craved the stability I have with mine. I see the way you watch them, there's a longing in your eyes to be a part of something like that."

True. Who wouldn't? Their perfect family in the perfect home overlooking the ocean right here in Florence. "You have such a wonderful family. It's just that… We're polar opposites."

"But we make it work. Our backgrounds haven't defined who we are today. You can't deny our connection." He gazed up at the clouds, now dappled with shades of pink beyond the canopy of trees. "I haven't imagined the chemistry between us, have I?"

"I do love you. I've never lied about that."

His face brightened. "So, what's the problem? Love conquers all, right?"

With her free hand, Bella picked at the blades of grass surrounding her skirt. "Can't we stay as we are?"

"You mean date forever?"

"When you say it like that, it sounds ridiculous. I've never been one to plan ahead too much."

"Maybe I blindsided you this evening. I should never have assumed you were thinking the same as me."

"Doesn't my weirdness freak you out a little?"

Adam smiled. "I don't think you're weird at all." He kissed the back of her hand. "I adore your obsession with lighthouses, I think it's kind of cute that you refuse to learn to drive a car and insist on riding your bicycle around town, and I admire your creative imagination and the way you get engrossed in your writing. Oh, and the bookworm thing makes you look super smart, which you are. Beautiful, intelligent, and intriguing. Nothing about you freaks me out."

No. This was wrong. She couldn't get caught up in the fairytale ending. That didn't happen to people like her. To people on the run. "It should, Adam. I should set off a dozen alarm bells in your head. I've been a fool to think I could have a regular life like everyone else, and I've been cruel leading you to believe we can have a long-term future together. It's too dangerous." How much was safe to share?

"Dangerous?" His breath caught. "Wait. How can it be *dangerous* for us to get married?"

She shook free from his touch and straightened her off-the-shoulder blouse. The one she had bought for this date night, when she thought it was a regular date night. Not a marriage proposal.

"Please, believe me. I don't want to drag you into something you may regret."

A branch snapped. It came from the wooded area to the right of them. Bella flinched.

"We should go." She stood, wrapped her arms around her body, and marched toward the trail which led back down to the beach and the parking lot.

Adam jumped up and fell into step beside her. "Your shoes—let me run down to the beach and get them? Your feet must be wrecked. Or let me carry you?" He raised an eyebrow.

Bella scowled. He knew full well there was no chance she would cave. He could carry her tiny frame in his muscular arms with no problem, but she was stubborn to a fault. She didn't need carrying. She'd learned that as a source of survival years ago.

"Thank you, but I'm fine." She continued walking, grimacing at the tiny stones underfoot. He took her hand again and it felt as natural as breathing. Over the past nine months or so, she'd grown accustomed to his six-foot frame towering over her. How was she supposed to do life without him now?

Adam sighed. "You can't leave me hanging like this. What's dangerous exactly? Don't you trust me?"

"No, I trust you. I do. I would trust you with my life."

"But not with your future?"

Bella winced. "I hadn't thought the relationship scenario through. We never sat down and discussed getting married or a wedding or anything." If only she hadn't craved what she could never have. She should have disappeared before it got too serious.

Adam slipped the ring back into his pocket. "I didn't realize I was so bad at reading people. At reading you."

Bella groaned. "Please don't beat yourself up. You're the kindest man I've ever met and you only see the good in people. I've become adept at keeping my life private over the years, and that means hiding a lot of my feelings."

"How much have you been hiding from me?" His smile didn't quite reach his eyes.

"Too much. Not enough." Strands of wayward hair blew across her face. "I don't even know."

10

This was not going well. Leaving him now would be the most painful experience imaginable, yet what were the options? She really should have run earlier. Left sooner. Moved on again, before both their hearts were broken. Or worse, her past caught up with her.

"Bella, I hate to sound cliché but you're the answer to my prayers. I felt sure you were the one for me. I still do—you should know I have zero intention of backing down. I've spent the past month dreaming of this evening. The candles and the champagne picnic, the sun setting at just the right time, the view of the lighthouse from your favorite beach—I thought I'd done it all perfectly. I hadn't taken into account you running away at the sight of a diamond…"

Bella shook her head. "I'm sorry."

"No, you don't need to apologize. *I'm* sorry. Perhaps you need some time to think about it? I suppose I did surprise you—and I know you're not a fan of surprises."

"It's not that." A tiny rock dug into her foot and she winced. Let the pain come.

"Then what? Your childhood? Your family?" He furrowed his brow.

The off-limits territory. "No. I can't go there right now." Bella couldn't meet his gaze. She looked ahead at the lengthening shadows across the path. "Let's just say I know enough not to go digging into things—now or ever. There was trouble before. Things I don't want to talk about. And if I'm ever found…"

She stopped walking and glanced back at the lighthouse, standing like a proud soldier guarding the coastline. Its glow burned brighter as the sun set, warning of potential danger.

If only she had taken heed of the potential danger she would create for Adam.

He followed her gaze. "Wait, what? If you are ever found by whom?"

"I can't let my real name be made public." Her voice was a whisper.

A second branch snapped the silence above them sending another shiver down Bella's spine. What on earth? Every time she dared to share anything about her past with someone, it was as if there were a presence ready to silence her. Always the feeling of being watched. Followed. Her heart raced as she glanced at the overhanging branches, gnarly and twisted.

"Your real name? What are you talking about? Are you saying you're not Bella King?"

"Not exactly. I had to change my last name a long time ago for my own safety. It's complicated, and I've tried to put it all behind me, but when you got down on one knee and used my full name—I realized it's a sham. I've lied to you. And I don't want you to get involved in my past. I want to leave it there, where it belongs." Breathing came hard and fast as she fought back a dam of tears.

"You mean it's a legal name issue?" Adam turned her around to face him. A glimmer of hope shone from his eyes. "I'm sure we can figure something out. We can still get married. My dad's a lawyer, for goodness sake. He'll know someone who can get to the bottom of it—"

"*NO.*" Bella bit her lip. Too loud. The poor guy was only trying to fix the problem.

"Okay." His shoulders sagged, deflated. "So, what's your real name?"

It took several seconds until she could choke out the words. "Isabella Robinson." When was the last time she'd said that name? It sounded foreign to her ears. She turned back to the lighthouse.

The gleaming white structure shone in the fading sunlight. It exuded such comfort, but how could she begin to share the reason? "The name is the tip of the iceberg." She rubbed her arms, as a chill passed through her. "Forgive me, but I can't pull you into my pit."

He took a step behind her and enveloped her in strong arms. "Too late for that. I'm fully invested, in case you hadn't noticed."

She spun back around to face him. "But I've always said you are too good for me, and it's true. You should have listened. My past is a disaster and I can't dig it all up."

"I'm far from perfect myself, you know." He reached over and tucked a stray wisp of her wavy hair behind one ear. "In fact, for the past couple of months, I've been trying to share some stuff with you from my own past." He stared out across the ocean. "Stuff that might affect the way you think about me."

"Trust me, whatever little hiccup you might think of as a big deal is nothing compared to the mammoth boulders I bring into this relationship."

"You don't know that..."

His eyes brimmed, and Bella pulled away. Too much. This was all too much. Her head pulsated like the surf's relentless pounding on the shore.

He let out a sigh. "I'll never allow anyone to hurt you—I know you're more than capable of looking after yourself and

I love you for it, but I want to do life *with* you. Whatever your secret is, we can work through it together."

Bella's heart plummeted. Her secret? There were so many she wouldn't know where to start.

"I don't deserve you. You need a nice, regular girl who can fit into your cookie-cutter family and bring no baggage into the mix. Someone who'll give you everything you want in life—the white picket fence and a slew of adoring kids." She let the silence stretch between them. "I'm dangerous. And I've already said too much. I never meant to break your heart, and I'm sorrier than you'll ever know." Her voice cracked. "I'll meet you at the jeep."

She turned and broke into a painful jog past the bed and breakfast and down the trail. She scarcely felt the gravel puncture the soles of her feet when her very soul was being pummeled to pieces.

CHAPTER THREE

ADAM OPENED THE PASSENGER DOOR to his jeep and Bella climbed inside. Her trembling hand pushed back the hair from her tear-stained face. His heart ached. How had their romantic evening come to this? She shivered. Something was surfacing from her past and it wasn't good. It must be grave if she'd had to change her name. How much danger was she in?

He cleared his throat. "Honey, here are the keys. Why don't you go ahead and start the car so you can warm yourself up? I'll run down to the beach and get your shoes and my things."

Wait—was he even supposed to call her "honey" anymore? She was the sweetest woman he had ever known. Kind to a fault, generous with the little she had, caring toward every person—or creature—she met. Had she been hurt as a child? Abused even? He couldn't go there right now. He looked at her profile.

Bella nodded as she wept behind her curtain of blonde hair. She never cried. What had he done?

Disappointment, confusion, frustration. He bit the inside of his cheek and turned to face the beach. No way he would lose it in front of her now. How could he layer guilt on top of the mountain of issues she was dealing with? This evening was supposed to have been the best of his life, one they would look back on for years to come and tell the story over and over to whomever would listen. The perfect proposal.

What a complete and utter disaster.

A solitary, elderly gentleman plodded across the expanse of sand from the direction of the tidepools, his shoulders slumped with hands clasped behind his back. Deep in thought and alone. Did he have a family? A wife at home, perhaps, who had loved him for decades? Or was he still brooding over the broken heart of his youth?

Perhaps that will be me one day.

No, Adam had been drowning in a gulf of guilt for far too long until recently. No more. He shook his head and jogged over to the pile of his belongings. At least it was all still there. The wind had picked up, leaving only the ponderous gentleman on the beach. Adam rolled the picnic blanket scattered with red rose petals, most of which had already been swept away by the breeze.

Yes, he had thought of everything. Other than a possible rejection. His heart sank.

He stuffed the remains of their supper into his mother's wicker picnic basket, careful not to squash the chocolate-covered strawberries in his haste.

Perhaps his mom would like the strawberries. She suspected there was the possibility of a proposal tonight and now he would have to explain. Earlier on, she'd raised an eyebrow when she noticed he wasn't wearing the jeans and T-shirt he favored most evenings. A bit dressy for a picnic. Maybe she wouldn't ask. He hadn't shared his plans with anyone, he'd just wanted to borrow the basket as it had seemed a little more romantic than his backpack.

But yeah, Mom had known. How many times since he graduated college had she hinted for him to provide her with some grandchildren? At the ripe old age of twenty-five, he was apparently in danger of being left on the shelf. And she adored Bella as if she were her own daughter.

He glanced up in the direction of the parking lot. Goodness, whose daughter was she anyway? Were her adoptive parents the ones putting her in danger? Or was it something to do with her birth parents? Oh, Bella. The thought of her all alone without a loving family twisted his heart. *She has to open up to me. I'll do anything to help her.* If only she would let him be her family. Change her name once and for all to Lexington.

He went to lift the basket when he spotted Bella's brown leather journal poking out from underneath. A brief smile escaped. She never went anywhere without a notebook of some kind. She was a writer through-and-through, and took pure delight in capturing the wonders around her by scribbling details for future use, or simply to ponder. Sometimes she would share her musings—she was good. Really good.

He knelt in the sand as he stuffed the book into the basket, alongside the unopened champagne bottle. How long had she been working on her historical novel? The past year at least. In fact, she had been writing research notes for it the first time he caught sight of her—on the steps outside church, twelve months ago. So engrossed in her work, she didn't even notice him staring at her. Was it crazy to think it was love at first sight?

"Do these belong to you, young man?"

Adam looked up as the sound of a theatrical English accent projected through the wind. The elderly man trudged toward him, carrying Bella's sandals in one wrinkled hand.

"Yes, thanks. Well they aren't mine, of course, they belong to my—" The word stuck in Adam's throat. *My what?* She wasn't his fiancée, and was she even his girlfriend anymore? They hadn't reverted to "just good friends," had they? A knot tightened in his stomach.

"What's that you say?" Mr. English hovered over him now, his white, bushy eyebrows knit together in confusion.

"Sorry." Adam stood and smiled. "Yes, I'll take them for Bella. She's sitting in the car."

"In the car, you say? Everything alright, son?"

"Yes, thank you for spotting the shoes." Adam balanced the sandals on top of the basket. He wasn't about to bare his soul to a perfect stranger. "Take care in this wind—looks like it's blowing up for a storm."

The old man tilted his balding head to one side and looked out toward the caves at the edge of the beach. "Storms always blow over eventually, young man. Don't you worry about that. The sun will come out once again. God bless you." With that, he turned and ambled off toward Cape Creek Bridge.

Adam stared after him. He bore a striking resemblance to Clarence, the quirky guardian angel in *It's a Wonderful Life.* Bella's favorite Christmas movie. Or had she lied about that, too? He shook his head.

Oh, Bella, what now?

His chest heaved as he carried his burden across the sand.

18

Why, God? Why didn't she say 'yes'? How on earth did I get it all so wrong? She loves me, I know she does. And I was certain You wanted marriage for us. Surely, she's the one for me—You brought us together from such different pasts, but we have You in common. If there's a way for us, if You do want me to pursue a life with Bella, would You show me how? I'm willing to do anything for her, Lord. Anything.

Adam sighed as he reached the parking lot.

And if I have this wrong—if You have other plans for us both, would You somehow heal my breaking heart?

He opened the jeep door and stowed the picnic basket in the back. "Here are your sandals."

"Thanks." Bella took them from him and slipped them onto her dirty feet.

Adam jumped in, slammed the door, and set off for home. The air between them was thick with something— regret? Sorrow? The drive over the bridge and down the coast toward Florence was silent. Almost more than he could bear.

Usually, Bella was so full of life—ideas, dreams, wondering at creation and the beauty of the rugged coastline, chatting non-stop about the latest book she had devoured or story she had written. Their conversations were never stilted, but flowed from faith and the latest Sunday service at church, to his job as an architect, to what meal he should experiment with next.

Their love for God, food, the ocean, and each other had deepened over their time together. The first three months as friends, and then almost nine months of dating, until marriage as a next step seemed so right. To him, at least. Granted, they hadn't discussed a wedding specifically or

19

how many kids they would have, but Bella must have picked up on the hints as subtle as tidal waves. He glanced at her, huddled against the window. Apparently not.

The silence was deafening. This was going to be a long twenty-minute drive. Even the road was void of traffic. Adam turned on the radio, and a country tune blared its lament over a break-up. She hated country music. He flicked it over to the Christian station. Perhaps some inspiration would seep into them both.

He took a slow, deep breath. The subtle sweetness of Bella's favorite coconut body lotion wafted across the space. His favorite scent. He fought the desire to reach for her hand, and cleared his throat.

"So, do you want me to drop you straight home?"

"I think that would be best. Thank you." Her voice was barely audible.

"Can I come in so we can talk some more? I hate to leave it like this."

"Like what?"

"Like unknown. Like I don't have a clue what to do next." Adam glanced over at her. She looked gorgeous, even after sobbing and being windswept on the cliff. Beyond her profile, the ocean darkened and stretched out beside them. It was a picturesque coastal drive, one they both enjoyed. But not this evening. The sun had set and taken hope down with it. A ball of grief settled in Adam's gut.

Bella leaned her head back and sighed. "What have I done?"

He allowed the question to settle between them as the ocean disappeared and they were enveloped by tall cedar trees. The shade caused the air to cool, and he focused on the winding road and his answer to her question.

"How have we managed to come as far as this in a relationship with something so huge standing between us? I mean, I don't even know what the huge boulder is—is it a person, or your family history, or an incident that happened? I'm in the dark here. Your past has always been ambiguous and kind of a mystery, but I didn't for a second suspect it was so painful." *Who hurt you, Bella?* He gripped the steering wheel. "And I never imagined anything could ruin our future together. Why didn't you share it with me before?"

"It's not you. You have to know that." She twisted in her seat to face him. "I chose to leave the past behind. It was a conscious decision. It sounds wacky, but this place has healed me."

"Florence?" Funny how he'd always longed to escape his hometown as a teen—until he, too, learned how healing a place could be. The lure of the magnificent ocean and the comfort of a friendly town. Safe, familiar, charming. "I get it."

"Florence and the entire Oregon Coast. The ocean, the lighthouses, the people, the food—it's nourished me. I knew it was special when I moved to the coast six years ago. I was seventeen—a kid still—but God stepped in and showed me love like I only ever dreamed of before. His grace and mercy are still almost too much for me to comprehend some days. My breath catches thinking about it. He used people in my life to show me how to trust again. To trust Him." She reached over and squeezed Adam's hand. "To trust you."

"You trust me. But not enough to share your pain and your past?" *Come on, Bella.*

"That's exactly it—I was intent on leaving the past where it belongs, I guess I hoped I could make a new life and forget the old one. It was foolish."

"Did you *want* to make a new life with me?"

"Yes." A whisper more than a word of affirmation. "Deep down I did, somehow."

Adam winced. *Did* sounded like it was very much in the past.

"But I didn't figure out what that would look like."

He had to know. "Do you still want a future with me, deep down in your heart? If we could make a way?" He held his breath. This was risky.

"Yes. If there's a way, then yes." Anxious fear filled her whisper.

More silence as they approached the town. Adam hardly dared move. He went through the motions of driving, but his insides churned. *Thank You, God.* There was still a sliver of hope.

"Then that's all I need to know for tonight."

They turned onto the quiet road where Bella shared an apartment with her good friend, Juliet.

He forced his voice to sound normal. "Are you working at the bookstore tomorrow?"

"Not until midday. Pippa's taking the morning shift."

Yes, work was a safe topic of conversation. "She's a cool boss, letting you sleep in on Saturdays."

"Right? But she's more than a boss—she's like a mother to me."

Adam nodded. Pippa had a tender heart and went out of her way to take in lost souls. No wonder she encouraged

Bella to share the apartment with Juliet, her true daughter. "Pippa's the best. Can I call you later in the morning then?"

"For sure. I have a lot of thinking to do this evening."

"I understand. Sort of. Is Juliet definitely coming home from Seattle tonight?"

It was vital that Bella knew there were people around her who cared, and Juliet was a gem like that. The nurse in her oozed concern and kindness. She'd help Bella through her minefield of secrets and heartache.

"Yeah, I almost forgot. She texted earlier to say she was leaving Madison's place and would be home this evening. She's been housesitting for her all week while Madison and Luke honeymoon in Mexico, but she's more than ready to come home. You know how she feels about big cities."

"Especially Seattle." Juliet had lamented her Seattle nurse's training experience to all who would listen.

"Sounds like Madison and Luke's wedding was fabulous though." Bella cringed. "Sorry."

Adam pulled up outside the apartment. "What's there to be sorry about?"

"I shouldn't be talking about a wedding after the evening we just had."

Right. "Hey, I don't want to rain on anyone else's parade. I don't know Madison super well—we only met her when she visited Juliet at the beginning of the summer, but I'm glad she and Luke are married after all the drama they went through. They deserve their happily ever after."

"So do you."

The crack in her voice broke his heart.

"Why don't you think *you* deserve to be happy?"

She wrung her hands as she gazed up at the roof of the jeep. "It seems so... impossible. And I don't want to hold you back from living your dream. That's all."

"You *are* my dream." He slapped a hand on his forehead. *Man up, Adam.* "That sounded way cheesier than I intended, but it's true. I don't want to pressure you into anything, but you need to know it's *you* I love, not some generic idea of marriage."

"Thank you. I appreciate that. I'm a hot mess tonight and I can't think straight, but I promise I'm going to take time to process and pray and figure out what's next. For me. For us. But I'll still have to give Juliet time to decompress from the Seattle trip and tell me all about Madison's wedding. She's been looking forward to being a bridesmaid for months and I know she'll want to give me the blow-by-blow."

"I can imagine." He wrinkled his nose. "Better you than me. I'll leave it up to you whether you want to tell her about... tonight."

Bella pecked his cheek. "Thanks for being so understanding."

The brief kiss left a spark of encouragement. It took everything in him not to pull her close and share a real kiss. *Patience.*

Adam turned off the engine, opened his door, and jumped out of the vehicle. He hurried around to help Bella — not that she needed assistance, but his mother would never forgive him if he didn't do the gentlemanly thing. She hopped down and he shut the passenger door behind her.

The heady scent of honeysuckle permeated the air. With more courage than he thought possible after tonight's fiasco, he reached for her hand as they walked toward the front path. She clasped it in her own. A good sign. Even the stars seemed to shine a little brighter as he looked up at the darkening sky.

"I'm sorry to end the day like this. Not quite what you had in mind." Bella looked at him and offered a sad smile. In the orange glow of the streetlight, she looked almost angelic. "We'll talk this through, okay?"

"I can live with that." He patted his front pocket. "But I'm keeping the ring safe, just so you know." He caught sight of a cardboard box in his peripheral vision and pointed to the bright red front door. "Hey, what's that? Looks like one of you girls has a special delivery."

"I'm not expecting anything."

They hurried down the path and reached the porch, where Bella peered at the package on her doormat.

"Weird. There's no label on it or anything. Looks like it's not taped up." She squatted down. "I'll see if it's for me or Juliet."

With care, she pulled back the flap and glanced inside.

The next moment, her scream made Adam's heart slam in his chest. He reached down and pulled her away from the box and held her tight. "Hey, it's okay. What's in there?"

Bella trembled. Between her sobs he made out the words, "There's a dead rat and a note and a—"

"A rat? What on earth?" He walked her over to the garden bench. "Stay right there." He hurried back to the box and looked inside. He cringed. Definitely a dead rat. And a collar? A blood-smeared collar? Too big for a rat—more like cat-sized. Pink and sparkly with a tiny heart-shaped tag. He squinted. The name *Suky* was engraved on it. *Who is Suky?*

Adam shuddered. Maybe "Who *was* Suky?" would be more accurate. The third item was less gruesome.

"Bella, did you read this note?" A small white card had been placed between the rat and the collar. "It says, 'NO MORE CAT AND MOUSE'." He turned back to face her. "What does *that* mean? And who would do something like this?"

Bella wrapped her arms around her middle. "I know precisely who did it." She bit her lip. "The message is for me."

"Are you serious?" He closed the space between them and took her shaking hands in his.

She looked up with eyes so full of sorrow and fear it took Adam's breath away. "Deadly serious."

CHAPTER FOUR

BELLA ACCEPTED THE MUG OF steaming hot chocolate and willed her hands to stop shaking. *Safe. I'm safe and everyone's fine.* She glanced over at Adam in the armchair. His grim, protective expression reminded her of the danger that brought her here.

"Thanks, Pippa. Juliet's going to wonder why on earth you told her not to go anywhere near our apartment. I'm grateful you're letting us stay here tonight." She forced a smile. "At least if I'm staying right above the bookstore, I won't be late for work tomorrow, boss."

"For goodness sake." Pippa sat on the edge of the sofa and squeezed Bella's shoulder. "You would think I were a tyrant running some major corporation in the big city. The Book Nook is a quirky bookstore in a tiny seaside town. If you need to take tomorrow off, that's fine. Juliet won't mind covering in the afternoon. And if she's too wiped out from her trip, I can run downstairs and handle it."

Bella shrugged. "I think it might help if I stay busy."

Pippa looked her in the eye. "Please tell me you're going to report this to the police. Even if it was a rat, a dead animal in a box on your doorstep is not only cruel, it's creepy. Not to mention the message and the bloodied cat collar."

Pippa's black Persian cat chose that precise moment to saunter into the living room.

"Ebony, you don't want to be listening to this conversation." Pippa swooped her up into her arms.

Adam fidgeted in the armchair. "Actually, Bella decided not to report it yet." He gave Bella a subtle nod.

He trusts me. Thank You, Lord. He wasn't yet privy to all the gory details, but he was going to let her take her time with this.

He leaned forward, elbows on knees. "I'll let the police know a dead rat was found and I'll give them a description of the collar in case someone has a pet missing, but we want to keep the rest low-key."

"Why?" Pippa never minced words. "Let's not forget my daughter also lives in the apartment. I don't want either of you girls in danger. And if there's someone out there threatening our pets, I would want to know about that, too." She snuggled Ebony closer.

Bella's mouth went dry. The last thing she wanted was to put anyone at risk. Especially Juliet. She was the best friend she'd ever had. Ebony was quite safe, however.

At that moment, the door to the apartment above the bookstore burst open and Juliet appeared, her face even paler than usual and her mass of long, red hair windswept beyond repair. "What's going on? Is everyone okay?"

She parked her rolling case on the tiled floor at the entry and hurried over to the gathering by the fire, where she embraced her mother fiercely. Ebony jumped down, disgruntled.

28

"Why's the fireplace roaring? It's September. Bella, you look awful. And Mom, I got your message to come straight here—are you sick?"

"No, I'm fine, sweetie. Sorry to be cryptic." Pippa ran her fingers through her short, grey hair and sighed. "We didn't want you heading back to your apartment tonight."

"Why?" Juliet hugged Bella and nodded at Adam, then sat cross-legged on the colorful area rug.

"There was a dead rat on our doormat." Bella bit her lip. This wasn't going to be easy. "Along with a cat collar."

Juliet shuddered. "I hate rats. But why dump it outside our door? And what's with the cat collar? Some people are so twisted."

Bella's stomach flipped. "Actually, it was left there on purpose for me. It was in a box. With a note."

And a terrifying threat that just turned my entire world upside-down. She looked at Adam and widened her eyes. He'd better not say anything. She wanted to do this her way. Carefully.

She set her mug on the coffee table, and Ebony clambered onto her lap. Bella gave her sweet face a kiss. Who could be cruel to such darling little creatures? Yes, she knew who...

Pippa stood. "I'm not comfortable with this. You know I'm as free and breezy as the day is long, but when it comes to safety, I'm all mother and a stickler for playing by the book. Not to mention I'm a cat lady, in the good way."

"It's true." Juliet nodded. "Hard to believe, but Mom does have rules. But I don't understand, who would leave a dead rat with a note? What kind of a message was it?" She gasped. "Wait, this isn't necessarily about you, Bella. What if the message is for me? We've both lived at the apartment for the past year."

Adam set down his mug and joined Bella on the sofa. She leaned against his strong arm, in need of an ally. "That's just it. It was definitely for Bella. Are you up to talking about it now, honey?"

Why was this so difficult? These people loved her. Maybe sharing a small slice of her story would somehow ease the burden. Or increase the danger for all of them...

Bella grabbed a tissue from a decorative box on the side table and blew her nose. "Yes." She looked up at Adam's kind face. Would she have to leave this place and this man after all? Or did she have the courage to stay? "I'm sorry I broke down out there, but it was a huge shock after all this time."

"After all this time? So now I'm intrigued." Juliet shed her jacket and settled against the sofa.

How much did they need to know? Bella stroked Ebony's soft fur and looked at the three people she loved most in the world. Could she navigate the murky waters of her past without going into too much detail? How much was too much? So far, they knew nothing.

"I got myself into this mess and it's only fair I share some of my story with you guys."

She handed the cat to Adam and stood. Pacing always helped. She took a few slow, steady breaths. The scent of lavender permeated the room as usual—Pippa's signature fragrance. There were always lavender candles or oil burning somewhere, and right now Bella needed all the calming ambience she could inhale.

"Pippa and Juliet, you've been like family to me and you know snippets of my background, but nobody knows everything. Not even Adam." She glanced over and saw the pain in his eyes. Pain she continued to inflict as the evening progressed.

Pippa took Bella's place on the couch and curled her legs under her flowing tie-dyed dress. "Go ahead, sweetheart. You know this is a safe place and we love you. No judgment here."

Bella nodded. "There's lots you don't need to know, and some is a mystery to me even now, but I have to tell you about my adoptive parents."

"You've mentioned them before, but only to say they died in an accident. I never liked to pry, but I'll admit I've been curious." Juliet bit her nails as she waited for Bella to continue.

"The thing is, the accident never happened."

"What?" Adam's voice cracked.

Juliet's eyes bugged. "You mean they're not dead?"

Bella winced. Who made up lies like that? Her face heated. "No. As far as I know, they are very much alive. And after tonight, I'm certain of it." Bella stopped pacing and wrapped her arms around her middle. "This is despicable and I don't expect any of you to understand, but I haven't been truthful with you about my family."

"Why would you lie about something like that?" Adam's jaw was set. "I don't get it. You said they were in an accident years ago—that was a… lie?"

Pippa's collection of bracelets jangled as she placed a comforting hand on Adam's arm. "Give her a chance. Let her explain."

"I'm sorry. I knew it was wrong to make up such a lie, and even as I told you, I felt sick to my stomach. But the more people I told, the easier it became. Nobody likes to probe into your family details if they think you are grieving over loss. And I *am* grieving. I'm grieving a family I never had. A childhood I never enjoyed. A life I somehow missed out on."

Tipping point. The wretched tears came like a sneaker wave and coursed their way down Bella's face. No longer able to control herself, she collapsed on the floor next to Juliet and sobbed. If only she hadn't seen that cat collar. It brought back every single agonizing memory. So much for stuffing all the emotions away for good. She may never stop crying if she allowed everything to come to light.

Juliet's arm held her close and Pippa's soothing voice uttered some maternal musings about letting it all go.

Bella caught her breath. How long had she been crying? Headache pounded. Nausea roiled. She hadn't allowed herself to weep like this in years. So much bottled-up pain. "This is going to be harder than I thought."

Adam crouched down next to her. "Do you want me to stay?"

His broken voice caused Bella to look up. His eyebrows were knit together and those fathomless eyes looked so full of hurt. What had she done to him? "I... I don't know. Yes. But only if you want to. I understand if you need some space."

He touched her arm. "You look spent. Why don't you try to get some sleep? If you're up to sharing more in the morning, I'll be here." Adam's face was impossible to read. A mix of pain, sympathy, and confusion before he turned to

32

Pippa. "Are you comfortable with me sleeping downstairs in the bookstore tonight?"

"Absolutely. But do you think it's necessary? We have good neighbors on either side of the store here, and Mrs. Hutchinson is like a guard dog. Nothing gets past her. She'll let me know if anyone suspicious is lurking about."

He smiled. "I'm sure you'll be fine, but if anything happened to scare you girls, I'd never forgive myself."

"Always the protector. You look done in tonight, too. In fact, if you're up early in the morning, go on home and shower and do what you need to do. We'll look after Bella, don't you worry." Pippa walked past and patted his shoulder. "Let me at least point you in the direction of our camping mattress and a blanket."

"Thanks. Promise me you'll call down if you need me? For anything at all?" He kissed the top of Bella's head and stood slowly, like he had aged in the past five minutes.

"I'm sorry, Adam." How many times had she said that tonight? Bella's throat was raw and she had no other words. She'd disappointed him with her lies. What would he say if he knew everything?

"Hey, I'm not judging you." He reached down and stroked her cheek with a featherlight touch. "I know you well enough to believe you have reasons for keeping your past a secret. And I know you'll share when you're good and ready. In the meantime, I'm going to get my buddy down at the police station to be vigilant. I'll only give him the basics, don't worry. Now rest."

Bella's neck was sore and her eye sockets ached. "I don't expect you to understand," she whispered, "but I want to tell you."

"Everything?" He raised both brows.

She nodded.

Adam managed a smile before he followed the jangle of Pippa's bracelets in search of bedding.

Bella yawned. Exhaustion pressed in fast.

Juliet pulled her up and they sat together on the floral sofa, both of them silent and somber. Juliet was like a sister. A true friend. But now these lies had created a chasm in their relationship. Adam wasn't the only one she had hurt.

Pippa bustled into the room, followed by Ebony, and pulled a soft throw from the back of an armchair and tucked the girls in comfort. "I'll get you some hot chocolate, Juliet. Yours is right here on the table, Bella love. Although, I'm not sure how hot it is anymore. You two can talk in private."

Rain pelted against the living room bay window, the sky joining in the sorrowful atmosphere of the evening. Juliet bit her fingernails again—a habit she had been trying to break. Bella sighed. How much should she share?

"I've started you back on your nail biting issues." Bella smiled sheepishly. The cat pounced onto the sofa and settled onto Bella's lap.

"It's not just you." Juliet shook her head.

"Really?" Bella noticed the dark circles beneath Juliet's eyes. "What's wrong?"

"Nothing serious. It's been stressful housesitting for Madison in that big ol' mansion of hers while she was away on honeymoon."

The mere mention of a honeymoon caused Bella's throat to constrict. She would have to tell Juliet about the proposal. Later. But for now, she could use a distraction. "I realize this has been a massive downer tonight, but I do want to know

34

about Madison's wedding. The photo you texted me was gorgeous."

"You want to know? Now?"

Bella nodded. "I think I want my mind to be filled with something joyful for a while."

Juliet twiddled the fringe of the throw as she closed her eyes.

"It was perfect. The whole thing was in the beautiful grounds of her home—she's a private person and didn't want anything huge or over-the-top. Plus, she pulled it all together in three months, which is incredible. Her sister, Chloe, and I were bridesmaids and Madison looked like a princess in her gown. Luke is wickedly handsome and tanned—I guess the tan is a perk of being a missionary in Mexico—so he looked like a million bucks. The only sad thing was that Madison's parents weren't there."

"That's right. They died a few years back." For real. Bella bit the inside of her cheek. The guilt from lying about her own parents' death was going to take some working through. She took a few deep breaths and tried to concentrate as Juliet continued on with details about the happy couple. This could have been her reality—if she hadn't ruined Adam's proposal.

"And then they jetted off to Mexico for the honeymoon, and I was left on house duty." Juliet took Bella's hand. "But now I'm glad to be home. Well, sort of home. I realize you don't want to speak about it yet, but I have to tell you, Bel, that stuff in the box is kind of freaky. I feel like I've missed a huge chunk of your life, and I thought we were close. What's going on? What happened today? You know you can tell me anything."

"Well, let's see." Bella cocked her head to one side. "Today, I worked on writing my manuscript, did a shift at The Book Nook, turned down a proposal of marriage, discovered a dead rat, and confessed to my dearest people that I've been lying to them all."

"A regular Friday then."

"Totally."

"Hold on." Juliet sat up straight. "You turned down a marriage proposal?"

"Yes." Juliet *must* be tired to not jump all over that.

"From Adam?"

"Really? Who else would be asking me to marry them? Yes, it was poor, wonderful, devastated Adam."

"Wow. I thought he looked upset. I can't believe he asked you." Juliet's face fell. Was she jealous or disappointed Bella had turned him down? Strange.

Bella pulled her hair to one side and began braiding it. Anything to keep her hands busy. "Me neither. I was blindsided."

"That's quite the shocker. But you turned him down? Why?"

"It's a long story. The bottom line is: I lied about my family. I had my reasons—and I've wrestled with God about it for years—but I lied. What kind of foundation is that to build a future on?"

Juliet shrugged. "He'll get over it."

Bella shook her head. "It's complicated. My past is complicated—I even had to change my name. I can't drag his family into my mess."

36

Juliet raised a brow. "Listen, he's been smitten ever since he met you at church last year. I've known Adam a long time and, trust me, he's not perfect. Don't put him on a pedestal."

"I'm not." What was it he mentioned at the lighthouse? Something about his own issues. They had a lot of talking to do. He deserved to know the truth.

"And no family is perfect."

"Your mom is one in a million though." Bella broke into a smile.

"Yeah, she is. But it might have been nice to have a father figure in the picture at some point. Mom was pretty much an outcast when she got pregnant with me. No husband. No family support."

"She's feisty. And she's got a heart the size of Texas. But Adam's family is so... balanced and regular and respectable. It would crush them if Adam got caught up in something dangerous." The words of the wretched note came to mind. They knew where she was—this was serious.

"Dangerous? How dangerous?" Juliet squinted.

She couldn't share too much. Not yet.

Pippa whistled as she meandered into the room and set Juliet's mug on the driftwood coffee table.

"Thanks, Mom." Juliet blew her a kiss. "You don't mind us crashing here tonight?"

"My baby and my best employee? Are you kidding? You girls can stay as long as you like. You know I love the company. I'm heading to bed with a good book. Your old room is ready and you can pull the sofa bed out here for Bella. Shout if you need anything." She bent over and kissed each girl on the crown of their heads. "Sweet dreams. And try not to worry about everything."

Bella smiled. "Thanks. You're so kind. I hate to be this secretive, but I'll tell you as much as I can eventually."

"No hurry, sweetheart. We all have our secrets. As long as you're safe, that's good enough for me, and I think Adam is taking care of that aspect for us."

"Yeah. He's remarkable." Bella sighed. There had to be a way to be together. Her heart ached at the thought of ending their relationship, and yet there was so much at stake. "Good night. I'll make breakfast in the morning."

"Pancakes it is then?" Juliet snickered.

Bella elbowed her friend. "Sorry, my repertoire is still rather limited."

Pippa laughed. "I love pancakes, and yours are the best. I might just dream about them. Night, girls."

Juliet waited until her mom was out of earshot. "Tell me this, and then I'll leave you to get some sleep: Is someone after you? I mean, did you do something like—illegal?"

Bella rubbed her tired eyes. "I've been running for a long time. Too long. But not from the police."

"Then who? I know the box was some sort of sick message. I'm not stupid. Who are you running from?"

The old cuckoo clock on the wall ticked in time with Bella's pulse for several seconds.

"I'm running from my adoptive parents. I've seen too much, and I know they will do anything to get what they want. And I mean *anything*."

CHAPTER FIVE

BELLA LAY WIDE AWAKE. HER safe haven had been discovered, and the life she had built carefully in Florence was crumbling around her. The tick-tock from the cuckoo clock echoed around Pippa's living room, a steady cadence, solid and soothing, keeping watch and keeping time. But as the silence stretched into the early hours with everyone else sleeping in blissful oblivion, the gentle clucking sound of the wretched clock grated on Bella's every nerve, pounding in perfect time with the rhythmic throb of her headache. Painkillers were required. Now.

Careful not to awaken Pippa and Juliet in their respective bedrooms, she peeled off the layers of blankets Juliet had used to swaddle her, and squinted in the direction of the kitchen. No need to switch on a lamp. Juliet's borrowed pajamas pooled at Bella's ankles as she stood—not surprising given their five-inch height difference. She hitched them up and tiptoed first to the window. She had to check.

Did they know she was here? It was possible. They had found her apartment address, so must have been watching her for a while. Or had someone else to do their dirty work. It wouldn't be the first time. She pulled back the sheer curtain and secured it behind the hook.

A streetlamp lit the quaint old town. It looked peaceful. Maybe there were fights and arguments and tears and disappointments behind closed doors, but for now, it appeared to be something right out of a picture book. Yellow haze provided a warm, magical ambiance to the storefront windows across the road. All was calm, as it should be.

Satisfied, she crept across the rug and onto the chilled tile of the kitchen floor. Blue light from the ice maker on the fridge and clocks on various small appliances lit the way. She knew this apartment like the back of her hand.

Pippa kept a selection of medicines tucked away in the drawer next to the stove, and Bella smiled when she slid open the drawer and spotted a bottle of painkillers. *Thank You, Lord.* Two would do the trick. She popped them in her mouth and winced as the faucet squeaked when she poured a glass of water. No way was she going to down those pills dry. She swallowed and then replaced the lid onto the small, white bottle.

Clasping the bottle in her hand, she stared at it for a second too long. There were plenty of pills in there. Enough to make the nightmare disappear for good.

No. No way. What was she thinking? Even when life with her adoptive parents had been desperate and she didn't know if she could go on, she'd always rallied herself. Made herself brave. Refused to surrender to the temptation of ending it all. And that had been before she'd found God. Now she had so much more to live for. He had been working in her life even back then. She just hadn't known it.

Forgive me for even letting my mind go there, Lord...

Bella dropped the bottle into the drawer as if it were on fire. It made one short, sharp rap and she held her breath for several beats, hoping not to have woken the other women from their sleep. Nothing. She exhaled and closed the drawer, praying the medication would work with haste.

Exhaustion drew her back to the couch, where she perched on the arm and looked through the window again, this time up into the starless sky. A sliver of moon showed itself above the buildings on the opposite side of the street. A dark, bleak night, in more ways than one.

But how bad could things get? She was a grown woman, for goodness sake. No longer a scared, secluded little girl who wanted only to be loved. She had found the greatest love imaginable in God, and nothing could ever take that away. Ever.

And then there was Adam.

She twirled a strand of hair around her fingers and sighed. He was sleeping downstairs on some makeshift cot in a bookstore, keeping vigil over her, when he had no idea what was going on. He was, in fact, in over his head and if he had any sense, he would send her packing. Or at least end things before he discovered the truth.

What did he think of her now? Had he not considered how her mysterious past could have major ramifications for their future? No, Adam was logical and analytical. He couldn't be blamed for not guessing there was something sinister from years ago. This was all her fault.

She stood and put one palm against the cool glass of the window. *I love this town.* It was unfair to be forced into moving again. She could have lived here forever, put roots down, maybe even raised a family here one day in the future. With Adam...

How can I let him go?

She didn't want to end their relationship, and yet what were the choices? Drag him into the fray with her, or continue lying. The latter had not gone well so far—that much had been clear from the look of betrayal on his handsome face when he'd discovered her parents were alive and well. And the lies had left a pit in the base of her gut for too long. They cramped and accused, painful and dark.

Ebony padded over and wound her fluffy tail around Bella's leg. The purring caught Bella's attention and she swooped the cat up in her arms.

"This is a perfect place," she whispered as she stroked Ebony's soft coat. "You're lucky to have this home with people who love you in a town that feels safe and cozy. But I don't deserve any of it."

A horrific image popped into her mind of The Book Nook being burned to the ground along with all its inhabitants, and she shuddered. "I'm going to ruin everything for the people I love most, and I can't do that, can I? How selfish would that be? I have to go. It's the only way I can protect these precious people I love."

Heart breaking in two, Bella kissed Ebony's velvet ears and set her on the couch. She peeled off the borrowed pajamas and replaced them with her own clothes from earlier. The clothes she'd worn when she rejected Adam's romantic proposal.

What is the matter with me?

As quietly as possible, she slid her purse over one shoulder. It was all she had. Everything else was back in her apartment, so that would be her first stop. She dug her hand into the oversized bag and located her keys. They jangled and she paused. No one stirred. Hopefully, Adam would be fast asleep downstairs by now, too.

This was it then—she would be on the run again in mere minutes. But this time was different. Before, she had always been running to something better, some dream of perfection. This time she was running *from* her dream of perfection before she destroyed it.

Scared she would talk herself out of leaving, Bella hustled to the door in the semi-darkness. Her sandals, where had she put them? She bent down to check underneath the little bench in the hallway, her fingers fumbling from cat toy to shoe to—yes, sandals.

A hand on her shoulder caused Bella to freeze. The gentle squeeze reassured her it was Pippa. Juliet would have flown off the handle by now, for sure.

Bella straightened and turned around. She flicked on the light switch and looked into Pippa's big brown eyes, filled with unshed tears. Similar height, they stood toe-to-toe in silence for several seconds. Bella dared not breathe.

"Sweetie, you know I respect your privacy and I can't begin to understand what you're running from, but could we sit for a little minute?"

Bella looked at the sandals and sighed. "Sure. I'm sorry if I woke you."

"I'm not."

Pippa took Bella by the hand and led her back to the couch. "And there's no need to worry about waking that daughter of mine. She's a sound sleeper—she'd sleep through anything, which is somewhat of a concern."

Bella smiled. "True. Sometimes I wonder if she's still breathing."

They scooted Ebony to a corner and sat side by side.

Bella fiddled with her purse strap. This was not going to be easy. Would Pippa even let her go? She might shout for Adam, which would make it near impossible to leave. Or she could go and shake Juliet awake and insist she come and talk sense. The guilt was suffocating.

"I'm sorry."

"For wanting to leave?"

"I don't *want* to leave. I think I have to."

Pippa tightened the throw blanket around herself and leaned her head to one side. "Now what on earth makes you say that?"

"I'm a mess. I've betrayed your trust as a friend—and a boss—by not telling you the truth about my past. I feel horrible about that. I've also broken Adam's heart and I feel like I've upset Juliet more than she's admitting. I've let you all down and you deserve better."

"Better than you, child?" Pippa's hand fluttered to her throat. "Sweet Bella, you have no idea. You have no idea how much joy and kindness you have brought us. As a best friend, roommate, girlfriend, and employee—you've touched each of our lives in such a beautiful way. How could you take that from us?"

Bella's mouth fell open. She hadn't expected to hear that. Was she being selfish by running? In trying to protect those she truly loved, was she hurting them even more deeply?

She hung her head and dropped her bag onto the floor with a soft thud. "But I don't want to put any of you in danger. I'm not sure how this is going to unfold. It could get ugly."

Pippa clasped both of Bella's hands in her own. "I could write the book on ugly. We don't have to let our pasts define us, you know. I learned that nugget of truth a long time ago and it's served me well. Please, please stay. I'm not the begging type as a rule, but I know we can help you through this—whatever it is."

Tears blurred the image of the loving firecracker of a woman in front of her. The woman who had raised a daughter alone and beaten cancer. Twice. Bella nodded as a solitary tear meandered down her cheek.

"I'll stay. I didn't mean to hurt you."

"No harm done. Lucky I'm a light sleeper. And how about we keep this little moment between the two of us? Put those pajamas back on and let's call it a nonsensical blip in the night. No use getting Juliet all riled up, and Adam seems like he's carrying the weight of the world on his shoulders as it is."

Sounds about right. "Thanks, I'd appreciate that. I'm not sure how much more disappointment Adam could take at the moment."

"Don't worry about that young man. I have a feeling he's going to be just fine."

Bella nodded and swallowed the lump in her throat.

He may not be so fine when he learns the whole truth.

CHAPTER SIX

HOW COULD THE SUN RISE on such a beautiful morning in the Oregon Coast, when there was a storm of pain brewing in the apartment above The Book Nook?

Adam stifled a yawn as he took long strides down the main street in Florence. Poor Bella. Whatever she was hiding, it was heavy. When he'd spoken with her earlier on the phone, she'd said she hadn't gotten much sleep either—no great shock there. She'd mentioned an argument with Juliet, which was hard to imagine. But Juliet Farr did have a temper. He'd found that out more than once over the years. Must have inherited that from her father's side, as Pippa was go-with-the-flow, and feisty rather than fiery.

The enticing aroma of freshly baked croissants wafted up from the paper bag he clutched in his hand. His stomach growled on cue. Last night, he had been too nervous to eat much of the romantic beach picnic. Then, after the devastating lack of acceptance and the dead rat drama, he hadn't had the stomach for anything at all.

A familiar throng of locals gathered outside the cafe, chatting and basking in the remnants of summer, even if it felt a little chilly this early in the day. He offered a wave and continued on past the florist and the swanky new restaurant, neither of which were yet open. Soon, the street would be bustling—Saturdays brought in more tourists on weekend breaks, especially when the weather cooperated.

He slowed his steps as he approached the bookstore. Bella would be upset—not only reeling from the information she shared last night, but the thought of Juliet being mad with her would not sit well. Bella was a quintessential people-pleaser and avoided confrontation at any cost. Adam grunted. Hence her running away last night at the beach.

Bella got on well with everyone, particularly her roommate, but she mentioned on the phone that stern words had been exchanged and he heard the slammed doors early this morning. It probably had something to do with the rat issue. He couldn't blame Juliet for being freaked out. It was more than a little distressing. Hopefully, it was the box on their doorstep and nothing else—like something he should have shared with Bella months ago.

Adam rang the doorbell. The bookstore wasn't yet open and the door had automatically locked behind him when he left earlier. Soft footsteps sounded and then Bella's face appeared through the glass at the side of the door. He held up the bag of croissants and she smiled. That smile could brighten up any room. It had brought hope and happiness back into his wounded world a year ago, and he would do anything to keep it that way.

She opened the door and poked her head out to take a swift glance down the street.

"You're safe here, unless the circle of snarky seniors outside the cafe is making you nervous." His attempt at humor fell flat. Her sky-blue eyes had lost their sparkle, but that was to be expected. "You doing okay?"

She pulled him inside and slammed the door shut behind him. "I had a rough night, but I'm fine now. I feel awful about Juliet being mad at me. I dreaded this. Life was normal for once—you, my friends, church, a job I adore." She glanced into The Book Nook. "It was too good to be true. I should have known better, but I let my guard down."

Adam pulled her close for a hug, the paper bag crunching in his hand. Her hair smelled of the familiar coconut scent. Warm and exotic. She tensed within his embrace and he stepped back.

"Are you going to let me in?"

She stood to one side and gestured toward the stairs. "Yes, of course."

He leaned against the wall. "That's not quite what I had in mind."

"Oh." Her brow furrowed.

"I mean are you going to let me into that head of yours? Let me help you?" He tucked a loose strand of hair behind her ear and gazed into her blue eyes.

Bella nodded and glanced at the staircase. "I want to explain some of it. You deserve to know. I didn't get a chance to talk about my past with Juliet this morning... She seemed fine last night, although she was surprised when I told her you proposed to me."

Adam shifted from one foot to another. *I'll bet she was surprised.*

"And then today, she was all fired up about something. Maybe she had chance in the night to stew about us not being at our apartment. I can't blame her for being upset. She's been in Seattle for the past ten days and I'm sure she wanted to sleep in her own bed. But she didn't even mention the box. Actually, if anything, she seemed to be mad at you."

Adam stared at his shoes. Juliet must be confused. Maybe hurt, too. But it had been years ago. "She's known me for a long time. So, you told her about the proposal?"

"Yes, it came up. Like I said, she was shocked to hear you'd popped the question, but then so was I." Bella's cheeks reddened.

"Fair enough." Adam's shoulders slumped as he recalled the disappointment from last night's rejection. "Was she surprised you didn't accept?" He held his breath. Was he the only one who thought their marriage was a good idea?

"I don't know. She seemed more confused by the fact that you'd even asked. Why would she have bad feelings about the proposal? I wondered if she felt a bit blue, you know, after being at Madison's wedding and now coming back to this. She hasn't had much joy in the dating world, has she?"

This could get awkward. He cringed at the thought of facing Juliet anytime soon. "It's Juliet, she'll be fine. I'm sure she's just exhausted. Did she have to go in to work today?"

"I don't think so. She gave me a piece of her mind and said she would be out all day. I get that she's stressed, but her reaction was so confusing."

"She didn't go back to your apartment, did she?"

"I told her not to go without us, but who knows?" She shrugged. "I'll call her when she's calmed down a bit. She missed my delicious pancakes, but there are some for you if you'd like."

"I bought these." He held up the bag of croissants. "But they'll keep for later. How can I resist your specialty?"

"It's the only thing I can make for breakfast and that's just because you taught me. We might need to build on my sorry repertoire."

He perked up at that thought. "If it means spending time with you, then it's no hardship." Cooking was his form of relaxation, and cooking with Bella was one of his favorite things to do. He gave her a wink.

That earned him a slight grin before Bella led the way up the narrow staircase to the apartment, where the inviting smell of freshly brewed coffee drifted through the open door.

"Adam, I thought I heard your voice." Pippa grinned and enveloped him in a bear hug. "How are you doing? Did you get any sleep at all on the cot?"

"It wasn't too bad, thanks. It's all folded away back in the storage room. I popped home for a quick shower and happened to pass the bakery. Croissants?" He handed her the bag.

"After Bella's pancakes, I'm not sure I have room. Maybe I'll grab one for my lunch though."

Adam laughed. It felt good to enjoy a light moment of normality before he dove into some heavy conversation with Bella. "Good plan. I hear there's a pancake left for me?"

"Help yourself." Pippa pointed toward the sunshine-yellow kitchen. Everything about Pippa was colorful.

Bella squeezed past and made her way to the breakfast bar where she loaded a bright blue plate with strawberries, three plump pancakes, and maple syrup. Strawberries—the picnic last night. The leftover fruit still sat in the back of his jeep. *I need to return that basket back to my mom. And face the interrogation, too.* Not a pleasant thought.

"Nice presentation."

"I learned from the best. You know I'm jealous of your mad culinary skills. Now, eat up while they're still hot."

He wasn't going to argue with that. They both sat on bar stools and Bella poured two mugs of steaming coffee.

"I'm heading downstairs to open up, loves." Pippa flitted past them. "Yell if you need anything. And don't worry about Juliet. Her hair isn't the only thing fiery about her. I don't know what got her so upset this morning, but she'll come around. She always does."

"Thanks, I appreciate that. I'll pop down in a while." Bella smiled at her boss. The world needed more Pippas.

"No need. I've got plenty of paperwork to keep me busy between customers. You get to the bottom of your ominous delivery and see what's eating that daughter of mine."

Adam took a swig of scalding coffee. This was not going to be easy.

"See you later."

With that, they were alone.

Food. He needed a distraction to put off the serious stuff for a few more minutes. He took a mouthful and chewed. "These pancakes are delicious."

They really were. Light, fluffy, and a perfect golden color. Bella had come a long way in the past year. She was a quick learner. Plus, she was always willing to be a guinea pig for his somewhat bizarre concoctions. Truth be told, she enjoyed eating more than cooking, but she was the most beautiful sous-chef he had ever encountered.

A ticking clock and the scrape of Adam's fork filled the silence. He waited. She twirled her hair around her fingers and leaned on the counter. *I'm in no hurry*. Time. He had to give her time. Even the air felt fragile and tenuous. How bad could it be?

Ebony wrapped her fluffy tail around Bella's leg and purred. Funny how animals could sense when a human needed a little love. Bella jumped down from the stool, picked up the demanding cat, and held her close to her chest. The purring amplified.

"I don't know where to start." Bella returned with the cat to her perch next to him, and looked up through wet lashes. "I want to tell you everything, but it's a lot and I'm not ready. I don't know if I ever will be, which is horrible. And that's why the idea of marrying you is absurd."

"Absurd?" He placed his fork on the plate as gently as possible. She was skittish and he couldn't chance her running again. But their marriage, their future together, was far from absurd.

"Look, I'm no expert on marriage—I didn't have a stellar example growing up, but I know there can't be secrets and there has to be complete trust. You have no idea what you would be getting yourself into."

"So tell me." He held his breath. She had to throw him a bone now.

"Okay."

Ebony took that moment as her sign to leap to the floor and give the humans some privacy. Bella ran her hands down her skirt, removed several stray black cat hairs, and then wrapped her arms around her waist. She was in protective mode.

"You know I was adopted as a baby. That part of my story is true."

"Go on." He pushed his plate to the side and swiveled on the stool to face her.

"Well, my adoptive parents, George and Susannah Robinson, were English."

"Ah. That explains some of the random words you throw out on occasion."

"Right? So before they adopted me, they came to the States as a means of escaping some suspect business dealings in the family company and—as I said before when we talked about extended family—they really did cut ties with all their relatives."

"Sounds extreme." As the son of a lawyer, he'd heard it all. *What kind of business dealings would cause a person to leave a country?*

"They rarely spoke of England or their lives back there. I asked once about my grandparents and was slapped so hard a tooth came out."

Adam's stomach knotted. No child should be treated like that. "What?" She wasn't kidding when she said they were dangerous.

"It was a baby tooth." Back to the hair-twirling.

He allowed the truth to settle in. This was dark. "You were young?" He recalled his baby sister, wide-eyed and innocent.

"Yeah. I didn't ask again." She shuddered.

Adam wanted her to stop. He didn't want to hear about her childhood after all. He pictured another young, innocent face in his memory. No amount of counseling could completely erase the guilt that still hung heavy like a cloak on his shoulders. But at least his family was full of love. And forgiveness. How did a child survive without love?

He had to know. "Were they always cruel?"

She bit her lip and turned away to gaze through the kitchen window. He gave her breathing room. In time, she twisted back to face him, her eyes glassy.

"I learned to stay out of the way. Fear will do that to you. I was rejected all the time, and as a child, I didn't understand any of it. I just wanted to be loved. There was never any sexual abuse, and for that I'm thankful. But yes, they were cruel. Hence the cat…"

Adam cocked his head to one side. Had he missed something? Was she talking about the bloody cat collar in the box? Surely not. But what had she said last night about it happening before? His stomach curdled at the thought.

She raised her eyebrows and shook her head. "I was ten years old when it happened. Shocking, isn't it? How parents could take their child's beloved pet, the most precious thing she had in the whole wide world, and allow her to find it dead in a box. On the doorstep."

"What?" Adam jumped down from the stool. He paced back and forth, running his hand through his short hair. "I don't understand. Why would they do that? What do you mean by 'allowed' you to find it?" He tried not to screech, but this was obscene.

"They told me to go and see what the mailman had left for me." Her chin quivered. "My cat had been run over and so they shoved her in a box and put it on the porch. And then they laughed like it was some huge joke. For all I know, they killed the cat themselves. I wouldn't put anything past them."

Adam found it hard to breathe. "That is disgusting." He leaned against the window frame.

"Suky still had her bright pink collar on and everything."

Suky? Adam pictured the heart-shaped name tag. They really were cruel.

"I knew it was my punishment, but it broke my heart. She was my only friend." Her voice cracked.

"Wait, punishment for what?"

Bella joined him over by the window. She held both his hands in hers. "I asked about my birth mother. The one and only time. I guess I was inquisitive because I'd found an envelope with my name on it, and another tiny envelope with a key inside. They were both together in my mom's desk. I didn't get to see the contents, although it was easy to feel the key. My parents were furious and forbade me to ever mention my birth mother again, which only piqued my interest further. I knew I had found something important."

"Wow." It sounded more like sick fiction than reality.

She exhaled. "They said she didn't want me and neither did they, but they were doing me a huge favor and I should be grateful, otherwise I would go to an orphanage."

What kind of monsters were the Robinsons? "Sounds like an orphanage would have been a kinder option."

"Tell me about it. I must be the only kid ever to fantasize about living in an orphanage."

Adam pulled her in for a hug and she stayed there for some time. He looked through the window onto the coastal town he loved so much. Welcoming, comfortable, cozy. No wonder Bella felt its charm. It offered everything she had missed as a child.

Even with the tragedy that cast a painful shadow over his own family, he had no comprehension of what it would be like to grow up unloved. What could he say? There was no way he could relate to the woman in his arms. To the abused little girl who'd longed to be loved. No wonder finding the cat collar had upset her last night. But what did it mean? He hated to open wounds, but he had to know what was going on. He had to protect her. And then he would spend the rest of his life loving her the way she deserved to be loved.

"I know this is painful for you, but do you think, since the details were so spot on with the collar, that this means your parents sent the awful box yesterday? And what did that note mean? Help me understand here. I know they're not dead—but I'm getting a clearer picture of why it was easier for you to consider them that way." He clenched his jaw. "How long has it been since you saw them last?"

"Years. Six years, to be exact. If they've found me after all this time, which is obviously the case, then I'm in serious trouble. Whether they're tormenting me or intend to confront me, it's not good. The question is what they would want from me now that I'm twenty-three, and how they're going to approach me. The reminder of my dead cat wasn't a promising start and it could escalate from there." She stared through the window. "I've seen a lot worse."

The hairs on Adam's neck stood to attention. What in the world was happening?

Bella's phone vibrated on the wooden kitchen table. "It may be Juliet." She picked it up, looking almost relieved at a change of focus. "Yes, it's a message from her." She gasped. "We need to go to our apartment right now."

"She didn't go in there alone, did she?" Was Juliet that stubborn?

Bella tapped a quick reply on her phone, and headed for the door. She looked up at him, her face grim. "There's only one way to find out."

"And I'm with you every step of the way." *Lord, help us.*

CHAPTER SEVEN

BELLA JUMPED OUT OF THE vehicle as soon as it came to a stop outside her apartment. She ran past Juliet's car to the end of the driveway, and embraced her friend in a hug. "What's wrong? You shouldn't have come here alone."

Juliet's green eyes were wide with fright and her wavy hair tangled about her face. She shivered in Bella's arms, even though the sun was now out in full force and there was no breeze at all.

Juliet started to speak and then stopped.

Adam joined them. "Are you okay? Have you been inside yet?"

She shook her head. "No, I didn't get that far." She pulled back from Bella. "I know I shouldn't have come, but I can be pigheaded at times. I was mad and frustrated and I wanted to be in my own place." She looked up at Adam. "Don't even think about lecturing me."

He put both hands in the air. "I wouldn't dare."

Bella looked toward the red front door and gasped. "What's that?"

"That's the issue. Looks like we've had another delivery. I was going to ignore it, but then I thought it might be important. And then I got scared and texted you."

"What is it this time?" Adam rushed past the girls and bent down at the door mat. "Well, it's not quite as sinister as last night. A white rose." He looked back and tilted his head. "Does one of you have a secret admirer?"

What? Bella hurried down the path to join him. She picked the rose from the cardboard box, careful to avoid the thorns, and stared at it. If only it had come with a message attached. What did this mean? She was receiving such mixed signals. How had life become so complicated?

"Umm, would you care to share?" Juliet waved a hand in front of Bella's face. "You look like you've either seen a ghost or won the lottery, I'm not sure which."

Bella shook her head to clear the jumble of thoughts. "Sorry, I spaced out there for a minute. I know this is crazy, but I'm confused myself. Can we go inside? I think I need to share something with you both." She caught Adam's eye and he gave a subtle nod. He was ready to hear whatever it was.

"Yes, if you think it's safe enough." Juliet had her keys out in a second. "Adam, you want to let your pal at the station know we're here in case they do a drive-by or something? I'd hate to cause a false alarm. I think the police have more to deal with than rats and roses—not to be insensitive, but I have no idea what's going on anymore."

"No, you're right. Although, he'd know it was us with our cars parked outside." Bella touched Adam's arm. "Could you fire him a text? Let's not mention the rose yet, just tell him we're in the apartment."

"Sure, I think that's smart. Give me two seconds." He typed on his phone and slid it back inside his pocket.

"Let's go." Juliet unlocked the red door. "We need to make sure nobody's been in our place. This is freakish.

Nothing like this ever happens in Florence." Her earlier upset was replaced by curiosity.

Bella's stomach lurched. She looked up at Adam as he took her hand and gave it a squeeze.

All three of them entered the shared foyer space and marched up the stairs to their second-floor apartment. "We should ask our neighbor downstairs if she's noticed anyone hanging around and looking suspicious. I hate to worry Mrs. Templeton, but imagine if she had found the box last night…"

Bella chewed on her lip. Sweet Gladys. Surely, she hadn't put the dear old lady in danger, too?

"I'll chat with her later," Adam called from behind. "I've know her for years and I can at least be subtle about making enquiries."

"Isn't he the perfect Prince Charming?" Juliet muttered under her breath.

Bella frowned. "What's wrong with you, Jules? He's trying to help."

"Nothing. Forget it. Don't mind me, I'm in a foul mood and I miss my own bed."

Juliet unlocked the door off the landing at the top of the stairs and they all spilled into the apartment. It was a light, airy space, modern and cozy at the same time. Juliet had said she'd been dying to live here since her mom's friend had moved out. When Bella came to town and they met up at church, they'd hit it off so well it seemed like the ideal opportunity to become roommates. Bella was thrilled with the cheap rent and it was the most beautiful place she had lived in for years. She shuddered at the memories. There had been some awful digs along the way.

But maybe this comfortable season was coming to an end? Maybe it was all too good to last? If it came to it, what would she leave behind?

"Everything seems to be normal, as far as I can tell." Adam peered into each room. "What do you think, girls? Anything look out of place to you?"

Bella wandered from room to room, but nothing appeared disheveled or tampered with. After the constant chatter and general hubbub at Pippa's place, the silence here was overwhelming. Her footsteps echoed on the old hardwood floors as they paced the area. Something had shifted, not physically, but their welcoming home had lost its sparkle overnight. A shiver crept up her spine, and she rubbed her arms at the sudden chill, still clasping the white rose.

"Does something feel off to you?" Juliet pulled up the blinds to let in extra light.

"What do you mean?" Adam stopped pacing.

"Just *off*. I don't know, maybe I'm overanxious and I need more sleep."

Bella nodded. "It doesn't feel like home anymore." The words shocked her. "I'm sorry, Juliet, I didn't mean that. It'll all be normal again in no time. We're a bit tender today, that's all. I can't see that anything's been touched here, though. And the door was locked and all the windows are fine. Right?"

Bella's white, old-fashioned bicycle leaned against the wall in the small hallway, exactly as she'd left it. Her bath towel lay on the tiled floor, but it could have fallen from the hook. It wouldn't be the first time. She winced and let out a short gasp as one of the rose thorns bit into her thumb. Blood oozed from the tiny hole and she looked away. Blood was not her thing.

"Careful." Adam took the rose from her and led her to the bathroom sink.

"I'm the nurse here." Juliet nudged him out of the bathroom and held Bella's thumb under a stream of cold water. "I think you'll live. I'll fetch a little bandage so you don't have to look at it."

Bella tapped her foot and turned away. "You have no idea how grateful I am to have a nurse for a roomie. You've saved my life so many times."

Juliet snorted. "Bel, I've patched you up after a few kitchen incidents with a knife. I'm not sure I've ever saved your life."

"Well, you've stopped me from fainting."

"All part of the training. I'm glad for the practical experience you give me. Now here, let's say bye-bye to the boo-boo, shall we?" Juliet wound a bandage around Bella's thumb and they all headed into the kitchen.

Nausea roiled in the pit of her stomach, but it wasn't only from the sight of blood. How was she going to explain this next part of her story without appearing like a delusional fool? She looked at the rose now lying on the glass kitchen table, and tried to collect her thoughts. Yes, she had to just say what was on her heart. It was going to be shocking but they needed to know.

She looked up to see Adam and Juliet were glaring at one another, arms crossed. What on earth?

"You two, what's going on? You both look like you want to punch each other's lights out."

Adam's face softened. "I'm sorry. It's my fault. Juliet's only being protective of you and that's kind of what I want to do, too."

"Not to mention your surprise proposal last night." Juliet's face reddened.

"What's surprising about that?" He held both hands in the air. "Forgive me for wanting to make Bella happy. But as I'm sure you were delighted to know, she didn't accept."

Bella blanched. Why was Juliet upset about the proposal? Was it plain old jealousy after all? This was not going well. "You guys, there's so much happening right now, I don't know what your issues are, but I want to get to the bottom of all this craziness and I need *both* of you to help me through it. Is that going to work? I mean, can you get along?"

Adam groaned. "I'm sorry. We're both here for you. And we'll put any weirdness aside so we can help any way we can. Right, Juliet?"

She nodded. "Absolutely. For Bella." Juliet gave Adam a quick, awkward side-hug, which he reciprocated.

Better. They even smiled. Or grimaced.

"That's more like it. Thank you. Now I want to go and dig something out of my bedroom to show you. I wasn't going to go into this much detail, but now with the rose and all, I feel as if I kind of have to." She touched Adam's cheek. His dark stubble was already evident and it wasn't even midday. "Could I ask a huge favor of you?"

"Anything, you know that."

"Would you mind telling Juliet the stuff I already shared with you this morning? About my childhood, I mean."

He flinched. "Yeah, I can do that."

Bella stared at her punctured thumb. "Are you sure? It's just that I've got to get my head around the next nugget of information before I change my mind." She sighed. "I'm sorry to drop all this garbage on you both."

"Hey, don't worry about us." Juliet walked over to the sink. "I've been tying myself in knots trying to imagine what you haven't been telling us. Take your time. I'll put the kettle on and make some tea."

"Thanks. I'll change and grab some of my things to take to your mom's." Bella glanced one more time at the white rose and her heart fluttered for a second. "I'd love some cinnamon apple tea, if we have any left." She turned and trudged to her bedroom, closing the door behind her. Listening to her boyfriend rehash the details of her dysfunctional childhood was more than she could endure.

Bella opened her closet and selected a few articles of clothing to last a day or two if necessary. Something for church. A couple of casual items. She threw them into her overnight bag and changed into her white jeans and a grey T-shirt. A book and a few toiletry items were stuffed down the side of the bag, and she was packed.

One more thing: she picked up her worn, leather Bible from the bedside table, its familiar smoothness an instant source of comfort. It fell open at the lighthouse bookmark, the one Juliet bought her last month. John 8:32 was highlighted in luminous yellow: "Then you will know the truth, and the truth will set you free." That was her ultimate dream. She claimed it as her life verse. Freedom was in Jesus, and she was so grateful to have found that—it had transformed her life forever.

But somehow her past... it plagued her still, the unanswered questions, the desperate desire to discover the truth, no matter how painful the journey and outcome. She placed the Bible on top of her other belongings and zipped up the bag.

With a fresh infusion of determination, Bella knelt on the sheepskin rug next to her bed and slid a shoebox from underneath. She sat back on her heels and reverently lifted the lid, inhaling the musty odor, not dissimilar to The Book Nook. This one little box had been with her for as long as she could remember. Like an old friend. The vague recollection of black patent shoes clawed its way into her memory.

Yes, this was her actual shoebox at one time. Susannah Robinson had been somewhat obsessed with having proper shoes—she would bring a pair home and insist Bella wear them, even if they didn't fit properly. Most likely why she loved flip-flops and simple sandals now.

Focus. Her entire history was right here in her hands. This was huge. Adam and Juliet were trustworthy, no question about that. But should she draw them into her complex web? Did they want to get involved? Adam did. That much was obvious. But Juliet could walk out of here now and accept Bella had a lousy childhood, end of story. The rat-in-a-box incident would remain a mystery, Bella would move on to yet another town, and Juliet would live her wonderful nurse life. They could part friends.

But no, Juliet wouldn't walk away. She was a hothead sometimes, but she was also tenderhearted, a caregiver, and fiercely protective. After Adam explained her story, she would be like a dog with a bone and would have a thousand questions. This was going to be rough.

Bella stood and set the lid on the cornflower-blue bedcover, tucked the little box under her arm, and took a deep breath.

Here goes nothing.

"I'm sorry—I had no idea." Juliet's mascara streaked down her face. She stood and embraced Bella until she had trouble breathing. "How did you manage to survive such dreadful stuff as a kid? I can't even imagine."

"You shouldn't have to either. Your mom is the complete opposite."

"Goodness, yes. No wonder you think she walks on water." She pulled Bella down onto a kitchen chair, next to Adam, and then sank down opposite them. "But we're still confused about the whole rat and cat collar thing from last night. It's disgusting and it's cruel, but why not just follow you and confront you if they have something to say? I realize they're sick and twisted, but why the drama? I mean, why would they even be looking for you if you haven't seen them in so long? You're not a child anymore."

Bella set the open box on the table and reached for Adam's hand. She soaked in his supportive gaze for a moment, and then looked across the table to Juliet. "I'll try to explain as best I can, but there are some things even I don't understand. You know how much I love you both, and I'm sorry I lied about my parents. It's ironic that all I want to do is find out the truth from my past, but in the process, I've not been truthful with you. Maybe I've been protecting you or protecting myself, but it was wrong. I don't know what I was thinking, imagining I could have a regular life here. I guess I got caught up in the beauty of the place and I felt so at home.

And then I went and fell in love." She looked down at her hand in Adam's.

He brought Bella's fingers to his lips and kissed them. "Sorry about that."

Juliet groaned and threw her hands in the air. "But the cat collar?"

"I know. It caught me off guard. I haven't had any contact with my parents in over six years. And if I had my way, I would never have to see them again."

Adam whistled. "That's crazy. I can't imagine you having to leave home at seventeen."

"Yeah. I ran away. I had to."

Adam squeezed her fingers. "I know. I get it."

Juliet gasped. "You mean you've been like, on the run for *six years*?"

"A game of cat and mouse, right?" Adam whispered.

Bella's stomach dropped. "And now they've caught up with me. The dead rat was a clear message." *I could be next.* She shifted on the chair. "I'm not going to lie, it's been exhausting. But I felt like I had no choice. I was basically a prisoner in my own home up until that point. We moved around every couple of years anyway, so I was used to not having roots or a family to speak of." That's why Adam's family seemed idyllic. *And the notion of raising children in a place like Florence is beyond my wildest dreams...*

"But what about schools and friends?" Juliet leaned across the table. "Couldn't any of your teachers help you with your home life?"

I wish I'd had the chance to seek help. Someone may have stepped in. "I was home schooled. I did online courses and Susannah was incredibly bright."

"She didn't work outside the home?" Adam's forehead wrinkled. "You were together all the time?"

"Pretty much. She was an artist so she painted from home. Sold her pieces privately. She was talented, for sure. And disappointed that I preferred writing over painting. George did something with finances and stocks—I never understood what. Looking back, I suspect a lot of it was illegal, and I knew he had a gambling problem. I'd hear them fight about it sometimes."

The kettle whistled and Juliet's chair scraped on the tiled floor as she stood. "I forgot about the tea." She stepped into the kitchen area and leaned over the breakfast bar. "So, were you rich if he was in finance?"

Bella took a strand of hair and twirled it between her fingers. "Not in the beginning. I remember the early years being lean. I recall being hungry often. But I suppose things went well in his financial circles, because by the time I was a teen, they were quite flippant with money. We never owned a home though since we moved about so much."

"They were really something." Adam rubbed his chin. "Why do you suppose they even adopted if they claimed not to want you?"

Bella dropped her head back and closed her eyes. "That's the strange thing. I think in the beginning they did want a baby. I don't have any strong recollections of my toddler years, but I know from the sparse collection of photographs Susannah kept in her dressing table drawer that we at least looked like a proper family at the start. There were shots of the three of us smiling and snuggled up together at a beach. There was one in particular of Susannah and I laughing in front of a lighthouse."

"Is that why you have such a love of lighthouses, do you think?" Juliet poured boiling water into three mugs.

"Maybe." Yes, lighthouses had always felt like home. "I can't help but believe we had some pleasant memories at the coast when I was tiny. But something changed, and in time, I became a burden neither of them wanted to carry. That was clear. The older I got, the more they detested my existence."

Adam set his jaw. "That had to hurt. I'm guessing you had no siblings?"

"No, it was just me." Bella fiddled with the lighthouse pendant of her necklace. "A brother or sister would have been nice, but I wouldn't have wanted anyone else to go through some of the stuff I endured. Trust me, you don't want to know the rest. And I was never allowed to have friends over. I would barely get to know a neighbor and then we would leave. It was my normal."

He squeezed her hand. "Is that where your love of books comes in?"

She grinned. This man got her. He knew her heart and the thought of losing him was unbearable. "Absolutely. I lost myself in books all the time. I could be free and happy and have birthday parties and visit anywhere I wanted in a book."

Juliet returned to the table. "Tea is steeping." She sank back into the chair. "This is heartbreaking—no child should ever have to put up with that kind of abuse and neglect. But what made you run away? That was gutsy."

It was time. Bella let go of Adam's hand, reached into the box, and retrieved a yellowed envelope. "I knew George and Susannah were up to something. The last year I was with them, they were super jumpy, and I had an ominous feeling something was brewing. I was done being fearful all the time and I decided something had to change. Somehow, in that time I grew from being weak to being strong with a fierce urgency for independence. I began waking in the early hours when they were fast asleep so I could look in their files and paperwork. It was risky, but I hit the jackpot." Her breath caught in her throat. "I found this again." She held up the envelope.

"What is it? It looks old." Juliet peered closer.

"It's a letter. Something I had come across when I was younger." Bella turned it over and over in her trembling fingers and shared a sad smile with Adam. The pain in his eyes said everything—he remembered her cat story.

Juliet tried to read the name on the envelope. "Who's it from?"

Bella took a deep breath.

"My birth mother."

CHAPTER EIGHT

"I THOUGHT YOU DIDN'T KNOW who your birth mother was?" Adam's head was beginning to ache. *Focus.* The envelope contained something crucial. He had to take in every shred of information if he had any hope of figuring this nightmare out.

Bella stared at the sheet of paper in her hand. "I don't know her."

What?

Juliet stood. "But you have a letter from her? Keep talking while I dump the teabags." She hurried to the breakfast bar.

Bella slid the letter out of the envelope. "This precious letter is addressed 'To whomever chooses to love my Bella…'" Her eyes brimmed with tears.

Juliet snorted. "And it ended up with your crazy adoptive parents?"

"I know. In a way, it makes me feel better. My mother didn't know George and Susannah or what they were like. And I think maybe they were even kind at the start. She must have presumed they would be desperate to love a child and would give me a happy home."

This was hard to stomach. Picturing Bella as an innocent baby being placed into the hands of monsters was almost too much to handle. Adam sighed. "If only she'd known. What's in the letter? Can you tell us?"

She lifted her chin. "Yes. I'm hoping it'll help you understand my dilemma, and explain why I had to make plans to run away once I read it." She opened the letter and read aloud.

Please help my baby.

I cannot keep her — it's too dangerous.

If my father or her father ever find her, she will be running forever, like me.

There will be a sizeable reward for your loving care when she turns eighteen. Legal documents have been secured with the bank to that end.

She is from a family of affluence, but they must not know of her existence.

Would you keep her safe and love her for me, please?

I will be watching from afar.

"And it's signed *Rose*."

Adam's eyes dropped to the flower on the table. Coincidence?

"Wow." Juliet set glass mugs of fragrant tea in front of Bella and Adam and then grabbed one for herself. "That's so — beautiful and mysterious. You have no idea who she is, this Rose? Your parents never gave any hints? I would be beside myself with curiosity if it were me."

"Trust me, they were tight-lipped about it all. I was slapped hard when I asked about their family, so it was no surprise they took it to another level when I asked about my birth mother."

Adam grimaced.

"But Rose consumed my thoughts for years, and I caught George and Susannah talking about her a few times when they presumed I was asleep. Little snippets. But I know they were biding their time until I turned eighteen. I was scared what they would do with me after they claimed the inheritance or reward or whatever it is."

No wonder she ran away. And sending a dead rat made their intentions crystal clear. Adam blew on his tea and pulled his thoughts back to their current motive. "So, it's all about money. Like you said, maybe at first they were doting adoptive parents who planned on loving you, but the incentive of the money messed with their heads."

Juliet leaned back in her chair. "Wow. This has the makings of a movie. Stuff like this doesn't happen in real life."

Adam scowled at her. "At least it shouldn't. But it did." He took a calming breath and turned to Bella. "Do you have any clue where to even look for your birth mother? I mean, do you know where you were born?"

Bella set the letter on the table. "Not really. From what they said in private, I got the impression she was originally from California. I know my parents lived along the Oregon Coast for many years—I have some fuzzy memories before we moved inland and ended up in Seattle. I'm not sure where we lived exactly when I was a child, but I remember the lighthouses and how they made me feel safe just looking at them. I loved what they stood for and thought of them as my own beacon of hope, I suppose." She fiddled with her pendant necklace.

"And that's why you always wear the silver lighthouse around your neck." Juliet smiled.

Of course. Had he ever seen her without that pendant? She wore it every single day.

"I guess so. When I finally ran away from home, I made my way to the coast. I was independent but always fearful my parents would track me down. I found my first lighthouse and decided to stay in the little town nearby. I faked my way into getting a casual job at a church."

"You did?" Impressive. *Sounds like the Bella I know and love.* "You must have been scared though, being on your own for the first time."

Bella nodded and stared past him through the kitchen window. Were the memories too painful to recall, or was it a whirlwind of excitement and adventure?

"It was bleak in the beginning. But even then, God was working in my life. I see that now. An elderly pastor and his wife took me under their wings. They knew I was in some sort of trouble with my family, but I convinced them I was eighteen and fine on my own. They introduced me to God, and gave me a little Bible. I was confused and anxious, but I would take that Bible up to the lighthouse and read it for hours."

"How long did you stay there?" Juliet nibbled a fingernail, transfixed with all the new information.

"About six months altogether. They loved on me, let me earn some cash, and even bought me this lighthouse necklace. And then when I told them I had to move on, they promised to pray for me every day. They were instrumental in my journey to find God."

The power of prayer. *Heavenly Father, thank You for revealing Yourself to Bella in this way.* Adam stretched an arm around her shoulders. "That's awesome. Did you stay in contact with them?"

Bella's eyes brimmed. "No. I couldn't chance that. I would be putting them in danger. But I hope they trusted I was safe in God's hands and were content in that knowledge."

"No wonder the necklace is special to you." Juliet cupped her hands around the steaming tea. "I thought it was a weird obsession—you spend so much time at Cape Cove and a bunch of the other lighthouses. Now it all makes sense."

"Yeah, the lighthouse is where I do my best thinking. And writing. Not to mention the amazing workout I get from cycling there. I know it sounds weird, but it does make me feel safe and grounded."

"It makes perfect sense." It was where she gravitated. His stomach dropped. *I hope I haven't ruined it for her after my proposal last night.*

Bella picked up her mug. "Smells like fall. Thanks, Juliet."

Adam inhaled the fragrant mixture of apples and cinnamon from his own drink. Delicious.

"You're welcome." Juliet slipped off her cardigan and draped it on the back of her chair. "But going back to the letter, what do you think Rose meant by watching you from afar? Do you think she's been keeping tabs on you all this time?"

"How could she?" Adam squinted at Juliet. What was she thinking?

Bella took a sip of tea. "When I was young, I wished someone would come and rescue me. I didn't know any details about my birth family, but anyone had to be better than my life with George and Susannah..."

Adam pulled her in closer to him. He longed to protect her with every bone in his body—if he couldn't help her before, he would do so now. He glanced up to see Juliet glaring at him. What was her problem?

"As I got older, I imagined my real family a lot, and dreamed about my mom or dad saving me from such a horrible life. After I read the letter and was able to give her a name, I wanted Rose in my life more than anything else in the world, but I was scared for her, too. And then after I ran away from home in Seattle, I always had this sense of her watching over me." She put one hand in the air. "Nothing freaky or anything. But I wasn't afraid anymore. I got as far from Seattle as I could on my limited resources, and made my way down the Oregon Coast. It felt like coming home, which, in a way, was probably right."

Juliet peeked into the shoe box. "What else do you have in here?"

Adam watched as Bella emptied the contents onto the table. "Sentimental stuff mainly. A diary I made when I was ten years old, a bookmark a kind librarian once gave me, a bunch of lighthouse postcards I collected when I was little." She shuffled the items around and smiled. "Silly treasures I've collected and carried around all these years."

76

Adam scanned the shoebox's contents. He could learn a lot about this woman he loved from this eclectic mix of paraphernalia.

Juliet picked up a small plastic bag. "Okay, but what's with the rose petals in here?"

Bella took the bag from her and held it up for them all to see. "My birth mother's name is Rose, as you now know. Once I lived on my own, I began randomly finding white roses. At first, I was creeped out. I thought maybe it was a secret admirer or something, but I couldn't imagine who it might be. And no guy ever materialized.

"And then... I found the roses comforting, somehow. One would be on the handlebars of my bicycle after work or propped inside my mailbox. Sometimes it was after I had been at a lighthouse and felt sad—they were always timely." She put down the bag and lifted the white rose to her face. She inhaled and closed her eyes. "It must be six months since I received my last one."

Curious. Adam folded his arms. "Why not make herself known to you, if it is Rose? Why not come into the open and make contact? Especially once you turned eighteen."

"Because she wanted to be Bella's guardian angel, right?" Juliet's eyes were the size of saucers.

Adam bit his tongue. Best not to make any snide comment.

"I can't believe I've been your roommate for a year and was oblivious to all this. How self-centered am I?" Juliet's face was flushed. Her frustration was nothing compared to Adam's.

He took the rose from Bella and studied it. *Lord, I know I prayed that I would do anything to have this woman in my life, and*

I meant it. Show me? Please? "I wish you could have trusted me with all this. But I get it. I see you were trying to protect yourself and all of us. But now? You need to let us help. Do you think your birth mom's here? I mean with the rose on the doorstep and all?"

"Oh, my word." Juliet's hands flew to her face. "If she's here in Florence, she may be warning you about your adoptive parents." She gasped. "You may even get to meet her at last."

Adam pursed his lips. "If so, she's a bit late with the warning. I think the note with the dead rat and cat's collar gave that message." But could Rose be in Florence? "What do you think? She could be here, couldn't she?"

Bella's eyes leaked tears down her cheeks. "It would be a dream come true. I've imagined meeting her so many times. But I can't get my hopes up yet. Just in case."

"Who else would it be?" Adam had to blink to keep his own tears at bay. "This could be amazing."

Bella exhaled. "I don't know what to think. I have to keep a level head and remember I'm being followed, or at least sent a message. A bad one." She gulped. "They might have been following me for a while, so there's the possibility they know about my roses. I can't rule that out."

Juliet looked directly at Adam. "They could have been following all of us. I feel like we're in this thing together, like it or not."

And who knew how dangerous it could get? Adam ran a hand through his hair. "Juliet, do you have anywhere you could go and stay for a while? Any family or friends in another town? Maybe a vacation?"

She stood and the chair clattered to the floor. "Are you kidding me? No, I can't take off and disappear, I just came back from a week in Seattle and I *do* have a job at the hospital. They sort of need nurses sometimes, you know. Good grief, we don't all have the money to take a random vacation. Besides, Bella is my friend and I want to help. Why don't *you* take off somewhere?"

Simmer down, hothead. "I was trying to look out for you..."

"Whoa." Bella picked up the chair and settled Juliet back into it. "Nobody has to do anything they don't want to. I hate that I've made your lives unsafe and I hate that I've turned you against each other—I never wanted any of this to happen."

Juliet's jaw was fixed. "I'm fine. I guess I don't like being told to go away. Okay, Adam?"

An awkward silence filled the kitchen.

Adam folded his arms across his chest. "I'm sorry. I'm trying to protect you and your mom." His downcast eyes fixed on the shoe box. There was something still in the bottom, another envelope, this one tiny. He picked it up and dropped it in Bella's hand. "What's in this?"

She turned the envelope upside-down and a key slid into her hand. Her face broke into a sad smile.

"A safe deposit box key?" Adam took it from her and turned it over.

Juliet squinted across the table. "How do you know it's for a safe deposit box?"

He shrugged. "My parents have one. And there's a serial number engraved on it. This looks pretty old—do you have any idea where the box is?"

"No clue. But I think this could be what they're after. George and Susannah, I mean. I believe this holds the apparent fortune they feel entitled to."

Adam tapped his chin. *Think.* "But the legal document Rose mentioned in her letter would most likely require them to be in possession of the key. Which is why they need you. They know you have the letter and the key, and they can't get their money without those items."

"Exactly. That's why I changed my name and haven't stayed in the same town for more than a year up until now. I hoped they would give it up. Move on and forget about me. Maybe even go back to England. But now with last night's box, I have to think the worst."

Juliet groaned. "They've found you."

Adam let out the breath he had been holding. He pressed the key into the palm of her hand and shook his head. "You have to let the police in on this. At least let me speak with my friend there and see if he can get you some security or something. Do you think George and Susannah are still capable of causing serious physical harm? How far do you think they would go now that you're an adult?"

Bella hugged herself. "I wouldn't put anything past them. They didn't like to get their hands dirty. But they knew people." She glanced at Adam. "This could be worse than we imagined."

A loud knock on the door caused Adam to jump.

"Who could it be?" Juliet held her phone, as if ready to call 911. "And how did they get in through the front door?"

"I can't imagine an axe murderer would knock first." Adam smirked.

Juliet grunted. "Whatever. Let's pack these things away."

While Juliet stuffed the items back in the shoebox, Adam took hold of Bella's shoulders and looked into her eyes. "You need to have that key with you at all times. They may search your apartment now they know where you are."

"Good idea." Bella grabbed the letter and folded it into her jeans pocket along with the key. "I'll thread it onto my necklace later."

Another rap on the door made Bella's whole body tense. The girl was petrified.

"You're going to be fine. You're not doing this alone anymore." Adam planted a kiss on her forehead. "I promise."

CHAPTER NINE

BELLA HELD HER BREATH. SHE watched as Adam looked through the peephole of their front door, while Juliet clasped her hand. They both froze in place.

"Don't worry girls, it's my buddy from the police station."

She exhaled and smiled at Juliet. "Thank goodness."

Adam opened the door and stood back. "Hey bud, nice of you to drop by—although a phone call would have sufficed. Come on in."

A guy with spiked blond hair stood in the doorway. He was built like a tank—a sporty tank. *Not quite what I expected.* Bella smirked. While the man wasn't in uniform—a white T-shirt stretched over his muscular frame—it didn't take much imagination to envision how intimidating he would appear as a police officer. *Nice to have him on our side, at least.*

"Sorry to stop by unannounced. Mrs. Templeton downstairs let me in when she saw my car pull up outside. I got your text as I finished my shift and wanted to make sure everything was okay before I head home for some shut-eye." He poked his head around Adam's slim frame and grinned at the girls. "Hello."

"Max?" Juliet's hands flew to her face. "When did you move back to Florence?"

"Hey, Juliet. I got here last month." Max dug his hands deep into his pockets.

What was happening here?

"Really? I was just in Seattle the past week or so." Juliet's cheeks were pink. "Madison and Luke got married. My friend from church in Seattle—do you remember meeting her? Must have been a year ago last summer."

Bella glanced at Adam. Was all this talk of marriage pouring salt on his wounds from last night?

"Yes, I remember her. That's fantastic news." Max grinned. "You look great."

"Thanks. But I'm a mess—you haven't caught me on my best day."

Bella raised a brow. Was Juliet blushing?

Adam closed the door and ushered Max further into the apartment. "It's about time you officially met my... girlfriend. Max, this is Bella King."

Bella's heart sank. Adam would have been introducing her as his fiancée if last night had gone as he planned. She stepped forward. "Hi." Her petite hand was enveloped in his meaty one and she tried to hide a slight grimace at his firm grip. "I'm surprised I haven't met you yet. I thought I knew everyone in Florence by now."

"It's nice to meet you. I wish it were under better circumstances. And it's my bad that I've been slow in meeting back up with friends. It's an adjustment, moving back."

Adam slapped his shoulder. "It sounds like you and Juliet have reconnected since high school, though. What am I missing here?"

Juliet leaned against the wall. "We happened to bump into each other, what eighteen months ago?"

Max nodded.

"In Seattle?" Adam put a protective arm around Bella's shoulders. Did he think the mention of Seattle would bring back horrific memories? She leaned against him.

"Yeah, when I was doing my nursing stint there. Max came into the hospital on some case, and we recognized each other straight away from the old days."

"Couldn't miss that long red hair, even tied back in a ponytail." Max grinned. Yeah, he liked her alright.

"Anyway, we had coffee, I took him to the church I attended…"

"And that's when you introduced me to Madison. I think we had brunch at her amazing house."

Juliet chuckled. "That's right. But then, between our shifts, we never got to see each other again, did we?"

"No. Unfortunately. Then I heard you'd moved back here to be with your mom. How's she doing, by the way?"

"Good, thank you. Cancer is in remission, and she's her usual self. So much so that I got this place with Bella. But how come you're back in Florence?"

"Honestly, I burned out. A small town and some ocean air seemed like a great idea when the opportunity for a transfer came along."

Juliet flashed a smile. "I think you'll find it's a good deal quieter here than Seattle on the crime front." She glanced at Bella. "Well, it was until yesterday."

Bella reached up to touch her lighthouse pendant. So much to process. The proposal. The threat. The white rose. It was all too much.

"Let's sit, shall we?" Juliet led the way into the living room.

Adam joined Bella on one loveseat, leaving the other one free for Max and Juliet. Juliet curled up on one side and Max balanced on the opposite arm. Adam gave Bella a subtle wink. She would have to grill him later on what he knew about this relationship.

Max cleared his throat. "What can you tell me about the package last night? Any idea who might have sent it? Adam was brief with his explanation."

Bella's mouth was bone dry. No, she couldn't do this again. A wave of exhaustion and queasiness came over her. "I'm sorry. I know you've come here to gather information and I appreciate it. But I can't do this right now. You'll have to forgive me." She stood and gave Adam a pleading look. "I'm going to stash my box, but then I think I need some fresh air."

Adam helped her up. "You are looking pale. I think that might be best."

Bella disappeared into her bedroom with the shoebox while Adam covered for her. She caught sight of herself in her dressing table mirror. Not great. Her face was white and her eyes were vacant. Not enough sleep and too many tears. She smoothed her hair, grabbed a denim jacket, and picked up the overnight bag from the floor.

"But we need to go and chat with Mrs. Templeton downstairs, if Bella's up to it." She caught the end of Adam's conversation as he hovered by the door. "Juliet, do you mind getting Max up to speed on the basics and we'll catch you later?"

"No problem." She jumped up from the loveseat and put an arm around Bella's waist. "You going to be okay?"

"I'll be fine. Some ocean air is all I need." She bit her lip. "But I told Pippa I'd work later this afternoon."

Juliet gave her a light squeeze. "Forget about it. I'm taking your shift. I want to chat with Mom anyway. She's dying to know everything about Madison's wedding."

Bella sighed with relief. Her mind wasn't going to cooperate in work mode today. "Thanks. I owe you one."

"It was nice meeting you." Max joined them by the door. "I want to help in any way I can, but I understand you want to keep the details quiet for now. I had a word with the sarge, and he's happy for me to monitor everything and fill him in as needed. You good with that?"

"I appreciate it. Thanks. We'll leave you in Juliet's capable hands." She winked at her friend and turned to Adam. "Ready?"

Adam took Bella's overnight bag from her and guided her out of the apartment. They left Juliet to play hostess.

"I think we may have found a good match there, Cupid." Bella squeezed Adam's hand on their way down the stairs. It was nice to have a distraction, even for a little while.

"I hope so."

"Why do you say that?"

"No reason. Max is a nice guy, that's all." He stopped outside Mrs. Templeton's front door and knocked. "This won't take long. I don't want to alarm her, but it makes sense to see if she's noticed anything suspicious outside."

"I agree." Bella looked into the eyes of the man she trusted more than anyone else in the world. "I'll let you do the talking."

"I've got you." Adam put his arm around her shoulder, and she felt her body relax. If only he could protect her like this forever.

***

Thirty minutes later, Adam pulled his jeep into their usual parking spot at Cape Cove Beach. The brief visit with Mrs. Templeton downstairs hadn't been fruitful in any regard, and since that conversation, Bella hadn't uttered a word. He turned off the engine and looked over at her. She was miles away.

"Want to go for a walk?" Adam reached out and pulled a strand of hair away from her face. She wasn't crying yet, but her jaw worked furiously as she tried to maintain control.

"To the lighthouse?" She clasped the delicate pendant around her neck and smiled with some effort.

"Sure. The fresh air will do us both good. I know we didn't have the best time here last night, but it is your favorite thinking spot." *As long as I didn't ruin it for you.* Adam grabbed a hoodie from the backseat and jumped out. By the time he reached the passenger side, Bella was already out and walking toward the pathway leading up to the lighthouse. He pulled the hoodie over his head, caught up in a few strides, and took her hand in his own.

"Thanks."

"For what?" He waited for her to answer.

Silence filled the air between them for a full minute, accentuated by the constant barrage of waves crashing against rocks down below. The afternoon sun was warm as a light breeze rippled the foliage on either side of the path.

"Thanks for understanding, even though I don't understand most of this myself. I haven't been fair to you, and I get it if you need some space for a while."

Adam held his breath and took a moment to compose himself. Surely, she knew by now he wasn't going anywhere. "I don't need space from you. Not at all. I want to be here for you. Now more than ever. I know you're a strong, independent, ravishingly beautiful woman…" He winked and she rewarded him with a smile. "But here's the thing. I want to protect you from whomever is causing you to run, and help you heal from whatever pain you're dealing with." *And then I want to marry you and build a lighthouse home for us to live in for the rest of our lives.*

She nodded and smiled as they passed an older couple hiking down from a trail. "Can I ask you something?"

"Anything."

"Don't you have *any* skeletons at all in your closet?"

His heart skipped a beat. "What do you mean?"

"It's just that your family seems perfect and you had an ideal childhood and your future is all figured out—don't you have any baggage? Is it even possible to be as squeaky clean as the Lexington clan?" She raised a brow. "Last night when I unloaded on you, it sounded like you had something of your own to share."

Adam forced himself to take a breath. The tang of ocean air revived him. He could tell her now. He *should* tell her now. It was an ideal opportunity—nobody would interrupt and she would be in her happy place, at the lighthouse.

"Are you alright?" She stopped walking and reached a hand up to touch his cheek. The electric current was instantaneous. She had this effect on him right from the start and didn't seem to even notice. "You're bunching up your eyebrows and that usually means there's a problem." She pulled her hand away and he could think again.

Should he say it now? Or was there too much going on? She didn't need another issue to deal with. Not today. There would be plenty of time later on to discuss everything. They had to focus on her safety and the mystery surrounding her birth mother first.

He rubbed his forehead. "I'm worried about you, that's all. But for the record, my family and I are far from perfect. And I'm sure you've already caught onto some of my imperfections."

She grinned and resumed her power walk up the path. "Like your horrendously sluggish walking pace?"

Phew. Dodged a bullet. For now. "Yeah, like that."

Once on the bluff, they sat on the bench right next to the lighthouse for ten minutes or so. Bella was quiet. Adam draped his arm around her and they sat side by side, pensive, each lost in thought. He sensed her breathing next to him, felt her sigh from time to time. Should he share his secret after all? Or would it send her running? No, he couldn't chance her leaving alone. None of them knew for sure how much danger she was in.

He was distracted when a young family passed by, out for an afternoon stroll. The toddler raced around the grassy patch in front of the bench, her chubby arms outstretched like an airplane. Her pretty pink dress rustled in the breeze as she enjoyed a lighthearted moment of fun. Guilt stabbed Adam like a dagger in his gut. *Please God, not now.*

He recalled his breathing exercises and implemented them as subtly as possible. He tried to remember perfect, carefree moments from his own childhood, but everything was clouded by cruel, vivid memories. The hospital. Hysterics. Heartache.

A pair of seagulls took off in tandem from a nearby post, carefree and light as air. Gazing out at the open ocean glistening grey-blue in the hazy sunlight, Adam wished he could pick up Bella right now and fly away somewhere safe. The two of them. Forget about all the baggage, all the worries.

Bella chuckled as the blonde little girl wove between her parents on their way toward the path and made dubious airplane sounds blowing air between her lips. Bella would make a wonderful mommy. Perhaps not experiencing the love of a mother herself would make her an even better one. Adam swallowed down his insecurities. He couldn't fall apart now, not when she needed him to be strong.

"This is perfect." She pulled her denim jacket tighter around her trim waist. "Sitting and thinking. Praying. I needed this space—thank you for bringing me here."

"I've been praying, too. There's a lot to take in."

"I still don't know where to begin or how much to dig up. But I guess we should go." A gust of wind whipped her hair about her shoulders. "It's getting chilly, and we're the last ones up here. Plus, my stomach's growling."

He laughed at the sudden change in conversation. "That's one of the things I love about you. You're a food girl."

An appetite after everything that had happened? This was a good sign.

Bella stood and put a hand on one hip. "Thanks. I think."

"I meant it as a compliment, trust me. It's awesome that you're a foodie. You appreciate the time and effort it takes to create a good meal."

"I get a kick out of being your sous-chef—at least, when you're not being bossy. What are you going to make for me tonight?"

"If you want to come back to my apartment, I have ingredients ready to go. We can grill honey-glazed salmon, roast some Italian potatoes, and you can wow me with a blueberry Arugula salad."

"With walnuts?"

The only nut he hated. Adam was about to come back with a witty, defensive comment but Bella froze, her eyes almost bugging out of her head.

"What?" Adam jumped up and surveyed the area surrounding their bench. Something had freaked her out.

"Someone just called my name," she whispered.

"I didn't hear anything. It's windy up here—are you sure?"

She nodded, her shoulders were bunched up around her neck and her face was drained of color.

Adam took her hand and began marching. It was deserted, but he wasn't about to take any chances now that he knew about George and Susannah. Surely, they wouldn't show up here? Although, if they had been following Bella, they would know this was her special place. How dare they invade her life now?

"It's probably nothing, but let's get back to the jeep and head home." He attempted to keep his voice light, but he scanned the bushes on either side as they hurried down the path.

"Can we run? I've got a bad feeling about this." Her voice had risen in pitch.

"Sure, but let's watch for any loose gravel going downhill. Flip-flops aren't the best for running, so hold tight."

Their feet slapped the ground in unison as Adam kept his strides shorter. Why was the place desolate all of a sudden? A quick look over the cliff confirmed they were alone. The drop in temperature had sent everyone home in a hurry, including the young family from the lighthouse. He spotted a couple of vehicles in the parking lot up ahead, but no people. Maybe the owners were still on a hiking trail in the area.

"You hanging in there?" He tilted his head to make eye contact.

She nodded, her ashen face wet with tears. Nails bit into his flesh as she clung to his hand. This was not like the Bella he knew. She was the most courageous woman he had ever met—nothing fazed her. Until now. But who could blame her?

She was crumbling before his eyes, and there was a huge possibility her natural instincts could kick in again soon.

Bella might run.

CHAPTER TEN

THE BOOK NOOK HAD NEVER smelled so enticing. The bell jingled above the door and Bella breathed in the comforting scents of furniture polish and ancient books. Grounding. Familiar. Safe. She dragged Adam further into the bookstore.

Juliet appeared from behind a bookcase. "You're back." She dumped a stack of picture books on the desk and walked over. "What is it? You look like you've seen a ghost."

"More like heard one." Adam set the overnight bag on the floor and put a protective arm around Bella's shoulders. "She got spooked up at the lighthouse."

"And then some maniac in a red car tried to run us off the road." Bella's heart still hammered in her chest. "Maybe it was a coincidence, like you said, Adam, or maybe I'm in some serious trouble here." She looked at her best friend and then her boyfriend. "Which means you could both be in danger." Adam's arm tightened around her.

Juliet bit her lip. "Mom, too."

"Where is Pippa?" Adam craned his neck around the tiny store.

"She's upstairs making a start on dinner. Shrimp linguini sound good?"

Bella's stomach grumbled. "My insides are in knots but that does sound divine. We ditched the idea of going back to Adam's to make salmon. I needed to be here with all of you."

Juliet walked over and pulled her friend into a hug. "It's going to be okay. Those wretched deliveries on our doorstep have upset you. So if you feel safer here, then this is where we'll all hang out for tonight."

"Sure we're not intruding?" Adam looked toward the stairs.

Juliet put one hand on her hip. "You know my mom loves you both. She's worried about Bella and would be more than happy to have your assistance with dinner, Adam."

His face brightened. "You think she needs a hand? You know I can't resist the call of the kitchen."

Juliet shook her head. "You are the strangest guy I've ever met. Go knock yourself out. Mom will be thrilled. I'll lock up here. We'll be fine."

Adam chuckled and turned to Bella. "Coming up? You might feel safer."

Bella pursed her lips as her eyes darted around the bookstore. She needed to feel in control again. "I'll be up in a minute. I want to chat with Juliet first. You go ahead and put the kettle on if you feel so led." She grinned. Tea always helped.

"If you're sure." He checked his watch. "I guess it's closing time anyway."

"I'm all over it." Juliet saluted.

"In that case, the kitchen calls. I'll take your bag up with me."

Bella watched him disappear up the narrow staircase, and sighed. "He's too good for me."

"Nonsense. I'll close up and you come and sit behind the desk with me for a minute. Catch your breath before Mom gives you the third degree." Juliet flipped the "OPEN" sign to "CLOSED," double-checked the bolts on the door, and steered Bella by the shoulders to the wooden chairs behind the desk. "Now, tell me what happened to get you this shaken up. You look worse than you did last night after getting that box."

Bella shrugged out of her jacket and held it close to her chest. "I'm sure it was nothing."

"Doesn't look like 'nothing' from here." Juliet began packing picture books into mailing envelopes.

"There was an idiot in a red car who almost ran us into the side of the road, but that may have just been someone in too much of a hurry. What really rattled me happened up at the lighthouse. I think maybe someone was watching us." A shiver shook through her body. She couldn't place the voice but it wasn't her imagination. "He said my name."

Juliet sat bolt upright in her chair. "Who did?"

"That's the thing—I don't know. A man's voice for sure. It was a little louder than a whisper, and I know it wasn't the wind."

"Did Adam hear it?"

Bella's shoulders slumped. "No. He must think I'm crazy." Yet he had been keen to get out of there. Had he felt the air change, too? "Poor guy had no idea what he was getting himself into when he started a relationship with me."

"In all fairness, you seemed like a regular girl who loved books and lighthouses up until yesterday."

"Juliet." She placed her hands on her hips.

"It's true. He thought he had the perfect catch—a gorgeous, blonde, slightly feisty bookworm. No wonder he proposed."

Bella groaned. "Do you think he's having second thoughts now?"

Juliet reached over and squeezed her arm. "What do you think? He's besotted. Besides, I've told you before, Adam's not perfect."

A few seconds of awkward silence caused Bella to bristle. Something was fishy and she needed to find out what the issue was. She squared her shoulders. "What is it about Adam that bugs you? You weren't happy when I told you he proposed and now there's an underlying tension between you guys."

Juliet blew a long strand of hair from her forehead. "There is? Well, Adam and I go back a long time. I should have told you, or he should have told you."

Bella's heart dropped. "Told me what?"

"We dated for a while."

Bella fiddled with the lighthouse pendant around her neck. Strange. Strange that neither one had been forthcoming with the information before, but not beyond the realm of possibility. There were only so many eligible local guys in Florence. Adam was quite the catch—handsome, smart, athletic, a man of faith, from a solid family—what was there not to like?

"I'll admit, I'm a little surprised. How come you never said anything when I started seeing him?"

Juliet picked up another pile of children's books from the floor and set them on the desk. "I didn't think you would get serious. You took it slowly for months— way too sensible, if you ask me. Plus, you told me you moved around every year or two, so I figured you would just hang out together and then be on your merry way. Don't get me wrong, I hoped you'd stick around—you've become like a sister to me this past year. But you're not an open book. I had no clue you were even interested in getting married."

It was the furthest thing from my mind. "Is that why you were ticked when I told you he asked me to marry him? You were worried for Adam?"

"No. Not exactly." Juliet shuffled the books in front of her.

"Then why? Don't leave me in suspense, Jules."

"Fine. I was surprised because he told me he would never get married. Ever. He was adamant he never wanted kids or to have a family. That's the reason why we broke up almost three years ago."

"Oh." But hadn't he spoken of wanting a family? Or maybe he only implied it would include children. He was great with the kids at church. Weird. This was quite the revelation. She needed to have a conversation with Adam and soon. "I'm sorry, I had no idea. And who knows why Adam changed his mind. I guess… he's three years older now and maybe he just wasn't ready before?" She glanced at the staircase.

"Maybe. He was resolute at the time and claimed he had his reasons but, like you said, he's matured since then." She lifted a shoulder. "I guess."

"I hope this isn't going to wreck our friendship—you know you're like family to me." Bella pulled the long, red hair back from Juliet's face. Her eyes glistened. This was a bigger deal than she was making it out to be.

Juliet turned and broke into a smile. A genuine smile. "It's not going to come between us. I'm sorry I was touchy. You know how I get sometimes, especially when I'm hungry and tired. Besides, I might have a love interest of my own…"

Bella gasped. "I knew it! Max? He seems like a nice guy." *Thank You, Lord. Please let Juliet find someone who will love her as she deserves. Someone like Max.*

"He is. At least from what I've seen so far. He was full of himself when I knew him back in high school. Pumped iron nonstop and was always trying to impress the girls. That didn't impress *me* one bit. But he's changed." She leaned back in her chair. "Mellowed. When I met up with him before, he told me God changed him and that he'd turned his life around. Isn't it amazing?"

Bella hugged her friend. She hadn't seen Juliet glow like this before. How refreshing to have something pleasant to think about for a change. "I'm thrilled for you. You look good together. I have to admit, I hoped something might spark between the two of you." *I have to tell Adam about this. He's going to be ecstatic.*

"That much was obvious." Juliet wagged her finger at Bella. "But it's early days, so let's not get too excited. I've had my fair share of disappointments in the men department. I'm not holding my breath."

"You aren't?" Bella smirked.

"Well, maybe I am a *little* breathless. He's picking me up after church tomorrow and we're going out for lunch."

"He's not going to church with you?"

"Work." Juliet shrugged. "That's going to be a huge challenge for us if this dating thing pans out. Between his shifts at the police station and mine at hospital, it'll be a miracle if we ever get to spend any real time together. I think that's why we never progressed when we met in Seattle."

Bella squeezed Juliet's hand. "You'll work it out. I have a good feeling about this."

"I hope so. I'll admit he makes me feel safe with all this nonsense going on."

Bella shuddered. "I know what you mean. Half of me is tempted to run again, Jules. Melt into the shadows and give George and Susannah the slip. I did it before and I'm older and wiser now. Is that awful?"

"No." Juliet pulled her cardigan tight around her. "I think I get it. But I also know how tired you are of running, and this could go on for years. You have us here with you now to support and love you through whatever happens. Not to mention what a wreck Adam would be without you. Gosh, I hate to imagine you alone somewhere new, always looking over your shoulder."

Bella winced. "Me too. It's a horrid way to live, trust me. I don't want to run. I'd love to stay here forever and grow old in Florence. But what if George and Susannah try something stupid? I'm scared stiff you or Pippa or Adam could get hurt."

"We're in God's hands—even my mom, though she doesn't accept it. We're not going to put ourselves at risk or do anything crazy. But perhaps it would be a good idea for Max to alert the other officers. Give them more of the details. Put out a photo of George and Susannah, just in case they are here in person."

Not a bad idea. Bella's stomach flipped when she pictured her adoptive parents. She hadn't dared to look them up online in case they could trace her somehow, but there were sure to be photographs of them on the Internet. Unless they'd changed their names, too.

"Does that scare you? Seeing pictures of them, I mean?"

"Absurd, isn't it? I'm a grown woman and I feel like a little girl cowering in my room again when I so much as think of George or Susannah. It's like they hold some sort of power over me, even after all this time."

Juliet brushed a smudge of dust from her jeans. "I guess that's your answer then."

"What is?"

"If they're still causing you pain even though you're a grown adult, then you need to deal with it so that you can finally be free. You need to stay here and we'll figure out a way to catch them. I guess they're still after the money in the safe deposit box, and you literally hold the key."

Bella's hand flew to her necklace where the lighthouse pendant dangled next to the little key. "You're right. I have to stay and figure this nightmare out." *If I ever want a future with Adam, at least. God, help me find a way.*

"How much do you want my mom to know about all this? I don't want to put my foot in it, and I want to protect her from as much as I can. She puts on that independent, calm, nothing-fazes-me air but, to be honest, I would rather she wasn't privy to all the details. She'll worry herself sick. And I can't bear the thought of her cancer coming back again."

"I agree." Bella took a deep breath. She couldn't be the cause of Pippa getting sick. "I would feel more comfortable telling Pippa as little as possible—we all want her to be safe and healthy. And I know we can ask Max to be more vigilant keeping an eye on this place as well as our apartment. I hate being chased away from our little home, but Adam insists on sleeping down here again tonight. He says he won't be able to rest in his own place knowing we could have some safety issues going on. I have to admit, I do feel better knowing he's around."

"Not that we couldn't hold our own." Juliet inspected her biceps.

"We would be fierce. This is all for Pippa." Bella grinned.

"Yeah, right. For Mom." Juliet blew out a long breath. "This is surreal. Max said a few of the guys on the force are taking additional shifts here in town and on our street—this must be the most excitement they've seen in a while."

"Great. All thanks to me." Bella sighed. "We should get upstairs and see if our tea is ready."

"Sure. Listen, before we do, I've been thinking and I have an idea." *Sounds ominous.* "How do you feel about me doing some digging around for you?"

"I'm almost scared to ask, but what do you mean?"

"I think I know someone who can help find out more about your birth mom." Juliet bit her fingernail until Bella swatted her hand down.

"How on earth do you know someone like that?"

"I know Madison has some contacts in the private investigation world up in Seattle."

"She does?" Why would a sweet school teacher need someone like that?

"Yeah, a couple of years back when she was worried she was being followed, she employed some private investigator dude—someone her late father trusted. It happened when I attended her church and we started hanging out together. She was a nervous wreck most of the time, but I remember her talking about her private investigator looking out for her. She was impressed with him."

Bella grimaced. "Sounds awful. Poor Madison. She's been through a lot."

"But she's happy and settled now. And that's how I want to see you, Bel—happy and settled."

"With Adam?"

"Yes. With Adam."

Bella's heart swelled.

"So, what do you say? Can I call Madison later tonight and see if she still has her contact numbers? She's back from her honeymoon and I know she'd do anything to help. She has some time before she and Luke head back to Mexico and the orphanage. Her guy could do some subtle background work and see if we can't locate your mom. It's worth a shot, don't you think? Unless you want to chance tracking down your adoptive parents first?"

Bella's pulse raced. The thought of trying to find George and Susannah when she had spent years hiding from them was hideous. "No, they're dangerous. That sounds like a bad idea. But looking for Rose shouldn't be as risky." She tilted her head. "What about the cost? I know Madison is super wealthy, so I'm sure this guy is going to be pricey. I don't have any extra money to pay for this."

"Let me deal with that. Maybe Madison can pull in a favor or something. Or maybe this won't take him long to figure out. Will you trust me?"

Bella folded her arms. "But shouldn't we leave the detective work to the professionals?"

"That's the thing—you don't want to involve the whole police force and the real detectives too much yet, do you?"

"No. Not while I'm unsure of my next move." This whole situation could blow over soon. Was that naive? Probably.

"If we have a full name, he can do some poking around without being obvious."

"I'm not sure." But how cool would it be to find out where her mom was—or at least learn more about her real family. It was serious business. How many people should get involved? And what if it put Rose in danger? The letter in her shoebox was written by a woman who feared for her life.

Juliet huffed. "Listen, it's your call, but you need to know it's okay to accept help once in a while. And I have a feeling you would do anything to get in touch with your real mother. Am I right?" She wasn't going to let this go.

"Yes, I want to know her, presuming she's alive. I have a thousand questions and I want to share my life with her, including my faith. I think about that sometimes—does she even believe in God? I don't know. This weekend has thrown me in a tailspin." She buried her face in her hands. "I can't even make a simple decision anymore."

Juliet crouched down in front of Bella's chair. "What else is stopping you? I know you well enough to suspect there's something deeper here."

Bella exhaled. "What if she rejects me? Again?" Her eyes filled. "I don't know how much more rejection I can take, particularly by the one person who was supposed to love me unconditionally but gave me away to strangers."

"I'm sorry. I get that you're scared. But isn't it a risk worth taking? What if she's been waiting for you to reach out to her? You know, there's got to be a reason why she sends you her little rose deliveries every now and again. I'm not pretending to understand any of this, but I know how much my mom means to me, and I'd love for you to have a relationship with yours if it's a possibility."

How long have I dreamed of meeting my mother? "I should have done this a long time ago. I guess now I'm backed into a corner—find her before George and Susannah do something dangerous. As long as we won't get in trouble with the police…"

"I asked Max if he thought it would be a good idea if, hypothetically, we could find your mom with our own resources, or at least try."

"And?"

"And he said, hypothetically, it would be smart and he would do the same. But then he said we never had that conversation, so he knows nothing about it." Juliet pretended to zip her lips shut.

"Fine then. Yes, if Madison is willing to give you her guy's information, then let's try this. What harm can it do?"

"Awesome." Juliet rubbed her hands together. "I'll call her after dinner. Do you have any idea what her last name is?"

Bella gulped. She had whispered the name so many times into the darkness of her bedroom when she'd craved a mother's love. "I'm not one hundred percent sure, as I've never seen it in writing, but the name George and Susannah used is Blake. Rose Blake."

O Lord, help me find my mom before it's too late…

CHAPTER ELEVEN

ADAM GUIDED BELLA OUT OF the church building and into the parking lot, where most people congregated after the service. It was as if it were a regular Sunday and the past two days of revelation and devastation hadn't even happened. *There's something to be said for normality and routine.* Although, there was nothing normal about the crick in his neck after spending another night on that cot in the bookstore.

"Girls?" Adam's mother hurried down the path and zeroed in on Bella and Juliet, clucking like a mother hen with her chicks. "Girls, please say you'll both come back to our place for lunch?"

His mom was the most gracious host he had ever known, and refused to take no for an answer. Besides which, no one in their right mind would decline an offer of Lydia Lexington's lunch. She was his inspiration in the kitchen, and made the most of every opportunity to offer hospitality.

"I'd love to, Mrs. Lexington. Thank you." Bella looked up at Adam and he squeezed her hand. Yes, it almost felt normal, like last Sunday or the Sunday before.

"And how about you, Juliet? No shift at the hospital today?"

Adam glanced at the blushing redhead. "Umm, I'm meeting someone, Mrs. L. But thanks for the offer."

His mom gasped and clutched poor Juliet's arm. "A boy?"

"A man." She kept a straight face.

Adam grinned. His mom wasn't going to let this one go without some further information. She'd been desperate to fix up Juliet with a "boy" from church ever since he had ended their brief dating experience years ago. For whatever reason, Lydia now felt responsible for Juliet's welfare and wanted to make sure the someone was suitable.

"Mom, you don't have to worry about our nurse. She's going to be in good hands." He grinned at Juliet.

She scowled back.

"Well, why don't you bring the mystery man along, too?" She planted her hands on ample hips. "There's plenty of food, and both Adam's brothers are coming over, along with some extras from church."

Juliet scanned the church parking lot. "There he is. Thanks again for the invitation, Mrs. L. Next time, okay?" And with that, she scurried off as fast as her high heels would allow in the direction of a certain brawny blond.

"Is that Max Bennett?" His mom squinted into the sunlight as she tried to make out the identity of the man in the car.

"Yes, it is." Bella sounded way too excited. "Isn't it sweet? They reconnected yesterday. Max must have finished his shift at the police station. They'll be lucky to ever see each other between their working hours."

She sighed. "How lovely. I was delighted for his mother when she told me he's back from Seattle. And now there's a budding romance with our favorite nurse. I have a feeling things will work out well for those two. He's such a nice boy."

"Really, Mom? We're men now, remember?" Adam planted a kiss on the top of her styled hair. "See you back at the house."

"You'll always be my baby boy," she whispered. His heart sank. He shouldn't be the baby of the family.

With a burdened heart, Adam led Bella to his vehicle and followed his parents' luxury car out of the parking lot. He should tell her the whole truth soon, but it was just too much after the revelations of her traumatic childhood.

As they turned into the sweeping gravel driveway, he found a spot amidst several other vehicles parked outside. It looked like Michael and Reid were already here—his brothers rarely turned down free food. He climbed from the jeep and surveyed the gorgeous Lexington family home with fresh eyes. No wonder Bella considered it something out of a fairy tale. Amazing what one could take for granted.

Minutes later, he stood in the spacious foyer with Bella at his side. The sweeping staircase, gleaming hardwood floors, and sparkling oversized chandelier all screamed of his mom's elegance. Yet, the heart of the home, the rambling kitchen that opened out into the great room and dining area all oozed with her love. It was comfortable and charming, and the kitchen was any chef's dream. Probably why Adam liked to cook so much.

"I love this place." Bella broke into his musings. "I think it was a good idea to come. I always feel at home here—your mom has a real gift."

"I won't argue with you there." Adam breathed in the promise of roast beef and Yorkshire puddings as he took Bella's denim jacket and hung it in the closet. "Mom's always enjoyed having people over to love on for as long as I can remember."

Bella slipped off her wedges and smoothed her fitted skirt. He hadn't noticed before, but the floaty blouse she wore was sky blue, the exact shade of her eyes. His gaze travelled down her face to those pink, kissable lips…

"Are you staring at me?" She raised a brow.

"Guilty."

She chuckled and shook her head, oblivious to the speed at which Adam's heart pumped.

"So, tell me, has your family lived here since you were born? I've always presumed as much, since you've never mentioned any other place. I guess I can't imagine you guys living anywhere else."

Adam bit the inside of his cheek. "We moved here when I was nine years old."

"And before that?"

Before that, the nightmare happened. Please don't ask. Not here. Not now.

Adam cleared his throat. "We had a house a few miles down the coast from here. It was a bit further inland and didn't have an ocean view like this." He gazed through the windows and marveled at the stillness of the ocean today. Smooth as glass. It was unpredictable. Like life. His parents had sought refuge in this vista after the incident that had destroyed their lives.

Bella sighed. "It's so picturesque. I can't imagine waking up to the ocean every morning."

"Would you like to?" *Because I still have the ring.*

She nudged his shoulder. "You know I would. It would be a dream come true for me. The majestic expanse of water and the glory of a sunrise—it all points to a masterful Creator, doesn't it?" A hint of peace had returned to her eyes at last. This was going to be a good day. An uneventful day.

"It sure does. I don't think I could ever take it for granted."

"What are you taking for granted, son?" Adam's dad slapped a hand on his shoulder with a chuckle.

"Hey, Dad. Don't worry, I'm not taking you for granted." He grinned and then pointed toward the ocean. "Talking about this beautiful view."

"Ah yes, we sure are blessed to live in such a splendid part of the country. And how are you doing today, Miss Bella?"

Bella smiled, although it didn't quite reach her eyes. She knew how to mask her emotions. "Not bad, thanks. How's the golf this week?"

He growled. "Don't ask. I ought to give it up."

"Dad, you've been saying that at least once a month for the past ten years." Adam took Bella's hand in his and walked in the direction of the sofas while the rest of the family and friends congregated in the kitchen. There was always a crowd on Sundays.

"Shouldn't we go help your mom?" Bella turned and waved to Adam's eldest brother, Michael. He was surrounded by a crowd, including Reid and Jennifer—the middle brother and his wife, and a couple of familiar-looking faces from church, all of whom were fussing over Michael's baby boy, Tyler.

Adam pulled her down onto the buttery-soft, leather couch. "I already asked, and she assured me the others were due for some kitchen duty. Plus, she's worried about you."

Bella's blue eyes widened. "Why? What does she know? I hoped to put on a brave face and not cause a fuss."

"Don't worry. You're giving an epic performance masking your emotions. She doesn't know anything about your family or the packages." Adam leaned in close enough for the conversation to be for their ears only. "After the service, she told me you were looking a little pale and sad, and she thinks I've upset you."

Bella flinched. "Does she know you proposed?"

"I didn't tell her the details, but you know what Mom's like. She has a sixth sense when it comes to her boys. She knew we were having a romantic picnic on Friday, and I guess I haven't been around much since then."

"Oh dear. I'll bet she thinks we had a fight."

"At least she knows we're talking now." He lifted her chin and smiled. "We'll get through all this."

"I hope so. And I don't want to worry your sweet mom."

"How are the lovebirds this afternoon?" Michael broke the perfect moment as he sat on the arm of the sofa, bouncing little Tyler on his knee.

"We're fine, thank you, bro. Where's your better half today?" Adam pulled back from Bella and settled into his seat.

"Steph went out of town with her mom to visit some relatives in a seniors' home. She wanted to take this little munchkin, but I pointed out most of the old folks would be napping and a screeching one-year-old might not be ideal."

"Good point."

"Do you mind if I hold him?" Bella asked. "I love babies and I have no intention of taking a nap anytime soon."

Michael raised a brow at Adam. "Sure." He transferred the squirming bundle. "But keep your eye on him if he goes on the floor—he's in the bionic-crawling phase."

Bella laughed as she held the baby close. "He smells good."

"Not always." Adam grimaced. He'd witnessed diaper changing time too often.

Michael laughed. "True. This parenting thing is quite the adventure. Life's a blur these days. I can't believe it's our third wedding anniversary next week." He folded his empty arms. "And on that subject—isn't it about time you guys tied the knot?"

"Are you kidding me?" Adam felt his face flush. *I'll bet Mom put him up to this.*

"What? I'm sure big brothers are supposed to help out wherever we can. Bella, I know you're strong enough to survive being part of the Lexington tribe if this lug ever gets around to popping the question."

Bella focused on the baby and said nothing.

This was awkward.

"Michael, are you behaving yourself?" Their mom called from the kitchen. Thank goodness her sixth sense had kicked in. "You leave your brother alone and go see where your father disappeared to. Lunch is about ready."

Michael laughed and stood. "Sorry. I couldn't resist. And for the record, Bella, we would be privileged to have you join our family one day."

What a charmer. *Thanks a lot, brother.*

Michael stood and took a bow. "Enjoy my little guy here and let me know if he gets grouchy. I'm on the hunt for Dad." With that, he disappeared into the study.

"Sorry about Michael." Adam loosened his shirt collar. "He's lacks any tact or subtlety." He watched Bella tickle Tyler's pudgy neck. She was a natural with babies. Would they ever have children together or had that wave crashed into the rocks for good?

"No harm done. Poor guy has no idea what's been going on the past couple of days. At least I know he likes me."

"Everyone loves you." Adam cupped her face in his hands. "My family think you're the best thing that's ever happened to me. And I agree."

Tyler tapped Adam's arm and babbled some dialogue only he was able to comprehend.

Bella giggled. He'd missed that giggle this past weekend.

"How come we've never offered to babysit for Michael and Stephanie?" She allowed the baby to take a fistful of her long hair and inspect it. "They live close by, don't they?"

Adam's stomach tightened. He needed to share the truth with her, and soon. "I guess they have it covered." He stroked the baby's downy cheek. Would he ever have his own son?

"You should ask. I wouldn't mind one bit. Like I said, I love babies."

"Hmm." That wouldn't be happening anytime soon.

They wouldn't ask and he wouldn't offer. There was an unspoken agreement, which suited him perfectly.

***

Sunday afternoons in September were pure perfection, and now they were alone at last. Adam's chest swelled as they strolled in comfortable rhythm along the boardwalk in the downtown area. It was quiet, peaceful after all the excitement of the past couple of days. An occasional jogger passed by, and a group of seniors gathered around the entrance to the riverside restaurant. He chanced a sneaky sideways glance at Bella. The sunlight caught glints of gold in her hair—how could she be so unaware of her natural beauty? Adam had never been so captivated yet content in the presence of a woman.

"Today has been a good day." Bella smiled and squeezed his hand.

Yes. No drama, no tears. Just church, family, and food. Bella had successfully deflected some interrogation from his mother, and they had both managed to stay on the periphery of the conversation about marriage and parenting over lunch. No one had questioned them leaving right away, even if his mother's smirk had let him know exactly what she thought. The hope of a future daughter-in-law was on her mind. She'd never been more right... and wrong, at the same time.

"It was kind of nice, wasn't it?" Adam shrugged. "I mean, other than the not-so-subtle hints from my mom about weddings and all. You know she can't help it, she thinks the world of you."

Bella chuckled. "No harm done. I love your mom to bits, and I understand her wanting another daughter-in-law in the family. She wants all her boys to be happy. I couldn't help but smile when she started wondering how many cousins Tyler would have." She wrinkled her freckled nose. "I kind of messed up the *happily ever after* this weekend, didn't I? I mean, if I had accepted your proposal, today would have been an engagement celebration..." Her voice drifted off and she looked away, toward the river that flowed out to the ocean.

God, please let our relationship work out. I'll do whatever it takes. Just show me how...

"Hey, I understand—maybe not everything, but I get why you can't make a serious commitment right now. I want to help you find out what's going on with your family stuff. You've been going solo with all this weight on your shoulders for far too long. The love of others can make burdens easier to carry." *Trust me, I know.*

Bella let out a long sigh. "It's been okay. I don't want you to feel sorry for me. I can't handle your pity—I'm a big girl and I've been on my own for a long time."

Her voice held a slight edge. He'd stepped over a line. Man, she could be feisty. Not that he was complaining. He loved her for it.

"Besides, I've had God walking through it all with me. He's carrying my burdens, right?"

Adam nodded. "Yeah, I'm sorry, that wasn't what I meant. All I'm saying is I want to walk through this with you, too. So do Juliet and Pippa. And my whole family would be at your side in a heartbeat. You know that, don't you?"

She stopped walking and let go of Adam's hand. "I have people." She whispered the words as she stared ahead. "I've never had people before. I mean, people who were there for me long term. Never." She rubbed her arms and glanced up at Adam. His heart constricted. "Thank you." Her tears brimmed and then spilled over.

114

"Hey, why the tears?" Adam wiped her damp cheeks with his fingers.

"I hope I haven't found you all, only to lose you. What if I have to run again, Adam?"

His pulse increased. The thought of her disappearing or having to leave in order to escape danger? That was not an option.

"Do you want to run? I kind of thought we were back on track. Today felt so right."

Bella bit her bottom lip and remained silent for a moment too long.

"Bella?"

"No. No, I don't want to run. I'm done with it. It's been my life for years, but now I've found this place, and you, and my people. I have no desire to leave—unless I'm faced with no alternative. I want to spend the rest of my life with you, to raise a family with you by the ocean. When I consider the possibility of losing you, I can't breathe."

This. This was exactly what he needed to hear. Nothing else mattered. He wrapped her in his arms and kissed her lips.

She eased back and looked him in the eye. "I talked to Juliet about this last night. But, I'm staying. I'm fighting this. I don't know who or how or even why, but I'm staying to fight. I *won't* run. This is my chance to find freedom from my past, the lies, the secrets, the sorrow—all of it."

A sudden roar from behind caused Adam to turn and look. A motorbike appeared from nowhere and sped along the boardwalk toward them. Adam yanked Bella over to his side of the boardwalk, causing them both to topple into a patch of landscaped shrubs as the motorbike raced past. It missed them by mere inches.

Adam held her in his arms, thankful the foliage had broken their fall. "What on earth? Are you alright?"

"Fine. Other than a few spiky twigs." She shook out her wavy hair. "How about you?"

"Yeah, I'm good." He stood and pulled her up next to him as he tried to make out the license plate on the motorbike. No, it was too far away already. He glanced behind at the restaurant and the flustered seniors, and gave them a wave to assure them they were okay.

Bella put her hands on her hips. "What an idiot. Where did he even come from?"

"Who knows?" Adam brushed debris from his dress pants and noticed something on the ground. *No.* He pulled his phone from his pocket and snapped a few photos as surreptitiously as possible. "I'm calling Max."

Bella picked dry leaves from her skirt as she stared after the crazed motorcyclist. "I don't think we should overreact." The quiver in her voice said otherwise. "It was probably some kid goofing off." She attempted a smile. "I'm fine."

"I know you are, but let's get you to The Book Nook. I'll make tea." Adam put an arm around her shoulders and marched her onward toward Main Street, where they could recover at the bookstore—and avoid what the motorbike left behind. She hadn't seen what the crazy guy had dumped in his dust. There it was, plain as day:

A trail of white rose petals blowing away across the street.

CHAPTER TWELVE

"I SAID I WAS FINE, and I meant it." She kicked off her wedges and willed her hands to stop shaking. "Let's not make this into a bigger deal than it needs to be." Who was she kidding? First the car last night and now this? But she would not be consumed by fear. No way.

Adam set a mug of chamomile tea on the table in front of her and leaned against the living room wall. He pulled back the sheer curtain and gazed down at a smattering of people wandering along the street. "I don't believe for one minute it was an accident."

"You think someone was aiming for us?"

He shrugged. "I think he could have hit us if he planned to, but I'm sure he wanted to scare you. Send a message."

"Well, I'm not scared." She jutted her chin.

Adam bit his fingernail. Strange, he never bit his nails. Perhaps Juliet's habit was rubbing off on him. What *wasn't* he saying?

"What is it?"

"I phoned Max when I was in the kitchen making your tea."

Bella threw her hands in the air. "Why? It wasn't that serious and we could have filled him in tomorrow. The poor guy's trying to have an afternoon off work." *With Juliet.*

"I know, but he made me promise I would let him know if anything at all was suspicious. Even something small. I think this falls under the suspicious category." He craned his neck to see further down the street.

"What else?"

"Hmm?"

"What haven't you told me? I've never seen you this skittish."

He joined her on the couch. "There was something you didn't see after the lunatic sped off."

Her stomach dropped. "Tell me."

Adam pulled his phone from the pocket of his jeans and scrolled to his photos.

"I'm sorry, hon, but this screams suspicious to me."

Bella squinted and pinched the screen to increase the size of the image.

Why had he taken a photo of the ground? That was right where they had fallen into the shrubs. What *was* that? Paper? No, wait. "White rose petals?"

"Yeah." Adam hung his head. "I should have shown you right away, but all I could think was to get you inside as quickly as possible. Now you know why I'm sure this *is* a big deal."

"Right."

Bella gulped. Think. Don't fall apart now.

"Are the petals still there, do you think? Should we go back and bag them or something in case there are any fingerprints on them?"

He squeezed her hand. "That's why I called Max. He and Juliet were on their way here anyway, so he's gone to see if there are any remnants left on the boardwalk. I'm not holding my breath, but it was worth a shot."

"For sure."

The door opened and Bella shot up from her seat. "Oh, Juliet, it's you." She put her hand on her heart. "Thank goodness. Is Max with you?"

Juliet dropped her purse on the entrance table and slid off her shoes by the door. "He's downstairs calling the station."

Adam held his phone in the air. "I'm going to run down to him with these photos. Be right back." He rushed past Juliet and disappeared down the stairs.

Juliet strode over to Bella. "You okay?"

"Yeah. So much for the normal Sunday, though. I don't suppose there were any of those petals left? It's breezy down there this afternoon."

"Actually, we managed to find several petals caught in the shrubs. I couldn't believe my eyes. At least, we're presuming they are the right petals. I had a look and there aren't any rose bushes at all along that stretch of gardens by the boardwalk."

"I can't imagine whoever is doing this would be dumb enough to touch the petals with their fingers, but you never know."

"Let's hope someone got sloppy."

Bella flopped onto the couch, and Ebony leapt up onto her lap for some attention. Amazing how comforting the simple action of stroking a cat could be.

Juliet perched on the arm. "You realize you're Ebony's favorite. She knows you'll always make time for her."

"I love kitties." Bella swallowed the lump in her throat. "I always have."

Juliet huffed. "I still can't get over your parents doing that awful thing to you when you were just a little kid."

"I can't get over them reminding me of it again now, to make some point."

A tear fell onto Ebony's back and she glanced up with a scowl on her squished little face.

"But let's change the subject. How was your lunch date with Max?" Bella reached over the cat and picked up her mug of tea.

Juliet checked to see if they were still alone. She grinned. "It went well. He took me to that new little seafood place for clam chowder." Her smile faded. "But there is something I want to run by you."

"Sure."

"I know you've had a bit of a strange encounter, and the last thing I want to do is add to your worries."

What now? "Go ahead, you can tell me."

"It may be nothing and part of me didn't want to even mention it, but Max thought it could be important."

"Now I'm intrigued." Or nauseous. Or both.

Juliet nibbled on her thumbnail for a moment. "Okay. We stopped here after lunch so I could change before we went for a walk. Mom said she was spending the day at her friend's place down the coast."

"Where she usually goes on a Sunday."

"Yes. I'm always more cautious when she's not around. I worry about her living here alone sometimes, which is silly because she's Mom. Anyway, I checked the windows before we headed back out again, and Mom had left this one open in the living room." She inclined her head to the window they were sitting by.

Bella shrugged. "Understandable. It was a beautiful morning."

"True. But when I pulled back the sheers to lock the window, something caught my eye down in the street. Two people, in fact."

"Who were they?"

"I don't know. And I realize it's not unusual to have occasional visitors here in town on a beautiful Sunday in September, but something didn't sit right with me."

Bella squinted. "What do you mean?" Following Juliet's train of thought wasn't always easy.

Juliet stood and brushed the sheers aside, as if reliving the moment.

"It was a middle-aged couple. They looked out of place. And the woman took a photograph of The Book Nook with her phone."

Bella exhaled. No big deal after all. "Jules, you know tourists take photos of this cute little store all the time. A quirky independent bookstore is a bit of a curiosity for some. To be honest, I would take photos of bookstores if I were visiting a new place. It's what bookish people do."

Juliet stared down at the street. "No. They didn't look like they were sauntering down the street, snapping fun vacation pics on their way for ice cream. They were too well-dressed."

Bella put the mug down. Was someone watching her? Maybe it was a couple of innocent, stylish booklovers.

"Perhaps they came from church or something." She flicked a fragment of bark mulch from her skirt.

"Hmm. Or perhaps they were here on business. I'm probably making a fuss over nothing, but I wanted to run it by you."

"Okay. I know what you're thinking—could it be George and Susannah?" She shuddered. "But I don't think they'd have the audacity to show their faces here. They could have arranged for the motorbike dude to scare me—I wouldn't put that past them—but they used to get others to do their dirty work for them. This is a bit up close and personal for their taste."

"Fair enough. But the woman looked agitated when she saw me pull the sheers back and stare right at her. They took off down the road at a rapid pace, even with her stilettos."

Bile rose in Bella's throat. She stopped stroking Ebony's fluffy coat. It had been six years, but she couldn't have changed much. "Stilettos?"

Juliet turned from the window and sat next to Bella. "Yeah, they were black and matched perfectly with a classy-looking dress. Not what I would expect an artist to look like."

Bella's stomach knotted. "Did she wear her hair in a chignon, by any chance? Blonde?"

"Yes. She was attractive. From what I could make out, maybe mid-fifties? Almost as tall as the guy. Like I said, not your average tourist in cut-offs and flip-flops."

NO. Could they be here? Had they been tracking her moves from the apartment on the edge of town? Bella reached out and grabbed her friend's arm. "Was the guy grey-haired and in a suit?"

Juliet nodded. "Pretty nondescript. Typical businessman attire. It was the woman who caught my attention. Do you think it could be them?" Her face paled. "I could have been staring at those awful people?"

Fear prickled the hair on the back of Bella's neck as memories of Susannah's cruel behavior bubbled to the surface. The solitary confinement, and punishment by way of a leather belt. The bizarre insistence that everyone look immaculate, even if they were seeing no one at all. The designated clothes laid out every single morning like some weird obsession. The piercing glare of disapproval and verbal slapping she gave Bella every single day. The constant knowledge that no one could live up to Susannah's perfectionist standards. The sick, twisted woman who looked like a million bucks on the outside, but possessed a stench of death within.

As saliva filled her mouth, Bella ran for the bathroom. She barely made it in time, but managed to empty her lunch down the toilet. Gross, but understandable at the thought of her parents being in such close quarters. What were they up to? Was it the key they wanted? If she let them have the stupid key, would they leave her alone and let her live her life? Probably not. Besides, it was a link to her birth mother and she wasn't ready to give that up.

"Oh, Bella." Juliet was right there, being all nurse-like and the best friend imaginable. "I'm sorry. I didn't mean to make you sick."

"It's not your fault." Bella stood and rinsed her mouth at the sink. "I'd rather know."

"I can't even imagine how bad it must be to make you throw up." Juliet dug Bella's toothbrush and toothpaste from the toiletries bag on the counter and passed them over.

"Thanks. I guess the memories are still there. I can't believe they would show their faces here though. We should let Max know." *And Adam. He's not going to let me out of his sight after this. Although, that's not so bad…*

"The guys are still downstairs. Why don't I run down there and fill them in? It'll give you chance to catch your breath here and freshen up a bit."

Bella nodded, the toothbrush doing its work.

She watched Juliet leave and then set the toothbrush down on the counter. What was happening? Were they all in danger or did George and Susannah want to talk? If they did, they had a funny way of showing it with the message in the box and the motorbike. No, something evil was brewing.

Bella gripped the edge of the sink with trembling hands and stared at her reflection in the large, square mirror. Her face was pale and dark rings were beginning to form beneath her blue eyes. She looked young for her twenty-three years, especially since most of her make-up had been washed off. In fact, she resembled the petrified girl she thought she had left behind in Seattle six years ago.

God, what is happening? I'm losing it here. Why the Robinsons? Why now after all this time? I know You have it under control, but I'm frightened. I haven't felt like this for so many years. I know You are bigger than any issue I'm having right now and I trust You, I truly do. But I don't want my friends to get hurt—they don't deserve to be in danger and they have no idea how dangerous George and Susannah really are. I know Juliet can handle most things thrown her way, but she still needs Your wisdom and protection. We all do, especially where that evil couple are concerned.

Father, I don't want to scare my friends, but I have a horrible feeling my parents finally want me dead.

CHAPTER THIRTEEN

"HEY MAN, THANKS FOR TAKING a shift here." Adam slapped Max's shoulder and handed him a paper bag full of doughnuts. "Here's some breakfast for you. I've heard it's what you guys survive on."

Max closed the door and locked it behind them as they wandered into the bookstore. He chuckled and tore into the bag. "Completely false rumors. But I'll play along just to be cool. It was uneventful here last night. The way we like it. Plus, added bonus, there was plenty of reading material." He waved a hand around at the shelves of books.

"Good." Adam pulled out a chair behind the desk and slumped into it. "Can't say I got decent sleep even in my own bed."

"You have a lot on your mind, buddy. This is all kinds of crazy. But you need to carry on with life somehow, too."

"Don't worry, the plants in my apartment are all watered now, and I've managed to put off a project I'm working on at the office for at least a day or two. I need to be fully present for Bella."

Max bit into a jelly-filled doughnut and groaned with delight.

"Do you need to head home for a while, get some real shut-eye?"

"Nah, I'm used to functioning on sporadic sleep. Besides, I'm not super excited about living back at home with my mom, if you know what I mean. She's amazing, don't get me wrong, but once you've lived on your own for a few years, you get used to having no one at home to answer to."

Adam grinned. He had thought the same thing after college when he had to move back home. "I can't even imagine. My mom would love me to death. Getting my own apartment was the smartest thing I've ever done. Close enough so I can pop over to the folks when I want to, far enough away that she can't call in for a daily cup of sugar."

"Perfect. I hear your apartment is fancy, too. Will you and Bella live there when she says yes?"

Adam ran his fingers through his hair and sighed. "*If* she says yes, you mean?"

"She will. Trust me. You guys were made for each other. I can see that already. She has a lot to figure out, but she's smart wanting to get everything straight and out in the open with you before making a mammoth commitment."

She's not the only one needing to get things out in the open. "I guess. But I have lofty plans for a home with Bella. I've been working on a dream project for months."

Max grinned and wiped a glob of jelly from his chin. "No way, man. Do I get to see these plans?"

"I don't think so. Architect's secret."

Max shrugged and then furrowed his brow. "Speaking of secrets, does Bella know about, you know, what happened with Emily?"

Adam stood. His stomach churned at the mere mention of her name. "No, not yet."

"Don't you think you should tell her? I get that it's painful, but it's part of your past and she needs to know about it, in my humble opinion. It's bound to come out sooner or later."

Adam clenched his jaw. It was good to have a friend to keep him accountable, but this was hard. Really hard. "I will. I haven't found the right time yet, but I've come close. She's got too much on her plate at the moment with all her own stuff—I can't expect her to take on any more. My family has been nagging me to tell her for a couple of months now. I know I need to do it."

"No kidding. Hey, it's your call. But after all Bella's been through and the pain she's bringing to the table, it might even be good for her to know you're not as perfectly put together as she thinks."

"Thanks a lot." Adam stole the bag of doughnuts and helped himself to one.

"Sorry. But I have a feeling she imagines your life has been all rainbows and sunshine, when you guys went through an unimaginable storm."

Adam chewed on the doughnut and the words. "You're right."

"I usually am."

"I will tell her. Eventually." A creak sounded above them and Adam glanced at the ceiling. "But now it sounds like the ladies are up and about. I should go check on them and then see what this day will bring."

Max grabbed the bag and picked one more from the diminishing pile. "Here, keep those. My mom's bound to have breakfast waiting for me, bless her heart. I'm heading home to change and then I told Bella I would work on finding out about the key for the unknown safe deposit box. I'm going to start looking in Seattle as that was where they lived before she left home. I have some favors I can call in from my buddies there, plus I need to check on any leads for the Robinsons. I'm guessing you'll be here with Bella? Best to lie low if it was them outside yesterday."

"That scared her big time. She hoped this would blow over and she could move on, but that's not going to happen. I don't think she believed they would show up here in person. At first, she thought they might just need to communicate something to her, but there's the dead rat, the red car, and the motorbike... now I'm pretty sure she believes they are out to do her serious harm."

"True. I think we have to trust her judgment on this—she knows this couple well enough to have her guard up and we need to follow her lead. Hopefully, the extra cops around Main Street will be a deterrent. It's all we can spare from the station."

Adam shook his head and paced over to the window. Nothing much happening this early on a Monday morning. "I sure hope so. Whatever they want, I have a feeling they'll go to any lengths they deem necessary to get it." Although, they would have to go through him first. "If they wanted to talk, they would have tried that already."

"But they must know Bella will run, or maybe even go to the police."

Adam finished the last of his doughnut and swallowed. "I don't know. I'm guessing they're aware of the power they have over her, even after all these years. You hear about those cases of abduction where the kid grows to have some warped respect or even love for the captors."

"You mean Stockholm syndrome? It's possible. The Robinsons were the only parents she ever knew. Was Bella's childhood that traumatic? Juliet told me bits and pieces of what she knows, and it turned my stomach."

Adam spun around and balled his hands into fists. "I haven't heard the half of it yet but, from what I gather, it was a living nightmare. She needed to run away from it, but she never reported them. She's non-confrontational and I think she just wanted a peaceful life. Freedom. Without having to address her ghosts, so to speak."

"But now she's going to have to."

"Looks like it."

"That's intense. And we'll do whatever we can to stay one step ahead of those ghosts. Let me work on the safe deposit box and let's stay in communication today. Remember, anything suspicious, call me right away. The guys will be on high alert. We have the most recent photo we could find online of the Robinsons—the girls confirmed the likenesses."

"Perfect. I appreciate it. You know, I can't help thinking that you coming back here now is no accident."

"God works in mysterious ways." Max shrugged.

"Yeah. I know He's in control and I'm trusting things will all work out for good."

"Amen." Max turned to leave. "Say hi to Juliet for me."

"Hmm, that's another good reason for you to be back in town."

"She's a great girl and she needs to be kept safe, too."

"You're blushing. A lot."

"Shut up."

A few minutes later, Adam knocked on Pippa's apartment door. "It's me, can I come in?"

The door opened wide and Adam was rewarded with a beautiful Bella decked in faded skinny jeans and a lacey white blouse.

"Morning. You're a sight for sore, sleepy eyes."

"Hey, gorgeous. I'm guessing you didn't do well in the sleep department then?" He pecked her cheek as she pulled him inside.

"Sweet of you not to mention that I look like death." She sighed. "I'm hoping sleepless nights catch up with me at some point, and force me to finally get some rest."

Poor girl. On closer inspection, her eyes were puffy and she looked several shades paler than usual. To be expected given the circumstances.

"They will. I'm sure you're missing your own bed, too."

"True. But I'd rather be here. Even though George and Susannah know where I am, I feel safe enough above the bookstore. This whole street is on guard."

Adam stroked her cheek. "Your people are looking out for you."

She nodded. "Yeah. I like that."

"We'll get to the bottom of this—and in the meantime, I'm here to keep you company. With doughnuts." He held up the crumpled bag. "Minus the couple Max devoured downstairs. And maybe I tried one, too."

Bella's stomach rumbled. Perfect timing.

"That's embarrassing." Her cheeks turned pink and she took his hand. "Come and sit at the counter, I'll pour you a coffee."

"Sounds good. Did you do anything after I left last night?"

"No, not much. I'll admit I checked out the window a few times before I felt settled enough to hit the sofa bed. But I chatted with Juliet and I think it helped talking everything through with her again. I feel like we have an action plan. Sort of."

He placed the bag on the counter and perched on a bar stool while Bella poured coffee into two mugs.

"Everything good at your apartment?" She added cream to her drink.

"Yeah, the plants aren't dead yet and I threw in some laundry."

"You look nice." She winked.

Wow. That was worth making the effort to run an iron over a T-shirt and dig out his favorite jeans.

"Thanks. Do you have enough of your stuff here? I could pop to your place later if you need anything."

She shrugged. "I have all I need for now. Maybe we can head over there tomorrow if we're still in this holding pattern. I'll need more clothes at that point."

"Sure. Max thinks it would be a good idea to sit tight here today at least."

Her shoulders slumped. "I guess he's right, although I hate being forced to stay inside. Is Max still here?"

"He just left."

"It was sweet of him to sleep in the store last night. You guys are troupers."

Adam flashed a grin. Being her protector was no hardship. "And Max said he was going to start checking into the mystery key with his friends in Seattle today."

"Did someone mention Max?" Juliet appeared in a set of pale blue scrubs with a bag slung over her shoulder. She reached for a doughnut and took a bite. "Has he gone already?"

Adam took a sip of hot black coffee. "Yeah, but he said to say hi to you."

"He did?" Juliet blushed.

"You both have it bad." Adam shook his head.

Bella came around to sit next to Adam. "Don't tease. Max is adorable and they're perfect for each other. You have a good day at work, my friend. Pediatrics still?"

"Yeah." She checked her watch. "It's heartbreaking to see sick kids, but I love being able to connect with them as well as do all the regular nursing stuff. They're brave. You know, I think it's fast becoming my favorite."

"Like someone else is fast becoming your favorite?" Adam tried to hide a smirk.

That earned him a hard shove in the shoulder from Juliet. Yeah, he deserved that.

Bella cleared her throat. "Is there any word from Madison yet about that investigator of hers?"

Ah yes, the investigator they had discussed last night, while Max had stuck his fingers in his ears.

"No pressure, it's just that—"

Juliet wagged a finger at Bella. "Don't worry, I'm all over it. Madison said she left him a message yesterday, so for all we know, he could already be looking into details and tracking Rose. We may have to be patient. I have no idea how easy or impossible a task it is."

"I know." Bella sighed. "I've waited this long to find out about her, you'd think I could be a bit more understanding.

But George and Susannah have my nerves on edge." She bit her lip. "I hope we don't rack up a huge bill with him. Who knows how much this may cost?"

Juliet held up one hand. "Madison said to not worry about the bill. She wants to help and has it covered."

Bella groaned.

Adam looked her in the eyes. "What's wrong? You don't want Madison to help?"

She tucked her hair behind her ears. "Don't mind me. It's a pride thing. I know I should be grateful and appreciative for Madison offering to pay, but I'm used to looking after myself. I guess I don't do well with hand-outs."

Adam took her hand in his. "We know you're more than capable of looking after yourself. But don't you think, in this case, with your safety at risk, you could be comfortable with accepting a little assistance?"

Bella raised a brow. "That was subtle."

Her face broke into a smile. Adam's heart pretty much did likewise.

"Yes. A little humility won't kill me. It's kind of Madison. Besides, you guys are all helping me so much already. I'm sorry for being silly."

Juliet wiped her fingers in a paper napkin. "This isn't easy for you on any level. We know all about accepting help and love from others when the chips are down. It was hard for Mom when she got sick. She was used to running her life her own way. I could spend all day telling you about all the meals and cleaning and running around and a million other little things people did for us when she was ill. She had to get right down off her high horse and learn to accept it all as gifts and be grateful. And trust me, she was grateful. Me, too."

Adam swallowed. People had shown such kindness to his family when they were in the midst of their season of grief. Everyone needed help at some point. Accept it now, and pay it forward later.

Bella sighed. "I guess I do need help now."

Adam pulled her into a hug. "This is hard on you. But we'll get some answers soon, I know we will. We have Madison's guy looking into Rose, Max's colleagues helping with the safe deposit box, and Pippa's covering your shifts. Plus, we're going to look online to try to discover anything we can on George and Susannah Robinson today, and the police are stepping up their presence around Florence. It could all be sorted out in a matter of days. Maybe even less."

Juliet grunted. "Or, you know, we could end up with no leads whatsoever. Sorry to be a Debbie Downer here, but someone's got to keep it real. I don't want you to get all your hopes up for answers right away, Bel."

"I know. Patience isn't my virtue. But it feels good to at least be doing something rather than stay huddled inside in fear."

Juliet leaned against the fridge. "Except the motorbike incident yesterday was a little too close for comfort if you ask me. And the rose petals? Not so sweet anymore. I think Bella needs to stay here as much as possible. It's right in the middle of town and if we keep the apartment door locked at all times, that would be double protection. Plus, Mom would see anyone suspicious coming in through the bookstore." She bit her lip. "I hope we're not putting Mom in danger."

"Me, too. And let's stick to only telling her what is necessary." Bella frowned. "I couldn't bear anything to happen to Pippa."

"Did I hear my name?" Pippa flitted into the kitchen, the smell of lavender oil permeating the whole area. "I hope you're not worrying about me, love." She took Bella's face in both hands. "How many times do I have to tell you? I'm a big girl and I've survived more than you can imagine. I have a whole town full of friends here and they are all watching out for us."

That was true. It felt wrong in some ways to keep Pippa in the dark, but Juliet knew best when it came to her mother's health.

"Trust me, if anyone tries to give me grief, all I need to do is yell. *And* there are my black-belt skills I may or may not have been reminding myself of these past couple of days."

Adam choked on his coffee. "You're a black belt? For real?" He gawked at the spunky little woman who was five feet tall on a good day. Perhaps he didn't need to worry about her after all.

Juliet laughed. "Yes, mom is a black belt in Tae Kwon Do. She got it years ago when she decided we needed to be able to protect ourselves. I lasted a year or so in lessons, but Mom went all the way." She glared at Adam. "Don't mess with this woman."

"I wouldn't dream of it." Life was certainly full of surprises these days. "And it does make me feel a little safer up here…"

"Oh, stop it." Pippa batted her eyes. "Now I feel like your bodyguard."

"I have to get to work." Juliet grabbed a granola bar and a tub of salad from the fridge and stuffed them in her bag. "I'll call you later, Bella, in case there's news from… anyone."

They exchanged a knowing look. It was going to be a challenge keeping up with who knew what.

"Thanks. Please be careful, though. You're sure you're comfortable driving? I can call a taxi if you'd rather."

"Or I can get Max to drive you?" Adam gave her a wide-eyed look of innocence.

She scowled. "My car is parked right outside and security at the hospital is hot. There are cameras in the parking garage and everything. I'll be fine."

Bella sighed. "Please take care."

Adam tensed at the thought of Juliet being followed. "Yeah. Call us if you're concerned."

"I will. Bye, Mom." She kissed Pippa on the cheek, grabbed her keys from the wooden rack on the wall, and left for the day.

Pippa picked up a stack of files. "That girl of mine is fearless. I'm heading downstairs to the store. Help yourself to whatever you need up here. Ebony, you come with me." The cat jumped down from the sofa and followed her owner out the door.

"Thanks," Adam and Bella said in unison.

"Pippa's full of surprises." Adam picked up his empty mug and loaded it into the dishwasher.

Bella cleared her throat. "Did you find that out when you and Juliet were dating?"

What? Adam swung around.

Bella inspected her fingernails.

"Wait? You know about Juliet and I? That's ancient history. Did she tell you?" This was awkward. He stepped right in front of her and she lifted her head.

She smiled.

Phew.

"Yes, she did. And I know it's ancient history, but I don't know why neither of you ever thought to mention it to me at some point in the past year. It's strange, that's all." She folded her arms. "At least now I know why you two have a funky relationship."

"Funky?" They were more like squabbling siblings most days.

"Yeah, you're super standoffish with each other most of the time, yet there's some deep understanding that makes it acceptable somehow. I don't know how to explain it. It must be weird, though, having someone around who you were once in love with." A hint of hurt flashed in Bella's eyes.

Adam gulped. "Whoa. Slow down there. I don't know how Juliet felt, but I'm not sure you could ever say we were in love. We were friends for years, and then all of a sudden, we were a couple. It only lasted a few months and I knew we weren't right for each other."

Bella bit her bottom lip. "She said the reason you broke up was that you told her you never wanted to get married. That you didn't ever want a family. Is it true?"

Adam blanched. That was a painful time, before he'd dealt with the guilt of the past. "I was young and foolish. I didn't see us going anywhere. I didn't want to date for the sake of dating, so breaking up seemed the right thing to do. I thought she was good with it."

"She wasn't upset?"

Was she ever. He recalled the fiery redhead giving him a piece of her mind. "At first, sure. And my mom was furious with me, as you can imagine. But we were in the same friend group and we had to get used to seeing each other around all the time. I'm sorry. We should have told you. I guess in my mind we'd moved past it a long time ago and it didn't matter. Forgive me?"

Bella pulled him into a hug. *Thank You, God. The first hurdle over.* "Of course. It took me by surprise, that's all." Her voice was muffled against his broad chest. "What changed your mind about never wanting to get married?"

Was she kidding?

"*You*, Bella. It was you."

CHAPTER FOURTEEN

"MY EYES ARE GIVING UP on me." Bella leaned back against the sofa and blinked in an attempt to focus. "I'm going to need reading glasses after this."

"Can I get you anything?" Adam closed her laptop and jumped up. "The pizza sure made me thirsty."

"Water would be great. Thanks." Bella watched as Adam worked his way around the little kitchen, clearing the trash, scrubbing the countertops, sliding the box of leftovers back in the fridge. The man was domesticated, no doubt about it. How attractive was that?

She pulled herself up for a stretch and gazed through the window at the ashen sky, pregnant with moisture, heavy and still. Not much to see. A young family hurried down the street toward the ice cream parlor, while the owner of the toy store opposite swept the sidewalk in rhythmic strokes. A quiet Monday.

"Here you go." He handed her a glass of water with ice and a slice of lemon—because even water was special with this man.

"Thanks. And thanks for helping me out here all day. It hasn't exactly been fun and we don't seem to have achieved much, do we?"

He downed his drink in one gulp and sat back on the floor. "I don't know. Pizza for lunch was awesome. There's not much to show for our work, but we've done some elimination of sorts. I guess they're not into social media, unless they've changed their names. We have a few more photos of Susannah at those arts events, though."

Bella sank down next to him. "They were from a few years ago." She tapped her pen on her knee. "I wonder if she's still painting now. She was good."

"That doesn't excuse the way she treated you, you know."

Bella balked. What was that supposed to mean? "I realize that."

"Good. It's important you stay focused on Susannah the adoptive mother. The *cruel* adoptive mother."

"What are you getting at? I'm merely pointing out she was talented in her field. Art—yes, motherhood—no."

Adam shook his head. "I don't mean to be a jerk. I guess it worries me when I hear you say nice things about her. Like she still has some supernatural pull on you."

Unbelievable. "Look, I ran away from home and haven't looked back since. That should tell you enough." Her raised voice caused him to flinch.

He reached over and took one of Bella's hands in his own. "Hey, I apologize. I'm looking out for you, that's all."

Before she had chance to reply with a lecture about how she didn't need anyone looking out for her, he held one hand in the air. "I know you're going to say that you don't need anyone looking out for you, but I have news for you, Bella. I *want* to look out for you. And right at this moment, you need all the people you can get to help you through this

141

nightmare. I'm still trying to wrap my head around what the Robinsons did to you. For years on end. Your entire childhood. I don't care how great an artist she was, I want to see them both put away for a long time."

Adam's voice level matched hers and Bella couldn't help a small smile. He was cute when he was exasperated.

He huffed. "What? Are you laughing at me?"

"No." She managed a straight face and squeezed his tense fingers. "I promise I'm not laughing at you. It's just I've never seen you this mad before. I kind of like this side of you." She shrugged. "It's attractive."

Adam's mouth dropped. "Oh." His blush only made him look more adorable.

"And I know you are only upset because you love me."

"Got that right."

"Are we good?" She kissed his stubbly cheek.

"Should I shout again and see how attractive I can be?"

His grin earned him a kiss on the lips.

Adam's cell phone burst into song, causing Bella to jump.

He sighed as he picked up the phone. "Lousy timing. But we need to take this, it's Max."

"Hey, Max. Seriously? Hang on, I'll put you on speaker phone so Bella can hear." Adam tapped the screen, then set the phone back on the table.

Bella's heart thumped in her chest. "Do you have news?"

"Yes, I think I do. You're not going to believe it, but one of my buddies was able to get hold of all the listings for the safe deposit boxes in the major banks up in Seattle."

"No way. That was quick." Breathe.

"Right? They're in the middle of some fraud case and were privy to a bunch of data. I have to believe God

142

orchestrated this whole thing. It could have taken days or even weeks."

"Of course." Bella smiled. God was always in control. Then why was it so hard to trust Him with her safety? Or her future with Adam?

"Anyway, we ran the data and the number on the key is matched with a safe deposit box right there in the city. And guess whose name it's registered under?"

"Not Rose?" Adam clutched her hand.

"I know we weren't sure if the name was even legit, but it seems it is. It's under the name of Rose Blake."

Whooshing sounds filled Bella's ears. Was this true? Could this be a connection to her birth mother at long last?

"You alright, honey?" Adam's arms were holding her up. When had she even stood?

"Yes, yes, I'm great. Oh my word." This was really happening. A solid link to her mother. She wiped the dampness from her cheeks. "She's for real. Rose has a safe deposit box in Seattle. I wonder why Seattle and not California or wherever I was adopted?"

Max cleared his throat. "I asked myself the same question. But then, going by what you've told us regarding George and Susannah Robinson, wouldn't they choose to be close to their reward as the time drew near for them to collect on it?"

"Yes, they would. If I remember correctly, we moved to the city when I was fifteen. Up until that point we were about two hours away. They were most likely biding their time. It must have killed them to be so close to the money yet not able to get their hands on it."

"Imagine how mad they must have been when you disappeared. With their key..." Adam squeezed her close. "You're one courageous girl."

Bella sank onto the sofa.

"Max, this is huge." Her voice cracked. "It could be a stepping stone in finding my mother—which is more than I ever dreamed of. There could be information inside that box which may lead me to her." *Please, God. Please.* "Would you thank your friends in Seattle for me?"

"Will do. So, what are you going to do with this newfound information?"

She was silent for a moment. "Pray about it."

"Good call." Adam stood at the window and looked down at the little town. Probably checking for any stray Robinsons. "Seattle's a big city. Do you want to go there and see what's inside this box? You're right, it might offer us some clues to Rose's whereabouts. Maybe even her family."

Bella closed her eyes and clutched the key and her tiny lighthouse charm in her fist. "For today, I think I simply want to enjoy the feeling of being one step closer to my mother. In case the box is empty or something equally devastating. I've dreamed of this key opening the box holding all my answers. Am I being silly to revel in the joy for a little while? Tomorrow, I'll decide what's next."

Adam turned and folded his arms. A smile appeared along with a dimple on each cheek. "Not silly at all. I think I like watching you happy."

"Hello?" Max's voice sounded from the coffee table. "I'm still here on the phone and it's starting to feel like three's a crowd. I'm glad I could help. Keep me updated and let me know if you decide to try for Seattle, okay?"

Bella giggled. "Sorry, yes. And thanks again, you have no idea how much this means to me."

"I think I could guess. You're welcome."

Adam chuckled. "Later Max."

"See you, bud."

Adam pocketed his phone and Bella fell into his arms. "Can you believe it? I can't believe it. Do you think this might lead me to my mother after all this time? What if there are no clues? What if we still can't find her?"

"Hey, hey, slow down." He smoothed her hair and breathed slowly and deliberately in front of her, so she couldn't help but emulate. "There, just breathe. This is a lot to take in. Let's not go down the 'what if' path yet. I don't want to pull the 'my dad's a lawyer with friends' card, but he is, and you know he would do anything to help you. There are plenty of options we can look into, but let's not get ahead of ourselves."

Bella's pulse rushed. This was all too much to take in. "You're right. I need to relax. But my heart is bursting here. And I must tell Juliet."

"Isn't she in the middle of a shift?" He picked up his phone from the table. "It's almost three. I guess you could leave her a message to call you."

"Yeah. Maybe I'll do that. I'm not sure what time she finishes today. But I could tell Pippa now."

"Wait. You have to be careful. She only knows that you are looking for your birth mother, right?"

True. "Right. And that my adoptive parents are being jerks. We've kept it as vague as possible."

"Sounds good. I think you might implode if you don't tell someone. How about I'll go down and cover for her while she comes up for a break?"

"You're going to work in the bookstore?" Bella raised an eyebrow.

"I think I've watched you enough times to know the lay of the land, and if someone has a bookish question, I'll text you."

She stood on tiptoe and kissed him on the lips. "You're awesome."

While Adam went down to relieve Pippa, Bella texted Juliet. This was the best news.

God, thank You for this glimmer of hope. You know how I've tried not to let my past consume me, but I'm desperate to meet my mother. Even after all these years. Would You help me now in this journey? Give me patience and peace...

"What's the news?" Pippa's bracelets jangled as she joined her by the window, followed by her fluffy black cat. "Adam looks pleased as punch. Can you believe he's down there in charge of my bookstore? Thank goodness there are no customers."

"He's resourceful. He'll be fine. I had to tell you about our phone call with Max. It's amazing, I can scarcely believe it. He found the safe deposit box which fits my key."

"No way. Where?"

"In Seattle. And it's under the name of my birth mother."

Pippa squealed. They hugged. They cried. Pippa rocked her back and forth. *Will I get to do this with my real mother one day soon?*

"Sweetie, this could bring you two together."

"I know. I'm trying not to get my hopes up too high, but how could I not? What if there's a letter or something for me?"

The door flew open and Adam rushed in, followed by Juliet who slammed the door behind her. Juliet's face was as white as a sheet and her hair was sopping wet, clinging to her cheeks. When had it started raining?

"Bella."

What was she doing home so early? And what was wrong? The hair on the back of Bella's neck prickled.

Adam steered Bella to the sofa and pulled her down beside him. How bad could it be? The people she loved most in her life were right here in the room with her.

"You're scaring me. Juliet, what's happened? Please tell me."

Rain now pounded against the window pane, angry and relentless. Ebony pressed in against Bella's leg.

Juliet knelt in front of her. "Bel, Adam just told me about your wonderful news. Your heart and your mind must be reeling from it." She sucked in a quick breath. "But I have to tell you something, too."

Bella struggled to focus. Adam, Pippa, and Juliet were too close.

Juliet's chin quivered. "I talked with Madison's investigator guy, the one who was going to do some digging on Rose?"

"Yes." Her mouth was stuffed with cotton. Where was the saliva?

"The thing is, he did find some stuff out. I'm sorry, my dearest friend, but it's not good news." Adam's arms hemmed her in, shielding her from what was about to come next. "I don't want to be the one to shatter your heart, but I have to tell you. It would be cruel not to."

Bella buried her head in her hands. She didn't want to hear this. No bad news. Please, no bad news. Please.

"It's about Rose. I'm sorry…"

"No." Her heart was breaking wide open.

"We're too late."

"No, I just found her today…" She couldn't think. Couldn't process.

"I'm sorry, but you have to listen."

"What?" Maybe it wasn't so bad. How bad could it be? She shivered and looked into her best friend's eyes.

"Bella, Rose is dead."

CHAPTER FIFTEEN

BELLA LAY HER HEAD BACK on the soft pillow. The rain was rhythmical now, pitter-pattering like tears on glass. She gazed up at the glow-in-the-dark stars on Juliet's old bedroom ceiling. Cold. She was so cold. Pulling the soft duvet around her shoulders, Bella sank deeper into the bed and stifled another sob. The sound of soft voices floated in from the living room—her dear friends were trying to figure out what to do next. What would become of Bella, the girl who had managed to turn all their lives upside-down in the space of three days?

"Honey, how are you feeling now?" Adam appeared at the doorway and took tentative steps toward the bed. He crouched beside her, brow furrowed.

How could she describe the numbness? Every movement seemed unnatural, forced, foggy. Senses dulled, mind muddled, heart shattered. How did she feel? She didn't feel a thing.

"Can I get you anything to eat? Some water?"

Bella shook her head and found her voice. "My stomach's churning. I don't think I could even keep water down right now. But thanks."

Bella focused on the compassion in his eyes, the color of the raging ocean on this stormy afternoon. His gentle kindness was almost her undoing. Did he still want to be her family? Her only family, in fact. If Rose Blake was dead, she had no blood relatives left to uncover, unless she decided to look into the mysterious Blake clan. But no, hadn't Rose warned they were trouble and it would be too dangerous? That was why she'd fled from them in the first place. She needed to know details. How had Rose died?

"I'm sorry." Adam knelt and clutched her hand like it was going to disappear at any moment. "I wish I could take all the pain away. I know you were hoping to meet her someday. This is a huge shock. You take as much time as you need."

She turned her head to the wall. This was foreign, this weakness. Flashes of her childhood and early teen years replayed over and over in her mind's eye. Yes, that's what this reminded her of, the utter helplessness she'd experienced as a child. Vulnerable, rejected, unwanted. The lies whispered to her by her own parents that she was unworthy, useless, unlovable. Like a groaning volcano ready to erupt at any given moment, the painful memories pushed their way closer and closer to the summit. Hadn't she dealt with these wretched insecurities? Hadn't she given it all over to God when she'd discovered He loved her unconditionally and wanted her to be His child? *Oh, God, help me...*

"You're shaking like a leaf, honey."

A hot tear dripped onto her arm. Adam was grieving right alongside her. Could she survive this anguish knowing she was not alone? He sat with her in silence. His hand, warm and secure, was wrapped around hers. If only that warmth could bring the dead parts of her back to life. Revive her enough to see clearly again, to find the strength to enter back into the world she had grown to love.

Please God. Don't let this sorrow consume me. You've given me hope—I cling to that.

Adam's measured breathing lulled her to sleep. Dreamless, desperate, and deep.

***

Onions. Someone was frying onions.

Bella opened her eyes. No headache anymore. That was a plus. She pulled her disheveled hair from her face and attempted to sit up.

"Hey, beautiful." Adam's voice came from somewhere in the room.

A light weight pressed against her feet but it couldn't be Adam. No, a sleeping, curled-up Ebony was the guilty party.

A small smile tugged at her lips when she spotted Adam. He sat on a bright pink beanbag in the corner of the room.

"How long was I asleep?"

Adam checked his phone. "An hour or so."

"You've been waiting?"

"Praying." He stood and moved over to the side of the bed. "You look like you have a little more color in your cheeks."

That must be code for "You don't look quite so horrific."

She took a deep breath and rolled her shoulders.

"I feel more human, I guess. Thanks for praying, I know it helped." Yes, knowing he was there and that she wasn't alone had calmed her fears, allowed sleep to claim her. "The news about Rose knocked the wind out of my sails and brought back all the fear I thought I'd gotten over. It scared me."

Adam sat on the edge of the bed. "Give yourself some grace. Grief can cause all sorts of reactions and it'll take some time for you to deal with. But I'm here for you. We all are."

"But am I crazy, grieving the loss of someone I never even met?" Bella leant back against the padded headboard. "Come to think of it, I've never grieved over someone's death before."

"You haven't?"

"No. Since I left home I've never stayed in a place long enough to get that attached to anyone, I suppose. Have you? I mean, has anyone you've ever been close to died?"

Pain crept across Adam's face. He gave a slight nod and bit his lip.

This was a conversation for another time. Maybe there were things she didn't know about this man. Interesting.

"I'm sorry. I guess it's not something we've discussed before."

"That's okay. We will, I promise." He attempted a smile. "But now I'm here to support you in any way I can."

"I know you are, and you have no idea how much that means to me. I've read about how grief can be all-consuming and hits you in stages. Maybe that's why I feel so… lost."

"Lost?"

How could she explain without sounding foolish? "Even the mere thought of my mother was like a comforting blanket I could pull over me when I felt alone or scared. When I was young, I would imagine what she looked like, what perfume she wore."

Adam swiped at his eyes. "I get that."

"Do you think she looked anything like me?"

"You mean gorgeous?"

She squeezed his hand. "I mean, do you think she was blonde with blue eyes? Did I get my freckles from her? Was she petite like me, or do I get that from my father's side? Who even *is* my father?" She exhaled. "Sorry, I'm not thinking straight. Don't mind me."

"Listen, if she was anything like you, she was blessed indeed. It's obvious you didn't get your big heart and kind thoughtfulness from your adoptive parents' actions and words, so I'm guessing she was much like you. She was also brave enough to run from her destructive, dangerous situation. Sound familiar?"

Bella's breath caught in her throat. "You know, I've never thought of it like that before—the fact that she escaped from whatever horrible circumstances she'd experienced and ran to safety, like I did."

"She ran away to save you."

"Yes. She loved me." A fresh tear fell down Bella's cheek, hot and fast. It was as if God were covering her with another blanket of love and peace with the memories of Rose. "She gave me up so I could have a better future. So I could be safe."

Adam shifted. "That must have been excruciating for her. Sounds like the kind of love God has for us, doesn't it? I mean, giving His own Son so that we might live. I see the parallels there. It's unconditional love."

A warmth stirred in Bella's stomach.

I'm loved. God, I know You love me immeasurably, and I'm learning more about You all the time—it never ceases to amaze me. But the reality that Rose loved me enough to give me a better chance of survival, or at least the hope of a happy life? This is monumental. Thank You for showing me.

She ran her fingers through her hair. "How much do you suppose she knew about the Robinsons? Obviously, she had no clue George and Susannah were heartless and ruthless in the beginning, but I wonder if she was aware of the way they treated me after time went on."

"Didn't the letter from her allude to the fact she watched over you regardless? And didn't the white roses start to appear after you ran away from Seattle?"

Yes. The roses. I have to find out what happened. I need to know.

Adam shrugged. "Someone had to be putting them there for you to find, and I'm guessing it wasn't your adoptive parents. Surely, if they had found you, they would have taken you back with them to Seattle—not left you a rose. Especially at the beginning."

Bella rubbed her sore eyes with the heels of her hands. "You're right, I guess. I don't know. Why didn't she make contact once I had run away from George and Susannah? I could have had a few years with her at least." A dull pain crept up her neck. "Did you find out any more details about how and when she died? I don't *want* to know because it makes it even more real, but I still need to have the details. I know I do. I'm going to need some sort of closure."

"You're right. I was going to head over to see Max at the police station. I want to see if there's any more information coming in and keep tabs on what's happening with the other stuff."

"I'll come." Bella pulled back the covers. She was still in her jeans and blouse. It wouldn't take a minute to wash her face and clean her teeth again.

Adam stood and gently swung her legs back onto the bed. "How about you stay right here?" He held one hand up in the air. "I know you're more than capable of coming with me and asking the questions, but you've experienced a horrible shock and look, you're trembling again. You should try to eat a little something."

He was right. Her hands were dancing on their own on top of the bedcover. How had she not noticed that?

He pursed his lips. "Please? Let us help you, just this once?"

"I smell onions and I don't think I could eat anything at all at the moment." Her stomach jiggled a similar dance to her hands.

"No problem. Juliet's making soup for later I think, but she's got some peppermint tea out there and I know she wants to come and sit with you while I'm gone."

"Maybe peppermint tea would be nice."

"It'll warm you up and settle your stomach. I promise to hurry straight back here with all the information I can gather."

"You won't leave out any details? Even if you think you're being kind? I don't need protecting." She stared straight into his eyes. Honesty shone back.

Adam tilted his head to one side. "I know you don't need protecting, but I can't help trying. It's in my nature—you know that by now. You are stronger than any of us can imagine. But you do need some loving. Let us show you

155

some love however we can? Can you open up just a little bit?"

His dimple flashed as he smiled. Goodness, he was handsome.

"Yes. I'll let you love me. And I do trust you. I know I've screwed up your lovely, normal life with all this madness and I'm sorry." She took a deep breath. "I'm only going to say this once, but I want you to know if you need to walk away from this, from me I mean, I'll understand. I know we still have a ton to talk through regarding our future—if that's still a possibility, and you want to do life with me in spite of who I am…"

"Wait." Adam leaned in closer. "I want to do life with you *because* of who you are, not in spite of it. These past few days change nothing for me. If anything, I love you even more—if that is possible—and I think our love will just keep growing." The thread of steel in his voice wove its way around her heart. He was serious.

Bella ran her fingertips over the light stubble on his chin. "I want to believe that. More than anything, I do. But, you have to know that rejection has played a major role my whole life."

"I know. But please hear me when I say I'm staying with you. I want to help you through your grief, through this mire of greed and deception and intimidation by the Robinsons. And I want to help you get some answers so you can move on with your life. Free from the past."

She sighed with a smile. "I'd like that a lot."

Adam bent down all the way and kissed her on the lips. "Will you get some more rest? I'll tell Juliet to come in with the tea, and I'll report back here as soon as I finish up with Max."

"Thank you."

Adam's tall form disappeared through the doorway. What had she ever done to deserve this guy? He must be crazy wanting to stick around. What if he was just being a gentleman? Giving her the sympathy vote? She couldn't live with that. But no, his eyes spoke truth—he was in this for the long haul.

"Knock, knock." Juliet poked her head around the door frame. She looked pale and drawn, precisely how Bella felt right now. "I have tea for you. Adam's orders."

"Thanks. That was quick, even for you."

"I already had it made before he came through the kitchen." She placed the steaming mug in Bella's hands. "There, this will help warm you up."

Bella inhaled the minty stream of warmth and cupped the mug like a life preserver. "You don't look so good. Are you okay?"

Juliet sat cross-legged at the end of the bed. "Umm, I think that was my line. That's so like you, always thinking of others. I'm fine, just tired. But you look a whole lot better than you did earlier, I have to say. I was getting worried and was about ready to speed-dial one of my doctors." She squeezed Bella's leg through the blankets. "I still can't believe it. I feel horrible."

"Why do you feel horrible? You went out of your way to help me find Rose. You couldn't have known she was... gone." Bella gulped and squeezed her eyes shut. "I felt positive she was with me, watching me. I felt in my gut she was very much alive."

"I'm sorry I don't have any more details." Juliet wrung her hands. "I don't think Madison's guy expected the news to be bad, so he didn't pursue it further. But I know Max is going to be able to help us out."

Bella nodded. "I want to know when she died. How long I've been an orphan."

"Oh, Bel." Juliet wiped her own tears from her freckled face. "You know you're family to Mom and me, don't you?"

"Yeah, I do. And you've no idea how much that means to me. Even more so now." Bella glanced at the door. "Where's Pippa? Is she okay?"

"She closed the bookstore and went to bed. She couldn't stop shaking. I think she was surprised how the news hit her. I guess it's a mom thing, but I'm glad she's sleeping now."

"Poor love. She went through the roller coaster of emotions with me. She had such an awful battle with her health. She's been good for a while now, though, right?" Bella sipped her tea, and savored the warmth.

"Yes, but I can never take it for granted after the rounds of chemo she endured. She's a walking, talking miracle, that woman. But still stubborn."

Bella's heart ached. Pippa was the closest thing to a mother she had ever known. "Why do you suppose she has such a hard time trusting God? With the cancer and everything, she had to consider that she might die and needed to know more about life after death? I mean more than the average person cares to think about the afterlife."

Juliet shook her head. "Stubborn as nails. That's when I took God seriously, when the cancer appeared for her the first time around. I guess I was eighteen, right after my high school prom. I was scared and, for me, finding hope in Jesus was the answer. At least that's how I started my journey.

But Mom is a hard nut to crack. Even when it went into remission and then came back, she didn't want to hear about a saving God. I know she's been through a lot in her lifetime, so she has issues believing there is a Heavenly Father who loves her. She's amazing at giving love out to others, but has a major wall up when it comes to letting love in."

"I love your mom."

"I know you do, and she's made an exception to let down her wall when it comes to you." Juliet stood. "Listen, I'm going to finish making some soup. It's my French onion."

"With the gooey cheese and French bread?"

"You better believe it. Give me a shout when you feel like some. Another little nap will do you good about now. Nurse's orders."

Bella set the empty mug on the bedside table. "I'll try. But please make sure Adam wakes me as soon as he gets back? I have to know what happened to Rose." She held back a sob.

"I promise." Juliet blew her friend a kiss and closed the door behind her.

Bella sank into the duvet again, disturbing the cat. "Ebony, I wish I could sleep soundly like you. In fact, sleeping for a solid week sounds rather appealing."

The kitty crawled up to the pillow and buried her flat nose in Bella's hair.

What happened to Rose? Was her death a true accident or part of the twisted scheme the Robinsons were now unravelling? The gaping, fresh void in her heart ached once again. She had tucked Rose in there for so many years, even without knowing her. Tears streamed anew. A fresh wave of grief crashed in, tugging her down and threatening to pull her far away in an unpredictable current.

Father, I need Your help here. I don't get it. Why did You have to take Rose? She loved me. I was so close, finally. And now I feel like I've been abandoned all over again...

CHAPTER SIXTEEN

"BELLA, ARE YOU AWAKE?" **ADAM** cringed as the bedroom door creaked like a screeching seagull. Now she would be. Apparently, so was the cat.

Ebony gave him a filthy look, jumped from the bed, and slunk from the room.

He closed the distance to Bella with three easy strides and watched her clear blue eyes drift open and focus on him.

"I must have dozed off again. What time is it?"

"Almost seven."

She sat up and rubbed her pale cheeks. "I don't think I've ever cried this much in my entire life. It's exhausting."

"I'm glad you got some rest." Sleep had removed most traces of grief. No puffy eyes or blotchy face. He winced. That would change in a matter of seconds once he revealed the information Max had presented.

"Did you find anything out about Rose?" Bella swung her jean-clad legs from the bed and dug into her overnight bag on the floor. She slipped a cardigan over her blouse, now wide awake. How wonderful would it be to wake up next to her every single morning? *Focus.*

"I did, but I wondered if you need some fresh air. The rain stopped hours ago. We could walk and talk."

Her blue eyes lit up. "I thought you'd never ask. I've been cooped up in here all day."

Adam reached out and touched her arm. "I kind of guessed. This isn't going to be easy no matter where we are. Max knows we're planning to head out. I cleared it with him so I think he'll arrive here soon to be with Juliet and Pippa."

"I'm bracing myself for whatever you have to say. But it can't be any worse than the news I already received today. My heart feels like a deadweight inside me. I'm hoping it'll help somehow to have the details, although half of me doesn't even want to know." Her eyes searched his. "Do you think we could go to my beach?"

Adam smiled. He'd presumed she would ask. "We can go wherever you like. It turned into a nice, warm evening. We might even get to see the sunset if we hurry."

Sunset? What was he thinking? Like a sunset was important on a day like today. But she would want to be at the place where she felt safe and secure, close to her favorite lighthouse. Cape Cove was like her private paradise—she went there to think and write and pray. Argh, it was also where he'd proposed. At least he hadn't completely ruined that place for her. And at least she hadn't been scared off by those whisperings she'd thought she heard on Saturday...

"And before you ask, that voice I heard up by the lighthouse on Saturday isn't going to keep me away." She planted her hands on her hips. Brave Bella was back.

"That's my girl."

Adam led her out through the living room. A somber Juliet was curled up on the sofa with a book, and presumably Pippa was still in her bedroom.

"I'm taking Bella out to the beach for some air. We'll be back later."

"Sounds good. Although, do you think you'll be safe?" Juliet frowned. "What if we're still being watched?"

Adam shrugged. "I ran it by Max. I'll text him when we get there and keep him in the loop. He should be here any minute."

A smile appeared on Juliet's face. No big surprise there. "Please be careful with our Bella."

"I will."

Bella cleared her throat. "I'm right here, guys. I might be a little fragile right now, but I'm not completely inept."

Juliet chuckled. "You don't have to tell me that. I just want you to be safe." She pointed to Bella's oversized purse on the floor. "Do you want to take your journal?"

"I don't think so."

She shuddered as if the thought of writing repulsed her. What was with that? Writing usually inspired her and soothed like a balm to her soul. *I guess not today.*

Bella wiped a lone tear from her cheek. "Maybe tomorrow I'll write in an attempt to process everything, but today, I simply need to be. I don't want to remember this day."

"Yeah, that makes sense. Listen, you guys go ahead. We'll save you something to eat."

The rich smell of French onion soup made Adam's mouth water. "Thanks. It smells fantastic. We won't be long."

"See you later, Jules." Bella's voice was small. "Call me if there's any problem?"

"Will do."

Adam took Bella's shaking hand, led her down the stairs, and headed to the jeep. It seemed she already knew she was about to get another round of bad news.

And he was the one who would have to break the devastating details about Rose's death to her daughter. How messed up was all this? A week ago, he'd been on cloud nine, dreaming about being engaged to the love of his life.

After a quick stop at his favorite coffee shop, they parked alongside a couple of other vehicles, and made their way over to the caves on the right side of the beach. Adam passed the skinny vanilla latte over to Bella and climbed onto the large, flat rock next to her. It was almost dry after a couple of hours of warm sunshine, not that either one of them would have cared about a damp rock. He took a sip of his bold-roast and savored the hot liquid, hoping it would give him the energy he needed to get through the remainder of this dreadful day.

Bella leaned against his side. "Thanks. Good idea to pick up some caffeine en route. I know I'm usually a coffee-only-in-the-morning girl, but this has been a long day."

"You're welcome." The longest day ever.

Adam watched the waves crash against the gigantic boulders, their regularity somehow comforting. The silence stretched between them as he sat at Bella's side, the breeze whipping their hair about their heads. They'd missed the sunset, and now only faint streaks of pink mingled in the sky with cool lavender and charcoal grey. He glanced at Bella. Her fingers were wrapped around her plastic coffee cup as she hunched over and closed her eyes. He let her take a moment. Perhaps she was praying, or trying to make sense of everything. She would tell him when she was ready to hear the details.

A seagull squawked overhead and her eyes flashed open.

He put a hand on her knee. "It's only a seagull." A quick shoulder-check revealed another couple walking hand-in-hand across the sand. Other than that, the beach was empty.

Her smile didn't quite reach her eyes. "I'm a bag of nerves."

"Don't be hard on yourself." He put an arm around her shoulders and pulled her in close. "Are you warm enough?"

"I am now." She blew out a stream of air. "I'm ready. Tell me everything."

To any passerby, they would appear to be a couple enjoying a romantic evening at the beach in the crevice of a cave, sipping coffees and looking out over the magnificent ocean as they shared dreams and whispered sweet nothings. The reality was painfully different. Adam set his half-empty cup on the rock beside him and turned to face her. He had to look her in the eye.

"There's no gentle way to tell you all this, so I'm just going to relay the information. Rose Blake was killed in a car accident. It was quite recent, too."

Bella gulped and searched Adam's face, as if for clues. "Where?"

He took her cup and set it next to his own. "In Northern California. She was driving alone. This is awful, I'm sorry."

"And when?" Her eyes squinted. She had gone into information mode.

"Three months ago. June first." He pushed a strand of hair behind her ear. "And I'm afraid there's more."

"You mean there were more killed in the accident?"

"No, I mean it was a hit-and-run."

"What?" Adam sensed Bella's breathing speed up as she considered the ramifications of this latest blow.

He held her close and stroked her long, silky hair. She wasn't crying yet. She was processing.

"Adam, there have to be more details." She pulled back. "Who found her? Was she dead right away? Why couldn't anyone save her? Who crashes into someone and drives away? Who does that?" She groaned. "Wait. George and Susannah?"

A strangled cry was muffled by sobs as the tears fell in torrents. Her shoulders heaved, and he held her as she wept. She needed to grieve and mourn and lament over the mother she loved yet never knew. All he could do was whisper how she would be fine, how much he loved her, how she was a child of God.

Time stood still as he watched the woman he loved almost break in two. His heart broke right alongside hers, further proof that his love for her was real. She took a ragged breath. Before she even uttered the words, he knew what she was going to say.

"Adam." She composed herself enough to speak. "If I hadn't run away from George and Susannah, my birth mother could still be alive. I'm right, aren't I?" She pressed her lips together and looked at him with swollen eyes. "They killed her because of me, didn't they?"

"I knew you were going to go there, but you have no way of proving that. Please don't beat yourself up for this. You ran for your life and Rose would have been the first person to support you in that. You couldn't have had any idea how all this would play out years later. Plus, we're jumping to conclusions. There were no witnesses to the car accident and the hit-and-run person could have been anyone. It happens more than we realize."

"It has to be George and Susannah." Her voice was a whisper. "The white rose on Saturday was a sick taunt, like the first box. All this time, all these years, I've tried to think the best of them, in spite of the way they treated me. Maybe they both had horrific childhoods or were abused or abandoned. They never spoke of anything from their pasts, but I wanted to give them the benefit of the doubt. Despite sometimes using a belt on me, they never hurt me physically enough to land me in hospital, so perhaps they weren't that bad."

Adam gritted his teeth at the thought of them laying a finger on her.

"They provided a roof over my head and food to eat, although I was sometimes punished by not being fed, but it was my own fault. Did I hurt them by running away? I was racked with guilt for years about that."

"Bella…" Adam's stomach knotted. How could she even think they had an ounce of good in them after all they had put her through as a child? *God, this is so wrong.*

She held up one hand. "I know, this all sounds insane. I'm seeing that now. Me trying to make excuses for George and Susannah. I guess a part of me hoped I had it wrong and they were good people somehow, deep down. They adopted me in the first place, after all. I've been such a fool. I may never know what went wrong or why they changed, but now, with this news about Rose, everything's different." She choked on a sob. "This is serious. I knew they were dangerous and cunning, but this? You can't blame me for thinking they had something to do with her death."

His shoulders slumped. It was his first thought, too. "No, I don't blame you one bit for thinking it. They're the obvious suspects here. But there's no proof. Plus, we have to consider what benefit they would have in killing Rose after all this time."

She had to see reason and not bear the weight of this death. He'd been there and done that in his own life. No way she was going to carry guilt like a sack of coal on her back for the rest of her days. It was beyond crippling. He had to tell her soon.

Bella pulled a tissue from her pocket and dried her eyes. "I don't know. Perhaps they knew she was going to contact me or something? We presume they still want the money, right?"

"Seems that way. From what you've told us, at least. I can't see what other reason they would have to contact you after all these years."

"Exactly. Here's what I'm thinking—they hired someone to find both Rose and I in one last ditch effort to track down the mysterious safe deposit box. They could have located Rose somehow, maybe even spoken with her and she brushed them off or threatened to go to the police or something. I don't know. Maybe they decided to tail her and crash into her, and then that eliminates her from the whole picture." She looked out over the ocean. "Now they only have me. Is this my fiction-writing brain going nuts or am I onto something?"

This was getting heavy. "They don't have you. They may be trying to scare you by sending you weird messages—"

"Like the rose. They must have known about my mother sending me white roses in the past—but how? Do you think they've been following me for years?"

"I don't want to speculate. They sound psychotic to me. I can't pretend to understand what they're up to." Goosebumps travelled up Adam's neck. He glanced around the deserted beach. Nothing ominous. In the parking lot, one of the original cars had disappeared and a new black truck was parked at the far end. "We should probably head home. It's starting to get dark. And you must be exhausted."

"I wish I could go and sit up at the lighthouse."

You have to be kidding me. Now? "Probably not the best idea. Not this evening."

"You're right."

Phew.

She eased herself down from the rock and retrieved her cooled coffee. "I can't believe all this. It's too much to take in. I never expected this day to pan out like a nightmare."

"I know. And my heart's breaking for you." They walked hand-in-hand toward the parking lot. "Anything I can do for you?"

"I'm not used to feeling needy."

"Umm, I think if there's ever a time you get to be needy, it's now. And you know you have me and Juliet and Max and Pippa. We're your people." He squeezed her hand. He couldn't resist the opportunity. "And I'm your man."

She stopped and turned to look back at the illuminated lighthouse perched on top of the bluff. "I bet that old structure has seen its fair share of drama and nightmares and heartache and joy over the years. I love how safe it makes me feel." She reached up and touched the tiny lighthouse

169

pendant on her necklace. "But I'm glad God has placed my people in my life to help me feel safe now. And I'm glad you're my man."

The sudden kiss she planted on his mouth took his breath away.

The tingling in his lips had finally faded by the time he had her bundled into his jeep. His heart might be aglow but a shiver indicated she was in need of some warmth. Adam dropped his phone in the cup holder, cranked the heating, and pulled onto the main road taking them back to Florence. He needed to get her home safe and sound.

Bella twirled a strand of long hair as she stared straight ahead. She had stopped shivering and was now deep in thought. What could he do to make her feel safe and loved and wanted? She still needed time to process all she had been told today, but there was a danger the voices of rejection and abandonment—and now even blame—would be whispering their lies to her. He didn't want to see her spiral again like earlier on.

God, show me what I can do...

A burst of light from behind caused Adam to glance at his rearview mirror. The guy was driving way too close. What was he thinking? Adam stepped on the gas to gain a little headway. Truck drivers. Always thinking they had priority with their gas-guzzling vehicles taking up half the road. Was it the truck from the parking lot? He had been distracted by the kiss.

A loud honk from the truck caused both Adam and Bella to jump. She sat up straight in her seat and spun around to see where the commotion was coming from.

"What's his problem?" Her voice sounded hoarse from all the crying.

"I have no idea, but he's been flashing his lights at me, too. I'm already pushing the speed limit, so it's not like I'm slowing him down or anything." *This doesn't feel right.*

"Do you know the driver?"

Adam squinted into the rearview mirror. "It's hard to tell with that baseball cap pulled down like that. Could be anyone." He eyed his phone in the cup holder. He didn't want to scare Bella, but they should phone Max if this guy continued acting like a jerk.

Other than an occasional vehicle coming the other way, the road was quiet. Until the truck driver blared on his horn once again.

Adam growled. Great, they were being tailed by someone with road rage. If he had been alone, there was no doubt he would have put his foot down and left the truck in his dust, but he had Bella to consider.

"Hon, I'm going to slow down and stop at this next pull-off. Let this dude pass us. I don't want to take any chances."

"Good plan."

Adam threw on his turn signal and tapped the brakes. "What?"

The truck did likewise. Did the driver need to speak with them?

"Bella, do you recognize the truck?" He tried to keep his voice light.

She turned back around. "I don't think so. But you know me with cars. It's a black truck and that's all I've got."

Something jolted Adam's insides. "The truck at the beach was black, but I didn't notice anyone sitting in it." Why hadn't he paid more attention? Right, the kiss.

Both vehicles stopped on the pull-off but Adam's foot hovered over the gas pedal.

Bella put a hand on Adam's tense arm. "There are lots of black trucks. Perhaps he's lost or something. Look, he's getting out now and coming our way."

"Hold on tight." He checked the side mirror to make sure no other vehicle was approaching, and slammed his foot onto the accelerator. They left a cloud of dust behind them and Bella let out a squeal as they sped down the open road.

Neither of them spoke as Adam maintained control and concentrated on the task at hand. The last thing he saw amidst the rising dust was the truck driver sprinting back to his vehicle. No way on earth that dude was merely asking for directions. He hugged the curve of the road and looked up at the mirror. No truck.

"What's going on?" Bella's voice was high-pitched and she clutched her seat with both hands.

"We're fine." Adam took a deep breath. He couldn't let Bella see how much that little encounter had rattled him in the light of Rose's hit-and-run. He eyed the phone again. Max. "Can you phone Max for me? To be on the safe side. He's on speed-dial."

Bella picked up the phone and found his number. "I'll put it on hands-free so you can speak."

Max picked up straight away. "Adam?"

"Yeah. We have a truck chasing us. I don't have plates. May have followed us from the beach."

"Is it still with you?"

Bella peered back between their headrests. "No. There's a blue car way behind us now. I think we can maybe slow down a bit..."

"I will, honey, as soon as I'm sure the truck isn't still following." *I have to keep you safe.*

"Adam? What's going on now?" Max's voice was clipped.

He checked the rearview mirror. "Looks like we're in the clear, man. We're about five minutes from home. You still at The Book Nook?"

"Yes. You need me to send a car out?"

"No. I think we lost him. I'll fill you in when we get there."

"Drive safe."

Bella disconnected the phone and held it in her lap.

Adam forced his shoulders to relax. There was a sizeable gap now between the jeep and the little blue car, and the truck was nowhere to be seen.

Thank You, God.

He reached over and took Bella's hand. "We're almost home. You okay?"

She nodded.

Silence.

"Are you sure?"

"No, if I'm going to be honest, I'm not. I know I usually say I'm fine, it's the answer I give even when I'm feeling like death warmed up, but if you really want to know? I'm not okay. Today I discovered my birth mother is dead. She was killed in a hit-and-run, and there's a chance it could have been orchestrated by my sick adoptive parents as a way of getting to the money. Money that might even be fictitious for all we know. And minutes ago, we were almost run off the road by some maniac in a truck who may or may not have been watching us at the beach. And may or may not be in cahoots with George and Susannah."

Adam bit his lip until he tasted blood. What could he say? It could be some weird coincidence, but there was a good chance the whacko driver may have been trying to cause them harm. It wasn't outside the realm of possibility, given the bizarre series of events of late.

God, some words of comfort would be great about now…

"Bella, I don't have all the answers. I wish I did. But I'm going to help you find the truth and get to the bottom of all this."

"I'm scared. For our safety and to know the truth." She sighed. "I know as a Christian I'm supposed to trust that God is in control, but it's not easy."

"I understand what you mean." Adam slowed down and pulled onto Main Street. "But a Bible verse just came to mind. It's one I learned as a kid, when I went through a phase of being afraid of the dark."

Bella took several deep breaths. Had she even heard him?

"You were afraid of the dark?" She tilted her head to one side. "That's kind of adorable. But yes, please tell me the verse. I need all the help I can get."

"It's Proverbs one, verse thirty-three: 'but whoever listens to me will live in safety and be at ease, without fear of harm.' I think we need to listen for God's voice in this. He's bigger than all of it, right?"

Bella nodded and looked up at The Book Nook. "I like that. The idea of being 'without fear of harm' is incredibly appealing after today. I really do love you, you know?"

Warmth crept up Adam's neck. It was wonderful to hear those words. "I love you, too. More than you'll ever know."

"Thank you for keeping me safe."

A muscle twitched in Adam's eye. He would have to tell her soon. Keeping others safe had become something of an obsession. But it would have to wait for another day.

CHAPTER SEVENTEEN

A STREAM OF SUNLIGHT WARMED Bella's face and welcomed her to a new day. Was it really only Tuesday? If only she could stay right here. Cozy and comfortable and oblivious to any further turmoil that might be waiting. She parted her eyelids and realized she hadn't quite pulled the curtains shut last night, hence the sunshine. What would this fresh day bring? *Lord, I know You say Your mercies are new every morning...*

A dull throb settled over her eyes. A headache was no surprise after yesterday. Last night had been a mangle of more tears, comforting, explanations to Pippa and Juliet, questioning God, eating soup, fitful sleep, and so much love. Talk about overwhelming.

She made a mental inventory of "her people." Juliet insisted Bella take her bedroom, as Juliet's shift at the hospital started early and she didn't want to cause a disturbance. Adam slept downstairs in the bookstore again on the makeshift bed they'd put together. Max promised to go into the police station first thing this morning to find out as much as he could about Rose's family. And Pippa offered to take the bookstore shifts again while Bella took some time off to get to the bottom of her plethora of family issues. Plus, the girls were not allowed back in their apartment until everything was back to normal.

What was normal? Bella stretched out like the satisfied cat beside her. Life had been good until the tsunami of disasters began crashing in on Friday. Unbelievable that last week, she had been writing at the lighthouse, working on another novel, reveling in how perfect her existence had become. Finally, after a childhood out of a Dickens novel followed by turbulent teen years, she'd been content. Her faith was strong, she had the best boyfriend she could ever imagine, she loved her work at the bookstore, and her writing was coming together to the point where she'd even considered submitting a manuscript or two. Almost.

Sure, money was tight, but that was how she had spent the past six years. Money was not a priority. Give her the glorious ocean view up at the lighthouse any day. What about Adam and finances? They'd never discussed money at great length. He came from such affluence, maybe he didn't consider it an issue. But it was important if they wanted to be on the same page looking forward. She raised her left hand and stared at her bare ring finger. That stunning diamond he'd pulled from his pocket had taken her breath away on so many levels. *Oh, Adam.* She eased herself from the bed. Everything ached, heart included.

One thing at a time. Focus. Today they had to check out any information on Rose's family that was available. Bella shuddered. What if they were dangerous people? Max would need to check on that. Should she try to make contact? Rose had warned her to stay away.

She pulled her hair into a ponytail with the elastic around her wrist and stumbled into the bathroom. Pain killers for the headache, shower to feel human again, and then coffee.

Fifteen minutes later, enticed by the aroma of freshly-brewed dark roast, Bella followed her nose into the cozy kitchen where Pippa was engrossed in her newspaper. Old school, she fought for all things paper. Her bright smile did little to disguise the dark shadows beneath her eyes. Bella's heart constricted. This sweet woman couldn't get sick again.

"Sweetheart, how are you feeling this morning?"

"I'm fine, thanks." Bella remembered her confession to Adam the night before and her decision to be honest. To stop hiding. To stop running from her feelings. "Well, maybe not *fine*, but I'm surviving. How about you?"

Pippa folded her paper and stood. "I'm ready for a day in my land of books. What could be better?"

"I, for one, know precisely what you mean. I miss the bookstore. I don't mind taking some shifts, you know."

"Nonsense. You have a lot going on at the moment, to say the least." Pippa jangled as she walked over and took Bella's hands in her own. "Give yourself time. You need to grieve and process and find your answers. Write. I know it helps, even if you don't write about what's going on in your head and your heart today. I don't pretend to have a faith like yours, but I do believe we were created with minds and bodies that take time to mend and heal."

"You believe in creation? I didn't think you believed in God at all."

"It's hard to cradle a miracle in your arms after giving birth and not believe in a Creator." Pippa winked. "Now I'm heading downstairs before you start preaching at me."

Bella smiled and gave her a hug. "Fine. But you can't stop me praying for you."

Pippa chuckled and Bella's phoned chirped. A text message from Adam. He'd run home to his apartment for a shower and was on his way back over with doughnuts. Max was meeting them here, which explained said doughnuts. Which would pair well with her coffee. Yes, a sugar-fix was allowed today.

She drained her mug, put on a fresh pot, and then sliced up some strawberries and pears. It was the least she could do in an attempt to give the breakfast a hint of nutritional content. While she waited for the boys, she perched on the barstool and thumbed through her worn Bible for some spiritual nourishment. Psalms. She would camp out in Psalms this week. As she focused on the words of encouragement, her tapping foot stilled. When had she even started with the foot tapping thing? Psalm 139 was like a warm, comforting blanket. She was no accident. She was intentionally created, even Pippa would agree with her there. It was in black and white, eternal promises that God would be with her wherever she went, that she was known intimately by the Almighty. That there was no running from Him.

Bella stopped reading and looked down at her bare feet, complete with soft pink nail polish. When she was a child, those feet were shoed with the best money could buy. Even when her body was bruised in the literal sense by her parents, her feet were well cared for. Those feet carried her away from abuse and ran toward a dream of safety. Those feet kept running from town to town, always ready to move on in order to stay one step ahead of pursuers. Yet there was no running from God. For the first time in her life, even with the shadow of danger hovering over her, Bella had no desire to run anymore. How strange. And how beautiful.

"Bella, are you here? It's us." Adam's rich baritone voice sounded from behind the locked door.

She put the Bible on the counter and padded over to let him in.

"Morning." The dimples in Adam's cheeks deepened as he smiled. His eyes were lit with caramel hues today—funny how they changed with the weather. This man was captivating.

Bella stood on tiptoes, kissed his cheek, and stepped aside while he strode in with Max on his heels. Interesting— Max had a blue file tucked under one arm. Could there be new information?

"Thanks for coming over again, Max. I guess this is feeling like a second home for you at the moment."

"It's all good. I like it here. Especially when my buddy brings doughnuts." He looked rather imposing yet dashing in his uniform. Juliet would be sorry to have missed out.

"Coffee?"

"Thanks." They both replied and settled around Pippa's kitchen table.

"Did you get some sleep?" Adam put a hand on Bella's arm as she set down the filled mugs.

"Yeah. Not the greatest, but I feel better this morning than I did last night." And looking into those fathomless caramel eyes helped, big time.

Max shook his head and placed the file on the table. "This is rough for you, I know. I called in the black truck to the guys at the station last night, but without a plate number, there's not much we can do."

"I presumed as much. I wish I'd had the presence of mind to concentrate on that plate number." Bella took a doughnut drizzled with chocolate frosting from the bag. "Maybe it was a coincidence after all. I think I'd be more suspicious if it were the same vehicle that tail-gated us on Saturday evening when we were coming back from the beach. But that was a red car."

"True." Adam blew on his coffee. "But we can't rule out the possibility that it was the same person, only in a different vehicle. We didn't get a decent look at either."

"It's a troublesome stretch of road." Max leaned back in his chair. "There have been a fair number of accidents over the years."

"I guess we'll have to stay extra vigilant when we're out and about." Bella cleared her throat. "I'm almost scared to ask, but did you discover anything more about my birth mother or her family?"

Max finished his mouthful of doughnut. "Not much, I'm afraid. Adam said you thought she was from an affluent family, but it appears there's not a great deal of information on the Blakes of California." He opened the file and read from it.

"Says here Rose went off grid for a few years—I'm guessing it was when she had you— and then decided to lay low to avoid her family or something. Looks like nothing really pops up until after Mr. Blake passed away in 2005, and then his wife died a year later. I wish I had better news for you."

Bella nodded. "It's heartbreaking to imagine she had parents but no real relationship with them for years. I hope at least her childhood was a happy one. I wonder what went wrong. I know she got pregnant, and that must have been an issue, but to never ever go back home and reconcile? That's too sad."

"Any siblings or other family?" Adam asked.

"None. And Rose never married or had a family of her own. At least not under this name. But there's always a chance she changed her name and flew under the radar."

Tears pricked Bella's eyes and she shivered. She'd been there, done that. But to be on the run forever? This could have been her life. Never settling down, always looking over her shoulder. It was her greatest fear and her mother's reality.

"I was her only child? And she never got to know me at all." Bella bit her lip. "I hope she made the best of her circumstances, whatever that looked like. What did she do all that time? Is there any way of finding out more?"

Max shook his head. "I wish I had some concrete details to give you. You can do some investigating yourself or hire someone, though. Don't give up all hope of finding out about your family history."

"Honey, I'm sure there are ways we can dig deeper. Find out more about the Blakes, if you'd like."

Or maybe she was better off not knowing the whole truth about her extended biological family. It wouldn't change the reality that Rose was gone. "No. No, I don't think I need to."

"Really?" Adam folded his arms on the table. "It might help give you some sense of closure."

How could she explain this? "Guys, I have to trust that Rose wanted the best for me. If there were any reason I should get to know my biological family, I believe she would have reached out somehow and told me. Sent a message or something. Written it in the letter." *Unless there's something in the box?*

"But I think she was protecting me. I have no desire to dig into an area of my family's history that will only bring pain. We don't know who my biological father was. He wasn't even named, so again, I think that's for my own good." She stood and paced around the table. "All I ever wanted was to be reconciled with my mother. I know she loved me. But now that can't happen."

Adam stood and opened his arms. She flew into them and dissolved. Again.

Max's chair scraped on the tile floor as he stood. "I should get back to work. Call me if there's anything else I can do."

"Thanks, man." Adam called over the top of Bella's head. "I'll catch you later. Take the rest of the doughnuts."

"If you insist."

Bella heard the door click shut as Adam walked across the room with her and lowered her onto the sofa.

"I'm going to drown in my own tears if I cry anymore. I hate this."

"Shhh. I know." He sat beside her and pulled her close. "This is a lot to handle. You have years of pent-up tears all needing to be released. I know you're disappointed—I would be. It might have been nice to have something to remember Rose by. A memory. A family member. Perhaps..."

She looked up. "Perhaps what?"

Adam paused and the cute little crease appeared between his eyebrows. He must be trying to decide whether he should say something or not. It was one of his charms, the way he mulled over his words before blurting something out.

"Just say it."

"What if there's something else in the safe deposit box?"

"I don't even care about the money."

"No, I mean something personal that Rose wanted you to have. Something to give you a sense of who you are. A memento. Another letter or a card explaining everything. You were supposed to be aware of the contents when you turned eighteen, of legal age. I don't know, maybe it's a dumb idea."

Bella sat up straight. "No, I think you might be onto something. It's too sad to think Rose's trail ends here and that I'll never know anything more about her. We could try to get hold of whoever is looking after her estate in California, too. But it might be tricky."

"Unless there's something in the box that will help."

"Dare I hope?" A flutter of nerves shivered in her belly.

"It's your call. You know I'm willing to take a trip to Seattle with you, if that's what you decide."

Bella rubbed at her eyes. "At least I could try to put this whole thing to rest once I've seen what's in the box. But what about George and Susannah? If they are following me, I could lead them right to the pot of money."

"I think they know where it is anyway. We could even catch them in the act of trying to take it from you. That's one way to put them behind bars, where they belong."

"A trap?"

Adam smiled. "That sounds a bit dramatic, but we can talk to Max about it. He has people in Seattle, remember?"

"Hmm. Perhaps I finally get to dig out the truth."

"Are you scared? You don't have to do anything, you know. There's no rush."

"But there is. I want to let the rest of you get back to your normal lives as quickly as possible before someone gets hurt." She looked up at him through her wet lashes. "If you want to spend the rest of your life with me, you have to know I'm determined."

"Well, I can see that…"

Bella wiped her cheeks with her sleeve. "And right now, I'm determined to get to the truth—no matter what."

CHAPTER EIGHTEEN

"COFFEE?" ADAM SLOWED THE JEEP as they approached their favorite coffee shop heading out of town.

Was he kidding? It was five o'clock on a Wednesday morning. Coffee was a non-negotiable.

"Yes, please. It's virtually the middle of the night still." Bella pulled her arms underneath her crocheted poncho and shivered. It was cozier than the denim jacket, but she would sooner be snuggled up asleep in bed. The early start this morning had *not* been her idea. Who left the house at five on purpose?

"It's not so bad. This way we'll be in Seattle by early afternoon, as long as the traffic's not too heavy."

She sighed and rubbed her eyes. "I know. But I'm not a bright-and-breezy morning lark like you. Plus, I stayed up reading until late. I think I got about three hours sleep."

"You can doze on the way. I managed to finish my work project and got a decent night's sleep, so I'm good to go. Here, I'll run in and grab the coffees. The usual?"

"Perfect."

Bella watched Adam rush into the coffee shop. His black T-shirt and black jeans made him look like he was more than ready for a mission. She smiled and pulled down the sun visor with the mirror. Ugh. Unruly curls and red-rimmed eyes. Five-in-the-morning Bella was not looking good. Especially running on three hours of sleep. But there was no way she could doze off last night after thinking about Seattle all yesterday.

They had spent hours finding a human to speak to at the Seattle bank, making an appointment, working out the best route to drive, and seeing what Max could pull together in the way of surveillance. Bella needed more clothes, so they'd stopped by her apartment. Thankfully, all was well there. Juliet had phoned her friend Madison, and arranged for Bella and Adam to stay with her overnight. It would be good to see Madison again and to meet Luke in person. At least that would be better than a random hotel in the city. Seattle still gave Bella the creeps. But she could do it for twenty-four hours, and then straight back home.

She dug in her oversized purse and pulled out some lip balm. She applied the layer of minty smoothness, pinched her cheeks, and pulled her long, disheveled, wavy hair to one side. It would have to suffice for now.

Before flipping the visor up, she peered in the mirror once more to check no other cars had pulled in behind them. Max encouraged them to watch for suspicious drivers, and in Bella's mind, anyone out at this unearthly hour was suspicious. And crazy.

The driver's door opened and Adam handed her a cup and a paper bag. "Here you go."

"Thanks. I'll eat the croissant later but I'll drain that coffee right now." She warmed her hands on the cup as the heat seeped through the cardboard sleeve. "How long until the sun comes up?"

Adam checked his watch and pulled the vehicle onto the road. "I'd say you've got a couple of hours until it's your kind of morning. Why don't you have your coffee to warm up and then take a nap. You won't miss much."

"Will you wake me up for sunrise?"

"I promise. I think it's going to be a nice day for travelling—no rain in the forecast."

"Ah, but do we ever trust the forecast?"

"No. Never." He grinned and took one hand off the steering wheel to brush a strand of hair from her face. "I think I like sleepy, first-thing-in-the morning Bella."

"I'm a bear before seven. I'm sorry."

"It's endearing."

Bella smiled in return. "Whatever, Mr. Morning Lark."

"It wouldn't be too bad marrying me, you know. Morning Larks can be useful. I'll bring you coffee in bed, have breakfast ready to go when you grace me with your presence in the kitchen, put the garbage out super early…"

She shrugged while her heart skipped a beat. "I guess it doesn't sound too bad." *Nice job at playing it cool.*

They were quiet for several minutes while Bella pondered their future together. She'd hardly had a chance to dwell on his marriage proposal since Friday, so much had transpired since then. What to do? There was no denying the love between them, and the thought of not having Adam in her future was more than she could bear. Truth be told, she'd never considered herself as a wife. It involved settling down, deepening roots, having a home. It both terrified and tantalized. Poor Adam. He was the most patient man in the world.

"Thank you."

He took a sip of his coffee and set it back in the cup holder. "For what?"

"For giving me time to process your proposal. For understanding. For being super patient. For driving me to Seattle. For risking your safety. You know, just a couple of regular things…"

He laughed and squeezed her hand. "You are worth all that and more. I'll wait as long as it takes, and I'm here for you one hundred percent. You can't get rid of me even if you want to."

"I don't."

"You sure?"

She took in his handsome profile, the strong, steady arms. "Positive." Bella sipped her vanilla latte and laid back her head. If only this would all work out and she could be Mrs. Adam Lexington. Bella Lexington did have a certain ring to it. Classy but approachable.

She gazed through her window in the morning darkness at the lush, green bushes and tall, imposing cedars caught in the headlights. It must have rained last night. The earthy smell was pungent. The air heavy with dew and dampness. How she loved this place. Could she truly settle here forever?

***

"You want to catch the sunrise?"

"Hmm?" Bella opened her eyes and took a second to remember where she was. Adam must have taken the cup from her hand at some point when sleep claimed her. She rolled her stiff shoulders. "Where are we?"

189

"Lincoln City. We could stretch our legs for a minute if you like?"

"Sure."

They pulled over to an empty restaurant parking lot and ran across the street. The morning breeze was bracing, but the view more than made up for any discomfort. Bella clutched the railing. The horizon stretched before her, tangerine with the promise of sunshine. Ocean and sky were the same grey-blue, each mirroring the other. The immense beach was deserted at this hour, and a peace settled over Bella in spite of her shivering.

Adam put an arm around her shoulders, doing his best to shield her from the wind. "Aren't you glad I made you into a morning person for today?" He raised his voice in order to be heard.

"It's breathtaking. I could stay here for hours." It was as if she had interrupted a Master Artist at work, yet was fully welcomed to be a part of the picture. "This feels like God telling me to keep going. Is that weird?"

"Not at all. He speaks to me loudest through creation."

"Really?"

"Yeah. I think He knows how to get our attention and hones right into where our heart listens."

Bella grinned. How awesome was this man?

They swayed back and forth, breathing in fresh dawn air for several minutes. At last, the sun made an appearance, colors building and reflecting off the clouds like an ever-changing painting, and the day officially began.

Bella pecked Adam on the cheek. "And now it's daytime."

"No more bear?"

"No more bear. And I suppose we should get going. It's a long drive." She turned to look at the jeep. "I'm sorry I can't help you out with that."

"Haven't you ever wanted to learn to drive?"

"Yes. But I don't have my birth certificate and it was always too complicated with my name and being registered and everything. I couldn't take a chance on George and Susannah tracking me down. Besides, the bike keeps me fit." She pulled Adam across the street and ducked into the vehicle.

He jumped in beside her and started the engine. "You realize that could all change soon? I mean if we can get to the safe deposit box and discover whatever information we might need to help you get some closure on your past, there's nothing stopping you from leading a perfectly normal life. Including learning how to drive."

"I guess so. We may need your dad to pull some strings to sort out my legal documents. I only hope George and Susannah are caught and put away. I'm positive they are involved in all sorts of illegal financial shenanigans. Goodness only knows what else they've been up to since I left home."

Adam shook his head. "They need to be held accountable. No one should get away with what they did to you. No one." His jaw twitched.

"I agree." Bella turned to check behind them. "Have you noticed anything suspicious yet?"

"Nope. Not many vehicles around this early. It'll start getting busier soon with work traffic, but I'm keeping my eye on anyone following us. Max said to call him when we're just

191

outside Seattle and he'll put us in contact with his officer buddy."

"Cam?"

"Yeah, Cameron Whitfield. He's expecting us."

Bella shuddered. "Why do I feel like we're in some crime show right now? This is bizarre."

"It is. But can you imagine what relief you're going to feel once you know the truth?"

Bella watched a seagull fly past them with graceful ease and swoop out across the ocean. "Freedom. That's what I want more than anything. And now I can almost taste it. Which makes me feel hungry—I think I'll have my croissant. Want yours?" She reached down and dug into the paper bag.

Adam grinned. "I had mine while it was still warm. Delicious. Way better than those doughnuts Max loves so much."

Bella giggled as she took a bite and caught a flake of pastry on her chin. "He's such a nice guy. He's gone above and beyond the call of duty with my stuff, hasn't he?"

"Yeah, but that's Max for you. And he has a vested interest."

"Ah, yes. Juliet. They make the cutest couple. This is the happiest I've seen Juliet in the year or so I've known her. She doesn't talk about guys much." She gave Adam the side eyes. "I still can't believe she never told me about dating you."

Adam pursed his lips. "Ancient history."

"It's not that ancient."

"I don't remember anything B.B."

"What?"

"Before Bella." He gave her a cheesy grin.

She slapped his knee. "You're incorrigible. Don't get me wrong, I'm glad you guys broke up. Otherwise, there would have been no *us*, but I'm not gonna lie, I'm still a little curious."

Bella finished up her croissant and eyed Adam as he focused on driving. His strong jaw, stubbly from a lack of shaving this morning, was set. His kaleidoscope eyes looked straight ahead. She sighed, safe in his presence.

She reached up and ran fingers through his thick hair, a little longer on top and super short at the back. He leaned into her hand and grinned. He had it all—looks, personality, career, faith, the whole dreamboat package. Her pulse raced a little. Juliet must have been devastated at losing him. Poor girl. She pulled her hand back to her lap.

"Can I ask—why did you tell Juliet you didn't ever want to marry? You must have had good reason if it meant breaking up with her."

Adam's jaw clenched and he said nothing for a few seconds. Finally, he took a deep breath and spoke without turning his head.

"Because I didn't ever want kids."

"Oh."

He didn't ever want kids? Her heart sank. Had he changed his mind since then like he had about getting married? Dare she ask? They'd never come out and discussed having children together, but that was because they hadn't even discussed marriage. One step at a time and all that. No. He loved kids. He adored his baby nephew. Although, it was strange he never wanted to babysit.

"Have you changed your mind since then? About having children of your own?" Her voice sounded weak in her ears. She held her breath.

"Yes."

Bella exhaled. "You sure? It's kind of a big deal, you know. You never mentioned this to me before. Why were you anti-kid back when you were dating Juliet?"

He rolled his shoulders. This was awkward for him. Should she back off?

Adam cleared his throat. "You have to understand life hasn't always been peachy for me. I know you have this idea I have never had anything bad happen, but that's far from the truth. Besides, since dating Juliet, I've had time to process a lot of things. I had to deal with some issues. I was immature back then."

Issues? Adam's voice was labored, like he didn't want to have this conversation but knew he must. For a second, she hesitated. Did she want to know details? Yes. She had to know everything about this man. He now knew everything about her, after all.

"What kind of issues?" Something about him losing someone? That was something he'd alluded to before.

He licked his lips and said nothing for well over a minute.

Bella swiveled in her seat to gage his reaction.

"Adam, is everything alright? You're worrying me a little bit here. You know you can tell me anything. For goodness sake, look at the plethora of issues I've thrown at you recently."

"You don't need any more heavy stuff to deal with right now. This can wait." His words were clipped.

Heavy stuff. What? This was getting scary. Adam's protective nature was sweet to some degree, but now she needed to know the truth. The week couldn't get any worse. She braced herself.

"Umm, hello, I don't think so. You can't tell me you have issues and then not explain. Please, won't you share it with me? I'm a big girl and you know nothing could ever shock me. Particularly coming from you. I love you."

He sighed and pulled over to an empty gas station. He kept his hands on the steering wheel and gazed ahead.

"I wanted to tell you a hundred times before, but I didn't know how. And the more you kept saying I had a perfect family and the ideal upbringing, the harder it became to admit you were wrong. The truth is, something horrific happened when I was a kid."

Bella reminded herself to take a breath. What was this? Some weird confession? A pain stirred in her stomach. She said nothing. He needed to tell her at his own pace. She rested a hand on his knee.

"I know you had a dreadful childhood, and I can't imagine feeling unloved and unwanted. The truth is, my parents have always been there for me and loved me, but there was a period of time when I wouldn't let them." He turned to face her. His beautiful eyes brimmed and he struggled to keep his lip from trembling.

Bella took his hand in hers. "Take your time."

He shook his head. "It happened so long ago, yet I can remember every sensation as if it were yesterday. Every scream, every breath, the sirens, the rushing. The pain, the guilt, the hate…"

A tear meandered down his face and splashed onto their hands. Bella was transfixed. She hardly wanted to breathe in case it broke the spell and he lost the courage to share his pain.

"I had a little sister. She was beautiful. A precious surprise to my parents and a gift to us guys. We all treated her like a china doll. She brought so much girly joy to a house of rambunctious boys."

Bella furrowed her brow. A sister? How had she never heard about or seen evidence of this sister in the past year of visiting his family home?

Adam shuddered and Bella felt it run right through her.

"I'm sorry I never told you about her before. It's a part of my past that I buried along with her."

She was dead? Oh, Adam. Her own eyes filled. "That's heartbreaking. But I don't understand why you couldn't tell me before." She squeezed his fingers.

"That's not it. Not all of it anyway."

"Oh?"

"She is the reason why I swore I would never have any children of my own…" He held her gaze. "I couldn't even consider being responsible for a child ever again. Not after she died."

"But why?" Bella barely heard her own whisper.

Adam waited a beat. "My baby sister is dead because of me."

CHAPTER NINETEEN

ADAM HUNG HIS HEAD. HE breathed heavily as he stared at his lap and Bella had no clue what to do nor what to say. She cranked her window down to let in some fresh air. *Lord, help me with this?*

"You killed her?" She had to get it straight in her mind.

"We were babysitting one evening. My parents were at some big gala event and they left my brothers and I in charge of Emily."

"Emily?"

"My baby sister." Adam shook his head. "Yeah, sorry, her name was Emily. She was always well behaved and my brother Michael had taken this babysitting course and everything, so it shouldn't have been an issue. Mom fussed before she went out, gave us a list of phone numbers in case of an emergency, and set out all the snacks and Emily's bottle of milk and stuff.

"As soon as my parents left, my brothers went outside into the yard to throw around a football. I said I wanted to join them, but they voted I give Emily her bottle inside the house first. She was almost two years old and loved her bedtime bottle. I'd done it a dozen times before and watched Mom each evening. But something went wrong."

"What happened?" Bella held her breath. She wanted to know. She didn't want to know. She needed to know.

"I gave Em her bottle, and she toddled off toward her nursery with one of my little toy cars in her hand. I followed and lifted her into the crib. I told her to go to sleep and kissed her pudgy cheek." Adam bit his lip. "She blew me a kiss, the way Mom taught her, and I went outside to join my brothers. I don't know how long we were playing outside, but at some point, Michael and Reid told me to go in and check on Emily."

Adam's face paled and his bright eyes were heavy with pain. "I sprinted into her room, hoping I could go straight back outside again, but right away I knew something was wrong. Em was lying on her back, her eyes were open and her face was blue. My little toy car was next to her head and one of the wheels was missing. She had choked on it right there in her princess crib."

Bella gasped and tears escaped. "What did you do?"

"I screamed and the boys came running in. We all just stared at her for a second, and then Michael picked her up and lay her on the floor to start CPR. He yelled at me to phone an ambulance and at Reid to phone Mom and Dad. The rest of that night is a mixture of vivid and blurred images. My mom's screams, us following the ambulance, the smell of the hospital, my brothers and I huddled in the waiting room. I carried her little stuffed bunny to the hospital for her to have when she woke up, but she never did." He exhaled. "And it was all my fault."

Bella blinked. "Wait, how old were you then?"

"Eight and a half."

"You were only a little child yourself. It was a horrible, heartbreaking accident, but it was exactly that—an accident."

"My head knows that now, but my heart still has its moments of doubt. And back then, I shouldered all the blame. My poor parents tried to console me, even though their own hearts had shattered. My brothers admitted they should have cared for Emily rather than play football in the yard, but they weren't the one who let her take a tiny car to bed with her and then left her in the crib to choke."

"Adam, no."

He attempted a sad smile. "Like I said, I went through a dark time and lived with guilt and shame for years. To say I carried the weight of the world on my shoulders would be an understatement. My parents did everything they could think of to help me, and most of the time I was fine. But certain things triggered me into a downward spiral, like little girls who looked like Emily. You have no idea how many toddlers have blonde curls and big, blue eyes. And even the name Emily. There were three in my class at school."

Bella picked up Adam's clenched fist and kissed it. "I'm sorry. I would never have guessed. I can't believe you've never mentioned such a huge part of your past to me before."

As soon as she said it, the truth hit her like a freight train. She bit her lip and closed her eyes. "That was a silly thing for me to say after me keeping my entire life history from you. I guess neither of us ever spoke much about our childhoods up until now, did we?"

Adam shook his head. "We found other stuff to talk about and managed to avoid discussing the excruciating experiences."

"But at your parents' home there's no hint of you ever having a sister. No photos or anything. Is it too painful?"

"Yeah, you could say that. We moved to that house soon after Emily died. There were too many agonizing memories for us all at the old place. My parents found the new house and we uprooted from our previous neighborhood. Nobody in the new area was aware of everything our family had been through at first, only that we had experienced a death in the family. We were quite private."

Bella nodded. "That's understandable. What about your friends? Did you ever tell them about it?"

"Max knows. A couple of other buddies in high school who have moved away since. To be honest, I'm not sure who is aware of how Emily died. I'm sure Mom has opened up to her friends, but those first years were tough. The new house helped, the ocean was healing for us all. God knew what we needed and he provided the perfect place. It was almost a physical reminder that grief comes in waves but God washes away the pain like footprints in the sand."

"That's beautiful." Another tear slipped down Bella's cheek.

"Then after a while, the family decided it was easier to keep all her photos and memories in my parents' bedroom. To be honest, I think Mom and Dad did it for us boys. We carried a load of guilt, which seemed to heighten when we were reminded of how sweet she was."

"Your brothers must have felt just as bad as you for the accident." The thought of Michael, Reid, and Adam racked with guilt as children was heartbreaking.

"They did. I think they managed to deal with it better than me. Mom says I was always the super-sensitive one, even before the accident."

"I love that about you."

Adam sighed. "It was hard work for my family. But we processed through most of the guilt and pain and everything. We all still think of Emily often, it's like an unspoken promise that we won't forget her. We visit her gravestone. It sounds strange, but it's how we cope. I talk to Mom about Emily now, and it's fine. But trust me when I say it's been a journey for me. I've come a long way in the past two years."

"You were still struggling with this when you dated Juliet?"

"Yeah. I thought I could tell her the details about Emily, but it was too painful. I couldn't even consider ever having children of my own, being responsible again for a little life. I decided I would never be a father. So, I broke it up with her before we got too serious, which I felt lousy about, for the record."

"She would have understood. You're a good man, Adam."

He shook his head. "The timing wasn't right, and we were better off as friends. After our break-up, I found another counselor and worked through the whole guilt thing thoroughly. It was hard work, but it was effective. I know I'll see Emily again one day in heaven, and I know now it was an accident. God's grace and mercy became clearer than ever before, and I believed He had a plan for me. And when you came along, I knew it had to include you."

Bella leaned across the handbrake and held Adam in a tight embrace. That poor, shattered little boy had

201

transformed into the most caring, kind-hearted man she had ever encountered. No wonder he was protective.

"Do you think less of me?' He mumbled into her shoulder. "I mean, knowing what I did, do you still think you could have a family with me? Because you have given me a fresh longing for children of my own. I never wanted it before, but I do now. With you."

Oh, Adam. "Is that why you couldn't tell me? You were worried I would think less of you?" She pulled him in tighter. "I love you, and maybe I love you even more now that I know your journey. I'm sorry I presumed you had a perfect childhood, I had no idea. I would be privileged to have children with you one day. The way you care for me, your protective nature—it makes sense now. But you have nothing to prove. You're *my* Adam. We both have our wounds, but we have One who took every one of them for us. Right?"

He nodded. "I'll be honest, the thought of parenthood scares me a little. Even the thought of babysitting someone else's kids makes me nervous."

That explains why we haven't looked after little Tyler. "It scares me, too. I haven't had many exemplary role models in my life."

"Until Pippa."

"Yes, dear Pippa." A smile split her face.

He leaned back and sighed. "When I think about the future, I see us living by the ocean one day, you writing your novels and me designing all sorts of cool structures. It'll be our creative space."

"Really? You'd live by the ocean to make me happy?"

"Are you kidding? I'd live anywhere with you."

"It's a sweet thought." *Dare I even dream?*

"You let me worry about the details." Adam tapped his chin. "I like the idea of you and me with the ocean before us and a few mini Bellas and tiny Adams running around."

"I think I'd love children one day."

"You're going to be a fantastic mommy. God will give us both the wisdom and courage we need for parenting, I'm confident of that."

"You're a brave man, Adam Lexington, taking me on."

"And you're a brave woman. The bravest I've ever known." Adam took a deep breath. "So, that's the past and the future discussed. I suppose now we should try to focus on the present. That was a heavy conversation, wasn't it?"

"Yeah. But I needed to know. Thank you for sharing."

"I should have done it a long time ago."

Bella tipped his chin up. "Hey, we're moving forward, right?"

"Right." Adam glanced at his watch and grimaced. "I hadn't planned for the detour; we should hit the road."

"Are you good to drive?" He must be exhausted after spilling his heart.

"Are you going to take over?" He grinned.

"Well, no, but I mean if you need to take a break and gather yourself, we can. That had to be draining for you."

Adam turned the key and flicked the turn signal. "You know, I feel kind of energized after telling you about Emily. It's like a weight has been lifted. I was worried you thought I was a complete jerk for breaking up with Juliet."

"I kinda did." She chuckled. "But not anymore."

"Good. Because now I feel ready for anything."

"That's a relief. Because the way this week is shaping up, who knows what's going to happen next?"

CHAPTER TWENTY

FIVE HOURS AND TWO NAPS later, Bella recognized the cityscape of Seattle. Had it really been six years since she'd left this place? Only six years, but a lifetime ago. She had changed so much—gone was the frail teenager. Now she a strong woman with faith in a stronger God. But the city still looked familiar, and not in a good way. The towering buildings appeared cold and imposing after living by the ocean in small towns laden with fresh seafood and old-world charm.

"Hey, Sleeping Beauty. We're here, in case you hadn't guessed."

"So I see." Bella stretched out her arms as much as she could in the confined space. "I can't believe how much I slept today."

"You needed it. Plus, I got to listen to my music." Adam chuckled.

"You made my sub-conscience listen to country? That's plain cruel."

"You were loving it. I could tell."

Bella raised her eyebrows. "I was obviously trying to be kind. And at the expense of my musical taste. Hey, did you speak with Max's buddy yet?"

"Cam? Yeah, I'm surprised you didn't wake up when I called him. He sounds like a good guy. Max filled him in on all the details and he'll be our go-to police officer here. Apparently, he's blond like Max, wearing a black leather jacket, and is going to be standing outside the bank reading a novel when we get there."

"Do we go and introduce ourselves to him or is this all cloak and dagger?" Perhaps she had read too many mystery novels.

"Definitely cloak and dagger. He wants to play it safe in case anyone's watching the bank, so I'll call him once we've parked nearby, then we'll walk right past him."

"Really? That'll work?"

"Yeah. It seems a bit overkill, but Max insisted. Nobody's expecting any trouble, though. I haven't noticed anything suspicious the entire journey."

"Well, that's a relief. I hope we can get into the bank today, grab the contents of the safe deposit box, and head back to Madison's to figure everything out. This time tomorrow we should be almost back home again, and with a few questions answered, too." *I hope.*

Adam shifted in his seat as he navigated the traffic. "Have you given much thought to the money that could be waiting for you in the box?"

"No. I know it sounds trite, but I don't care about that. I would trade any money in there for a clue to my mother's past or a way to find out more about her. Not that I would turn down financial help, don't get me wrong. I'm hardly rolling in it on my meager bookstore salary. The occasional short story I sell helps somewhat, but things are tight."

"Good thing my business is growing then. I want to be able to provide well for my family. Our family." He wriggled his eyebrows. "It blows my mind how you manage to live so frugally. I'm impressed."

"It's called survival." She let out a humorless laugh. "You should have seen me learning the ropes when I first left home."

"I don't know how you managed. I would have been clueless at that age. There are so many intriguing layers to Bella King. But you should prepare yourself for what may be in the box. It could be a whole stack of cash, or it might be nothing. Something could have happened since Rose originally made the deposit. It was a long time ago. She most likely had a key, too."

"I hadn't thought of her having a key." Bella ran her fingers through her hair, snagging a couple of knots in the process. "Maybe that's what George and Susannah were after when she got hit by the car."

"*If* they were responsible for the hit-and-run."

"I know. But it's a definite possibility." *Probability, more like.* Bella took a swig from her water bottle. "I'm grateful Max managed to get all this organized in time with Cam and the bank and everything. It's quite the operation."

Adam grinned. "Max always accomplishes what he sets out to do. He's a tireless worker."

"Do you think he'll miss the big city? I mean Florence isn't a hub of extreme crime, is it?"

"I don't know, to be honest. We didn't stay in touch while he was away, but I think he was close to burning out. A quieter pace will be good for him short-term. But who knows for how long?"

"Poor Juliet. I hope she doesn't get her heart broken if he up and leaves after a while."

"Maybe she'd follow him." Adam shrugged.

"You know Juliet's not the kind of girl who follows anyone anywhere. And she hated her time nursing in Seattle. She's small-town."

"What about you? If you had a choice, would you go big city or small-town?"

Bella pulled her hair to one side and leaned against the headrest.

"If I could choose, I would stay in Florence. Give me the ocean over a skyscraper any day." She tapped her chin. "Is that the right answer?"

Adam belly laughed. "Spot on. That's the answer I hoped for."

"I'm not a fan of being in *this* city in particular, given my history. Although, it's helped to put my mind at ease knowing we're not all alone up here."

"For sure. Would you still like to go to Madison's house first to freshen up? I have her address loaded into the GPS."

"If we have time. I'd really like to change into my nice clothes for the bank."

"Even the torture shoes?"

"My stilettos need to make an appearance at least once a year." Bella glanced at her watch. "It's almost one o'clock now and we have to be at the bank at three. I'd hate to get stuck in traffic and miss our appointment."

"Let me check how far apart they are." Adam pulled over and inspected the addresses on the GPS screen and his phone. "What did we do before technology?"

"I'm fairly sure we used maps." Like Pippa, Bella was a fan of paper anything. Technology caused her way too many headaches.

"Hmm. Well, it looks like both places are on the same side of the city. Madison's house is on the outskirts, but I can't see it taking more than thirty minutes to get from there to the bank. I say we go to Madison's and change clothes, grab a snack, and then head to your appointment."

"Perfect. I'm looking forward to seeing her. Juliet said Madison's not teaching anymore as she and Luke are planning to both be in Mexico as soon as they can work out the logistics. So, she should be around all day."

"Let's head there first then."

"Sounds good." *And then perhaps by tonight I'll get some answers to give me my freedom at last.*

***

"Wow. Juliet wasn't kidding when she said Madison's place was a mansion." Adam's mouth hung open as they entered through an automatic iron gate.

"It's stunning, isn't it?" Bella was mesmerized.

She took in the enormous grey stone home as they pulled into the circular private driveway. A trickling fountain on the front lawn and a theme of arches in the architecture emitted an Italian aura—warm, classy, and opulent. The property was enclosed by tall black railings, hidden by mature shrubbery and conifer trees. Safe. It felt safe, and that was a welcome sensation.

Adam stopped the jeep and Bella opened her door and jumped down from the passenger seat. She stretched her arms over her head as Adam jogged around the vehicle and closed her door. They held hands and made their way to the huge entrance.

"Welcome."

Madison walked toward them on the large front porch and enveloped Bella in a warm hug. She looked gorgeous, tanned from her honeymoon in Mexico and trim in her jeans and cream blouse. Even in bare feet with her long, brown hair tied in a top-knot, she looked put-together. She was "effortless chic" personified.

"I'm glad you found us. We're thrilled you could come and stay." She turned to Adam and took both his hands in hers. "It's wonderful to see you both again."

Bella grinned. "And we're grateful you could have us here. A hotel's fine but this is extra special. And congratulations on your wedding. Juliet sends her love and says to give Daisy a tickle on her belly."

"Daisy?" Adam's face scrunched up.

"My French bulldog. She's kind of a diva but she loves having her belly scratched."

With that, Daisy trotted through the front door and proceeded to bark ferociously at the strangers.

"Nice collar." Adam bent down and Daisy jumped up and attempted to smother him with kisses, her sparkly pink collar gleaming in the sunshine.

Bella laughed as the little pooch sought attention. "Here, girl, come and see me."

Daisy ignored Adam and sniffed out Bella, finally licking her hand. In one smooth motion, she rolled onto her back and all four legs protruded into the air.

"I guess you need that belly rub, hey, girl?" Bella obliged as Daisy groaned her appreciation.

"Looks like she's found a friend." Madison chuckled. "Careful, she may drool on your jeans."

Bella knelt down. "Not a problem. I'm changing before the appointment."

"I assume you guys are both comfortable around dogs then?"

"We are." Adam raised an eyebrow. "Bella would have a whole menagerie if she could."

"Maybe one day." She winked in his direction.

Madison shook her head. "One pup is enough for me. She's rather needy. But won't you both come on in? Daisy will follow us. She won't want to miss out on anything."

Bella took Adam's hand and they joined Madison as she held open the front door. She couldn't help smiling—it was an exquisite home. Windows lined one entire wall on the far side of the house, looking out onto the grounds. *Must be where Madison and Luke were married a couple of weeks ago.* The light, airy space flowed from one living area to another, each accentuated by colorful rugs, which popped against the dark hardwood floors and white walls. And the smell—something must have just come from the oven. It smelled like sweetness and autumn.

"This house is magnificent."

"Thanks. I moved back in here after my parents died and haven't had the heart to sell it yet. My sister, Chloe, and I have great memories growing up here. But now that we're both married, that's our next job, to put it up for sale and start downsizing. But come on into the living room and sit down. Would you prefer tea or coffee?"

"Tea for me, please." Bella looked at Adam.

"Tea is great. Thanks."

Madison smiled. "Make yourselves at home. I'll put the kettle on."

Adam glanced up the sweeping spiral staircase. "Is Luke around? I'm looking forward to meeting him."

"I'm sorry, you just missed him. He'll be here this evening though, whatever time you get back from the bank. Today he promised to help his parents with some yard work for a couple of hours. I think they're enjoying having him around for a change."

"That's fine. So, have you guys decided when you're moving to Mexico yet?" Adam sank into the black leather sofa and Bella sat next to him.

"Soon, hopefully." Madison blushed. "My Luke…" This girl was so in love. Bella slipped her hand into Adam's. "The poor guy had to go from living in the orphanage where he works as a missionary in a tiny town in Mexico, to hanging out here in this lavish house."

"Poor Luke." Adam chuckled.

"No, trust me, he'd go back tomorrow if we could sell the house and get my Visa arranged that soon. And I'm super excited about going there with him."

"Won't you miss Seattle? Or the States?" Bella glanced around at the breathtaking home. "Mexico is going to be quite different, isn't it?"

Madison flicked on the kettle and leaned across the granite island separating the kitchen from the living area. "I met everyone at the orphanage when we stopped by on our honeymoon. They're all so sweet. I'll miss it here for sure, especially my sister. But it's been a rough few years and I'm ready to start the next chapter of my life." Madison walked back around and perched on one of the sofas. "Bella, Juliet told me about your situation... I'm sorry about your birth mother. I know loss."

"Thanks." Bella looked at Madison through a blur of tears. "But I hope today we can start making sense of everything and, like you said, have the freedom to start my next chapter, too."

"I do hope so." Madison attended to Daisy, who was ready for the next session of belly rubs on the hardwood floor. "Juliet was such a trouper to come and look after this little pup while we were away. How's she doing? I hear she bumped into Max, that police guy."

Bella pursed her lips. *Did she ever.* "That's right. He's from Florence originally, so I guess it was only a matter of time until their paths crossed again. Do you remember meeting him?"

Madison nodded. "Of course. He came to the church Juliet and I were going to and we invited him back here for brunch with some friends. If I remember correctly, his work shifts never meshed with our church services, but he seemed like a sweet guy. I think Juliet was smitten."

Adam chuckled. "Consider them both smitten now."

"That's awesome." Madison clapped her hands together. "A nurse and a police officer seems like such a romantic notion. I'll have to keep tabs on her and see how things progress."

"I have a good feeling about them." Bella grinned.

"That's the best news." Madison stood. "Now, I know you haven't got too much time, but I'm going to make the tea and I have some pumpkin chocolate-chip muffins that just came out of the oven, if you're interested."

"Sounds perfect." Adam walked over to the open kitchen and groaned. "This could be my dream kitchen."

The girls laughed.

And you're my dream chef. "Don't mind Adam." Bella took her turn tickling Daisy. "He loves cooking, and I think he's fallen in love with the copper pots hanging from your ceiling rack."

"I'm sorry, hon. I totally have." He shook his head. "But back to reality, I'll pop out and grab our bags, if that's okay, Madison."

"Sure. Bring them in and head upstairs with them. You have the first two rooms on the left at the top of the stairs, go on in and get yourself settled." She chuckled. "And I know you're an architect, so feel free to go check out the whole house. Mom had some cool Italian designers who tapped into her inner *signora*." *Ah, that makes sense.*

"Great. I'll do that."

Bella followed Madison into the kitchen, Daisy at her heels.

"How are you feeling about your meeting? I'm sure you must be at least a little nervous about going to the bank."

Nervous? Try petrified. "Let's say I'll be glad when today is over. It's been the most surreal week of my life, and I'm desperate to get back to normal. My new normal."

Madison grabbed three mugs from an open shelf and pulled out a drawer of assorted teas. "Well then, first things first. Tea."

***

A knock on the bedroom door broke into Bella's daydream and she hurried across the plush carpet to open it.

"Hey." Adam stood with his hands in his pockets. He had changed into a black, collared shirt and smelled amazing.

"Hey yourself." She reached up on tiptoes to kiss his cheek. "How's your room?"

"This whole place is fantastic. I'm surprised Juliet wanted to come back to Florence after housesitting here for a week."

Bella leaned against the doorway. "She loved Daisy the Frenchie, but I think she found it a bit grand living here on her own. Although, I'm pleased she suggested we stay here. I'm already looking forward to climbing into that clawfoot tub at the end of today."

"You may need it. Are you about ready to go?"

"Can you give me five minutes? I still want to change."

"Don't tell me. You've been writing in here for the past fifteen minutes, haven't you?"

Bella bit her lip. "Maybe. There's so much ambience in this house, I had to try to capture it—you never know when I might need it. And it's been a while since I felt inspired to write anything."

Adam stroked her cheek. "You fascinate me. And you're right about this place." He produced two apples from his pockets. "You want an apple? Madison said I could help myself in the kitchen."

"So you did?"

"Only to apples. Although, I was tempted by the copper pots." Those dimples flashed beside his kissable lips.

"Sure, I'll have one. Come and sit for a minute." They each took a seat by the French doors next to her bed and gazed out over the grounds. She took a deep red fruit from his hand and bit into the sweetness.

Adam swallowed down a chunk of his apple. "Is it weird for you? Being back in Seattle?"

"It's not as bad as I imagined. I've moved on in so many ways, but the memories are hard to get over."

"I'm sure they are. Do you know if we're anywhere near where you used to live?"

Where was their last house from here? She'd never been great with getting her bearings. Juliet described her as being directionally-challenged. It was a miracle she'd ever found her way to Oregon without getting lost. Her only goal had been to keep moving south, close to the ocean. As far away from George and Susannah as possible…

"Hey? You still with me?" He smiled and bit another chunk out of his apple.

"Yeah, I was trying to remember. We moved around every couple of years until we hit Seattle and we didn't venture out often. To be honest, I don't know my way around the city at all. I recognize certain landmarks, but this area doesn't seem familiar. I guess I didn't pay much attention as a teen. When I left for good, I grabbed a cab to the bus station, bought a ticket south, and never looked back."

Bella thought as she munched. How on earth had she survived being kept prisoner in her own home most of the time? Granted, she hadn't known any different, but her heart ached as she recalled how lonely she had been. How she'd lost herself in books night after night. At least she'd been allowed that one luxury. Her beloved books.

Adam's phone lit up and he stood as he talked to Max. Bella decided to text Juliet and let her know they had arrived and were heading to the bank soon. She smiled when Juliet replied, saying she was with Max in the bookstore and that she was aware of their Seattle whereabouts. Those two were getting serious. Good for them.

"That was Max checking in. Do you want to get changed now?" Adam pocketed his phone. "I don't want to chance getting delayed."

"Yeah, I'll be quick. See you in the living room in five?"

"Five minutes. I'll go tickle Daisy's belly."

"You'll make her day."

CHAPTER TWENTY-ONE

ADAM'S MOUTH FELL OPEN AS she walked down the staircase. "Wow, you look fabulous."

Bella felt her cheeks heat up. She wanted to look professional for this momentous appointment, so she'd brought along her white silky blouse to wear with her charcoal grey pencil skirt and matching stilettos. Not quite the boho-chic look she favored at the coast. She would regret the footwear by the end of the afternoon, but it somehow helped to look put together, even when she felt like she might fall apart. Much hinged on the contents of one little box.

"Thanks. Is it me or is it unseasonably warm today?" Or maybe it was a major case of nerves.

Adam nodded toward the front door. "The sun's out and it's not raining in Seattle. I think that's something of an anomaly. Let's go and find this bank, shall we?"

Madison joined them from the kitchen and gave Bella a tender hug. "I'll be praying. And I'll have dinner ready this evening, but come back anytime that suits you. There's no pressure if you're not feeling up to it."

"Thanks for everything." Bella took a deep breath. "Here we go."

Her stomach flipped as she slid on her shades and they walked out to the jeep, hand in hand.

Adam opened the passenger door. "I'm sure I don't have to ask this, but you have the deposit box key, right?"

Seriously? Bella patted the chain around her neck. "Yes. Don't worry, I have the key."

She slid in and fastened her seatbelt. This was it. She had kept the little key safe for so long, hoping it would unlock something of her past, something to help her discover the truth, and now it was happening.

"All good?" Adam smiled from the driver's seat. He looked like a handsome movie star with his aviator shades on, and Bella's pulse picked up speed.

"Yes. All good here." She tried to hide her smirk.

He dialed the address for the bank into the GPS and pulled out of Madison's driveway toward the city. "Want some music on?"

"Sure. But please, make it something soothing? My hands are trembling already."

Adam found some classical music and she forced herself to take regular breaths.

Bella pressed her hand against the cool glass of the window as they joined the steady stream of traffic. Memories of her time spent living in this city invaded her mind. The occasional outing to an art gallery with Susannah, or if she were lucky, they would go grocery shopping. But always at night. Like everything was a huge secret, including her very existence.

How had they pulled it off? The homeschooling, the seclusion, the house moves up the coast and eventually into the Seattle area—it must have been exhausting for George and Susannah to keep up the pretense. They had no friends to speak of. Vacations had always been to private destinations where they wouldn't have to interact with anyone. And all in the name of greed. All to end up with Bella's apparent fortune.

What if there were a genuine fortune in the safe deposit box? What if there were simply a note from Rose? The note would be preferable. Time would tell.

As they took an overpass, Bella marveled at the sheer volume of traffic in the city. People and cars darted about like frantic ants—everyone lost in their own little world with their own secrets and sadness and joy.

"Do you want me to come in with you?" Adam spoke as he switched lanes.

"Hmm? Into the bank?"

"No, I mean into the actual room where you get the box. Would you rather have some privacy? I understand. This is kind of huge for you."

Bella adjusted the air conditioning vent. Should she be on her own to observe the contents of the box? Would she need time to process or cry or be alone with her thoughts? No. If this was the man she was thinking of marrying, then she wanted him by her side for all the important moments. Especially this.

"I'd like you to come in with me." She bit her lower lip. "Whatever's inside may affect you, too."

"Yeah? Really?"

She nodded. "I think we're in this together."

Adam concentrated as he slipped back into the outside lane. He kept glancing in the rearview mirror, and Bella had a flashback to the other night on the road from Cape Cove Beach.

"Everything alright? You're hopping around these lanes a bit."

Adam shrugged. "Just being extra careful. There's a black car that pulled out from Madison's street and has followed me each time I've changed lanes. Could be a coincidence..."

"You have to be kidding me." Bella swung her head around and craned to see the black car. "The one behind the red sports car?"

"Yeah. Can you see the driver?"

"Not clearly. Male. Shades. Can't see anyone else in the car. I wish I could catch the license plate, but it's not in my sightline." Her stomach dropped. "You don't think we're being followed again, do you?" A phone call to Cam might be wise.

"There's one way to find out for sure. Hang on tight."

She held her breath as Adam swerved at the last minute and took them off the highway to another road leading to an overpass.

"I don't see him behind us now. Do you?"

Bella leaned over and searched the trail of traffic. "Nope. If he was following us before, he isn't any more." She unclenched the death grip she had on the edges of her seat. "Nice maneuver, by the way."

Adam smiled and adjusted his shades. "Thanks. Any excuse for an opportunity to show off in front of you. Chances are it was some regular guy trying to dodge the traffic like I was, but it's better to be cautious. Argh. The GPS is going nuts. It should reroute us quickly."

"Or, I could pull out an old-fashioned map." Bella smirked and then settled back into the seat. Nothing like a false-alarm stalker emergency to tug at her already-frayed nerves.

"Try to relax. I'll have you at the bank in plenty of time. Listen to Mozart and I promise not to do any more amazing driving stunts."

"Thanks. I'd appreciate that."

***

"There it is, up on the right." Bella pointed to the large brick building and blew out a sigh of relief. "With that detour and the confused GPS, I thought we would never find it."

"And we still have ten minutes to spare. That'll give us chance to find somewhere to park."

"I see a sign for parking in the next block—what do you think?"

"Yeah, let's do it." They passed the bank where sure enough, a tall blond guy wearing a black leather jacket leaned against the low wall by the front door. He casually read a book, as if he had all the time in the world.

"Ha. That must be Cam." Bella smiled. "I do believe the plan is working."

"Like clockwork. Are you still feeling nervous?" Adam indicated and pulled into the parking lot.

"I'm shaking like a leaf. I don't know if it's nerves or excitement. I've waited such a long time for this."

"Let's get you inside the bank. The suspense is just about killing me."

"Really?" She wiped sweaty palms on her skirt.

"Sure." Adam reversed into a parking spot and killed the engine. "This is monumental. The trajectory of your life could change with the contents of this box."

Bella groaned. "I don't know if I'm ready for more drama. And believe it or not, I don't enjoy change. It seems to have been the story of my life—always moving, running, morphing with the circumstances. I would like some *boring* and *predictable* for once."

"At you service, ma'am." Adam tipped an imaginary hat. "I'm all about the boring and predictable."

"You are *so* not." Bella poked him in the ribs and picked up her purse. "I think this past week has proven that. Come on then, let's do this."

"I have to call Cam first. Let me put him on speaker phone in case he has any last-minute questions for you."

Adam punched in the phone number and Cam picked up.

"Cam?" Adam smiled. "This is Adam Lexington and I'm here with Bella King. We're parked in a lot about a half-block down from the bank on your right."

"Glad you made it, guys. Everything's quiet here at the moment. Have you had any trouble at all since we spoke earlier?"

"Not really. We thought a car might have been following us from our friend's place, but we pulled off the highway and he didn't come after us, so I don't think it was anything to worry about."

Cam clicked his tongue. "What make and color was the car?"

"It was a black Beemer." Adam slid off his shades. "Older model. I'm afraid we didn't get a license plate."

"No problem, I'm only asking as a precaution." Cam paused. "You come on in for your appointment and I'll get back to this scintillating novel."

Bella chuckled. "Thanks, Cam. We appreciate the extra security today."

"You're welcome. I'm going to stay out here and keep an eye on things. I'll watch out for any black Beemers for sure and anything else suspicious. If needed, I'll call for back-up. I have a few guys I can call in from within a couple of blocks."

Bella shuddered. "Did you receive those photos of George and Susannah from Max? In case they make an appearance, I mean."

"Yes, but I have a feeling they won't show up here in person. If there's anything unusual going on out here at any point, I'll get a message to you inside the bank. Please stay put and don't attempt to come out, if that's the case."

"Got it."

"And guys, don't forget to walk right past me. What are you both wearing so I know it's you without gawking?"

"Bella is the blonde stunner in a white blouse and grey skirt and I'm the regular-looking guy in jeans and a black collared shirt."

"Perfect. When this is all over and you're back in your vehicle, give me another call, okay?"

"Sure thing. And thanks again." Adam pocketed his phone. "Ready?"

"Yes." Bella jumped out of the vehicle and met Adam at the rear. "Do you think this parking lot is safe?" She glanced around at the concrete walls separating them from the busy street. "It might have been better to find somewhere in more of an open space."

He placed a warm hand on her shoulder. "Relax."

"I know. I'm paranoid." Deep breaths. Long, deep breaths.

Adam locked the jeep, took her hand, and they walked half a block. Right outside the large bank, a group of businessmen gathered in a huddle. Cam stood guard and, as arranged, they ignored him and entered the building.

The cool air hit Bella as soon as she stepped into the foyer. It was somehow soothing to see people milling about, doing their everyday banking, running errands and paying bills. *Nothing to see here. Just a regular day.*

Adam steered her in the direction of a semicircular reception desk. A brunette with a megawatt smile looked up.

"Hello, my name is Denise. How may I help you today?"

Bella cleared her throat. "Hello. I have an appointment at three to view my safe deposit box. Bella King."

"Ah, yes." Denise didn't even need to check her computer screen. Her gaze flickered toward the glass doors where Cam stood like a sentry. "Carol is expecting you. Won't you come this way?"

Bella took a deep breath and trotted behind the receptionist with Adam bringing up the rear. Denise punched some numbers onto a keypad and took them into the bowels of the building.

They came to a small office, where a grey-haired woman typed on a keyboard.

"Carol? Bella King is here to see you for her appointment."

The woman looked up with a kind smile, and Bella exhaled. A friendly face. This wasn't going to be so bad.

"Thanks Denise, I'll take it from here."

The receptionist clipped back down the corridor in her high heels and Carol picked up a file, stood, and beckoned Bella into the office. "Hello, I'm Carol Barnes. Won't you both come on in? I have a couple of things for you to sign and then I'll take you to your box."

Adam held out a chair and Bella sat next to him, her pulse whooshing in her ears. He rested his arm around her shoulders and she drew from his strength as she stared down at the paperwork spread on the desk.

"I know this is rather a sensitive case. The police in Florence forwarded your photograph and the details we needed to know." Bella felt her cheeks flush as Carol scrutinized an image on her computer screen and then considered Bella's face. She smiled again, apparently satisfied. "The box has been here unopened since the contents were deposited about twenty-three years ago, with explicit instructions that no one was to see the contents until your eighteenth birthday."

Bella nodded. That much she knew.

"The rent was paid up front for a total of thirty years, so feel free to continue using it until that time. I need you to sign where I've marked with an X on both pages, please. It's to prove you've been here. Here's a pen, dear. You have your key, I presume?"

Adam cleared his throat, and she nudged his foot with hers. Like she would forget the key.

"Yes, I most definitely do." Bella scanned the page. It all looked straightforward enough. "Am I allowed to take the contents with me?"

"Of course. You'll have to sign to say you have removed them all. Will you be taking everything?"

Bella nodded. "I think so. There's no reason for me to keep anything here. I live at the coast."

"We can do that. And if you need help in setting up another box in a city nearer to your home, please let us know." Carol handed her a business card.

Bella signed the forms. "This is it then." She glanced at Adam. "Can my boyfriend come with me? I'd rather not do this alone."

"Yes, that's no problem at all." She swiveled in her chair to a filing cabinet behind her, and produced another sheet of paper. "Here's a form for you to sign, sir."

Adam signed the bottom of the paper and they stood and followed Carol down the hall to a small room. A low mahogany table and two chairs were situated in the center of the space.

"You two get settled in here and I'll fetch your box. You won't be disturbed. Take as long as you like." She pointed to a black button on the wall. "You can press this buzzer when you've finished and I'll pop back in to collect the box. Any questions?"

Bella felt a chill pass through her. Either it was cold in here or this place held way too many secrets. "No, I don't think so. Thank you."

Carol gave a regal nod, and exited.

Adam put an arm around Bella's shoulders again. "You're shivering. I should have brought my jacket inside."

"I'm fine. It does feel kind of damp in here though. Like a cellar or something."

"Yeah, or a dungeon. It's not what I would call cheery."

Carol knocked on the open door of their room, carrying a steel rectangular box twice the size of Bella's shoe box.

"Here we are. The key should ease in and then turn it clockwise. Don't forget to press the buzzer if you need me for anything at all." She set the box on the table.

"Thank you." Bella mustered a smile and the older woman left.

Bella touched the cool metal of the box before her and savored the moment. Adam's hand was still on her shoulder, warm and safe. She could do this. She had dreamed of this revelation so many times over the years, and now it was a reality. Whatever lay inside this box could change her life. It could answer a lifetime's worth of questions.

It could reveal the truth.

Bella's hand trembled as she released the clasp on her necklace and allowed the key to fall into the palm of her hand.

"This is it."

"Here, let me hold your chain while you open the box. I'll slip it into my pocket to keep it safe."

Bella dropped the chain with her tiny silver lighthouse pendant into Adam's hand and inserted the key into the lock of the box in front of her. It fit with ease, so she turned it clockwise until it stopped and she felt the mechanism click open.

i

The hairs on the back of her neck stood to attention as she lifted the metal lid to reveal the contents. On first glance, it looked like paperwork and she sighed with relief.

"You okay?" Adam squeezed her shoulder.

"Yes." She didn't want to take her eyes from the box. "I suppose I'm grateful there wasn't a dead man's finger or something sinister in here. You have no idea where my imagination has taken me when I've considered this moment."

"It looks routine to me. Do you want to read it all in here or take it back to Madison's?"

Bella lifted the large, brown envelope from the box. There was another underneath. The smell of dust and paper hit her fast and she sneezed.

"It looks like there's a lot to go through. Maybe I'll have a quick scan and we'll get going. I don't like it down here. It feels like we're being watched." The chill sent a shiver right through her body.

"Whatever you like. We're in no hurry."

She tore open the end of the unmarked envelope and slid the papers partway out. "It's, it's from my mom. It's written by Rose. I recognize the handwriting without even reading it. It says, 'To my darling daughter...'"

That was enough. Tears blurred her vision and her hands trembled.

"I'm sorry, I can't read it here." Bella turned to Adam. "Please, can we leave?" She slid the papers back inside.

"Of course. Let me grab the other envelope for you." He leaned across and pulled the fat package from the box. "Whoa, this one's packed with something. Want to take a quick peek?"

Bella was beginning to feel nauseous. "No, you look."

Adam pulled open the seal and peered inside. "Wow. I don't know how much is here, but there's a pile of cash."

"There is?" Her mother had cared for her after all. She had made provision in her own way, and that made the tears fall faster.

"I even think there's some pieces of jewelry or something in these little velvet pouches. We need to be extra careful walking to the vehicle with this."

Bella stood and smoothed her skirt. "Okay, one envelope each." She slung her purse over a shoulder and hugged her envelope to her chest. "Let's ring for Carol."

Adam pressed the buzzer and they heard Carol's footsteps approach.

"Are you done already, dear?"

Bella nodded as she swiped at her falling tears. "If you don't mind, I think I'd rather go through these things at home. Or at least at my friend's house."

"I don't blame you one bit. It's not particularly cozy here, is it?"

"No, it's not. Thank you."

Carol observed the empty box. "Perfect. I have the form right here to say you've removed everything." She placed the paper on the table and offered a pen. "And don't forget, if you change your mind or want to put anything back in here, the box rent is paid for another six years at least."

Adam steered Bella from the awkward little office and Carol led them back through the corridors to the foyer. The kind lady shook both their hands and left them alone.

"You feeling alright? You look pale." Adam touched Bella's damp cheek. "Want me to go get the jeep and park outside? I'll bet Cam would let me pull it right up."

"Yes. No. I don't know." What was with the wooziness? This was not the scenario she had dreamed of for as many years as she could remember. A sudden wave of exhaustion hit from nowhere and caused her knees to buckle.

Grip the envelope. Don't let go of the envelope...

CHAPTER TWENTY-TWO

"I'M SORRY, I DON'T KNOW what's wrong with me. It must be all the excitement or something. I might throw up."

Adam shifted his envelope under one arm, and supported Bella's weight. He glanced around, and led her to a plastic chair in the waiting area. "Stay here. I'll get you some water."

She gripped her envelope, bent over, and put her head between her knees. By the time Adam returned with a paper cup filled with water, the world had righted itself.

"Thanks." The water tasted divine. "I feel human again. I think I'll be fine in a second." She set the cup on an empty table next to her.

Adam leaned close to whisper in her ear. "You know, I don't want to take any chances hanging around. Why don't I run to the jeep? I'll speak to Cam once I'm out of here to let him know what I'm doing and get him to stay right outside."

Bella hugged her envelope tighter to her chest as she watched busy people going about their banking business. Everything was normal, right? Another shiver ran through her. It wasn't in the plan to be separated at any point. Her stomach flipped.

"I don't know. I'm sure I'll be alright now. I think I'm feeling better already. I can come with you."

"You look white as a sheet, hon. Having you faint in the street is not quite the subtle exit we're hoping for. This way, Cam can keep an eye on you and make sure there's a place for me to pull up nice and close. Look, you'll be able to see me through these windows." He nodded straight ahead to the wall of glass. "I'll get Cam to help you from the foyer to the jeep and we'll be outta here. What do you say?"

"But you can't just go and speak with Cam, can you? What about all the cloak and dagger stuff? You'll have to call him from your phone."

"Exactly. I'll call him as soon as I'm on the sidewalk."

Bella glanced at her thumbnail. Not good. Juliet's stress-relieving habit was rubbing off on her. "Should I look after both envelopes here? I'll be safe—I'm sitting in a bank after all."

Adam stalled. He considered both options. Bella knew him well enough to recognize that squint.

"Sure. That's a good idea. There are cameras all over the place. Sit tight and I'll be as quick as I can." He handed the envelope to her. "It's going to be fine. You happy with this seat? You're close to the reception desk, in case you need Denise for anything."

Bella nodded. "I won't move a muscle until I see you pull up. Promise."

Adam bent over and kissed her on the lips. "I'm proud of you."

"For being pathetic and sickly?" She attempted a grin.

"No, for being brave enough to come here in the first place. It's been a draining week, no wonder it's all catching

232

up with you. We'll get you back to Madison's, have some food if you're feeling up to it, and you can spend as long as you like looking through these envelopes. Okay?"

That sounded good. "And tomorrow we can go home?"

"For sure."

Bella nodded. "Go on then. Don't be long. And Adam, I do love you, you know."

Dimples appeared. "I know. I love you more."

Before she could argue, he turned and paced to the door. She forced herself to breathe in and out, sipped a little more water, and attempted to blend in with the banking people as she clutched both envelopes on her lap. She sighed with relief when Adam pulled out his phone before he disappeared around the corner. So far, so good. She had a partial view of Cam as he stood nonchalantly reading his book. He tapped his ear and lifted his chin. The call had come in.

A sudden noise caused everyone in the foyer to turn toward the road. Was it a car crash? Bella's heart stopped for a moment as she tried to gage what was happening. A movement caught her eye through the window—Cam was sprinting away from the bank. *What?* He wasn't supposed to leave her here alone.

For several seconds, Bella froze on her chair. She'd promised Adam she would stay put, but now Cam had disappeared and her stomach knotted. Something was horribly wrong. A minute passed. She glanced at her watch—Adam should have reached the parking lot by now. He would be outside any moment. Should she wait out there alone or sit tight and hang on until Cam returned? She held goodness-knew-how-much cash in her hands.

She stood and rushed over to Denise.

"Excuse me, do you know what's going on outside?"

Denise shrugged. "I know as much as you, sorry. The traffic is awful along this road. Could be a fender-bender or something. Although it sounded more like a gunshot, don't you think?"

Bella didn't hesitate. She turned and ran to the door as quickly as her stupid stilettos allowed, and collided with a police officer entering the bank. The woman looked as surprised as Bella.

"Excuse me, officer, do you know what happened out there?"

The officer's face softened. "Are you Bella, by any chance?"

"What? Yes. How did you know?"

"I'm Officer Bingley. Come and sit down, dear." She started to steer Bella back to chair she had just vacated.

"Wait, no, I can't. I'm meeting my boyfriend outside any second…"

"It's alright, Bella. I know all about that. I'm with Cam."

"Oh." Bella shook her head. "Where did Cam go? One minute he was out there and the next he disappeared. He's supposed to be outside. My boyfriend was going to call him."

Everything began swirling in the foyer and Bella could think only to clasp her envelopes in a death grip. Adam. Where was he? Where was Cam? Why did this police officer have those sad puppy eyes?

"I was just around the corner when Cam phoned me. I'm afraid there's been an incident."

"No. Not Adam. Please tell me Adam's okay." Bella sank onto a chair. The officer crouched down next to her.

"The ambulance is on its way."

"What?" There hadn't been time for all this drama to play out. Adam was here mere moments ago, bringing her water and saying he loved her.

"*NO.*" Bella propelled herself from the chair and ran to the open door and into the bright sunlight, Officer Bingley at her side. She took a right and headed in the direction she had last seen Adam. A crowd had formed up ahead. People hung around, some trying not to look but staring anyway. Bile rose up in Bella's throat as she pushed through the crowd to the entrance of the parking lot where Adam's jeep was parked. She recognized Cam's blond hair and ran to the spot where he leaned over a body on the pavement.

"Adam?" It felt dream-like, as if cotton were stuffed in her ears muffling the sound of an ambulance and the many voices around her.

"Bella?" Cam looked directly at her now. "I'm sorry. There must have been someone waiting at the vehicle for you guys."

Bella collapsed over Adam's body and kissed his cheek, her fingers still clutching the envelopes. She heard herself scream—it was pitiful, more whimper than wail. "Is he shot?"

Stupid question. His eyes were closed and there was a slick pool of shiny blood all over the side of his black shirt, which had now transferred onto her own. *Don't think about the blood.*

"Yes, in the arm. It looks clean from what I can see, but he must have hit his head on the way down. He was out cold when I got here."

Confusing. This was all so confusing. "But how did you know he was in trouble?"

"He called me right as he walked from the bank. I heard the shot both on the phone and from down the street."

"Is he going to be alright?"

"You can go with him to the hospital. We'll have security there for you both." Cam wiped a hand down his face.

"Wait. But who shot him? Do we even know?" Bella tore her eyes from the man she loved and searched the area looking for—who? Susannah and George? A masked gunman?

Cam jerked his head toward another police officer who talked with some bystanders. "We will. There are witnesses and one had the presence of mind to snap a photo of the car with his phone as it sped away. Brave move."

"Oh." Bella was pulled up by Officer Bingley as two paramedics came in and maneuvered Adam's limp body onto a stretcher.

God, please let him be alright. He has to be alright.

They rolled him to the back of the waiting ambulance and slid the stretcher inside.

"Wait. I have to be with him."

"I know." Cam put a hand on Bella's trembling arm. "Officer Bingley will go with you to the hospital. If you have any questions, she'll help you out. I'm going to jump on this trail while it's hot. I'll let you know when we get news. Adam will be fine. You stay strong." He eyed the envelopes in her arms. One was now smudged with blood. "Do you want me to put those back in the bank for you?"

I want to go home. To turn the clock back and pretend we never even came to Seattle. How selfish am I to put Adam's life at risk?

It had been a huge mistake, and now the man she loved had been shot. Why? He wasn't even carrying the envelopes. How long had someone been following them?

A wave of fury overtook her fear and Bella straightened her shoulders. "Thank you, but no. I'll keep these with me. Adam could have been killed for these envelopes. There's no way I'm letting them out of my sight now." She bit the inside of her cheek. This was the right decision, wasn't it?

One of the paramedics leaned out from the back of the ambulance. "Miss, we need to leave."

Cam nodded. "I get it. You go with Adam. Hang on to your stuff—I know it's important. I'll call Max and fill him in, too."

Max would be worried sick. And Juliet and Pippa. And Madison—she was expecting them for supper. Adam's mom and family. They had no idea what danger Adam had been in and would be anxious when they found out the truth. As she sat in the back of the ambulance and held Adam's limp hand, Bella prayed as if her life depended on it. This guy would do anything for her, and he had been shot as a result. God had to hear her prayers. He just had to.

She looked down at her white silk blouse, now ruined with Adam's blood. Had it been worth it? Was the pursuit of truth worth the blood of the man she loved? The stained envelopes screamed from her lap and the truth became clear at that moment: the past was inconsequential. It was the future that mattered, and now she knew for sure she desperately wanted to share it with Adam.

CHAPTER TWENTY-THREE

ADAM'S HEAD POUNDED. HIS EYES burned in their sockets and he dared not attempt to open them, lest they allow in a sliver of piercing light. No way could he tolerate that right now. He took one slow breath after another and tried to detect the source of the pain. The back of his skull. Definitely there. He tried to move his hand up and check for a lump or a knot or blood. *No.* His left arm was not moving anywhere. Fire shot from his shoulder to his elbow when he shifted it even a fraction. Other arm might work—wait, his fingers were interlaced with something. Someone.

"Adam?"

Loud. The voice was a whisper but it still seemed unreasonably loud.

"Adam, can you hear me?"

Yes. Please don't ask me to move. I think I may have been run over by a truck. Maybe I'm still under the tires...

***

A female voice. Not as loud as before... "He hasn't woken up since his surgery. Yes, I know. I will. Thanks, Max."

Adam licked his lips. They were dry and he was dying of thirst. What had happened? He forced his mouth to move. "Max?"

A warm hand on his cheek. "No, it's me, Bella. I'm so relieved you're awake. You had me worried there."

The sweet scent of coconut. "Bella?" Adam forced his eyes open. In a haze, he saw the most beautiful sight he could imagine. Definitely not Max. "You look like an angel."

"Here, let me get you some water. You sound awful."

I feel worse.

As he concentrated on the straw Bella held to his lips, he looked into her big, blue eyes. They were wide with fright. Her face was pale and she had pulled her hair into a pony tail. She'd had it in long, loose curls before, hadn't she? As he sipped on the delicious coolness, she shifted and he saw blood on her blouse. He spat out the straw.

"Wait, are you hurt?" He went to sit up and collapsed back down against the pillow. Searing pain shot through his left arm. He was in a hospital bed. It must be bad.

"I'm fine." She took away the cup and shuffled her chair closer. "It's your blood. Do you remember what happened?"

It hurt to think. He scrunched his eyes closed in the hope it might help. Where had they been? They were in Seattle, he had driven most of the day, which was why he felt drained. No, he was hurt. There was blood. A car accident? No. A sound, a shot. He'd been shot?

Adam's eyes flew open. "Was I shot?" He looked down at his left arm—it was in a sling. He wriggled his toes and they seemed happy enough. He took a rapid inventory and decided the damage was solely in his arm. No, and his head.

"I'm sorry. This is all my fault." She wiped her face and attempted a smile. "You are my hero."

"I am? What happened exactly? We're in Seattle, right?"

"Yes. We were at the bank, remember?"

"The envelopes?"

"I have them right here." She turned and patted them on the bedside table.

Adam rubbed his forehead with his good hand. "And I was outside on my way to the jeep, wasn't I?"

"Yes, do you know what happened next?" Bella's lip trembled.

"Yeah. I was on the phone to the police guy."

"Cam."

"Right, Cam. I walked down the slope into the parking lot and spotted the jeep." A shot. There was a gunshot, but where had the shot come from? "I think there was a car—yeah, it was parked a couple of spots over. Someone opened the door and I looked up and that's all I remember. My ears hurt. I guess it was a gunshot, and then I must have hit my head. That's about it, I think. I'm all over the place with the details."

Bella stroked the hair from his forehead. "You have a concussion, you poor thing. You must have slammed down hard on the concrete."

That would do it.

"You lost a lot of blood. They had to clean the wound and sew you up. You've already been in and out of surgery."

"I have?" *How long have I been here?*

"They said everything went fine. It was a straightforward shot to your upper left arm. Ended up being a through and through, without causing any structural or vascular damage."

"Impressive. You know the lingo now?" He managed a slight smile.

Bella blushed. "I memorized it. All I know is I thought I was going to lose you and I've never been so scared in my life."

At that moment, a young male doctor breezed into the room and checked the chart down by Adam's feet. "Hello there. I'm Doctor Blair and I'm going to check you out for a second. You've had quite the adventure today, I hear. How are you feeling? Head booming and arm throbbing?"

"Yes, spot on." Plus a massive cloud of confusion hovered over the bed.

The doctor checked Adam's wrist and listened to his chest with great efficiency. "I'll get the nurse to keep you topped up with some meds for the pain, but otherwise, you seem to be in fine form. Surgery went smoothly and we don't foresee any complications. We'll keep an eye on your concussion, but if you have a good night, we might be able to send you on your way tomorrow. Also, you should know there's a police officer outside. I'll tell him to give you a couple of minutes to get your bearings before he peppers you with questions."

"That would be great. Thanks." He sank back into the pillow. *My head is so heavy...*

"No problem. I'll check in on you later."

The doctor hurried out and Bella gripped Adam's right hand.

He exhaled. So many questions. So little energy. It could have been worse, for sure. He needed time to process what had happened. Exhaustion. His eyes were so heavy... lids must be turning to lead...

"Do you need to rest? It looks like your body is demanding some sleep. I'll tell Cam you'll talk with him later."

"I should speak with him now, though, don't you think?" His words slurred and a thick blanket of sleep covered him from head to toe.

Maybe a little shut-eye would be a good idea.

***

Adam braced himself for the impact. He was falling fast and there was no way to stop. The darkness swallowed him whole and no air reached his lungs—

"Adam, wake up."

He sucked in a deep breath and opened his eyes. The sterile mix of antiseptic and sickness filled his nostrils. What was going on? His headache was no longer throbbing, but his shoulder was sore and stiff. He wasn't falling though, and that was good.

"Are you in pain?" Bella's hair tumbled over her shoulders and it tickled his neck as she leaned over to kiss his forehead. "I think you were having some sort of nightmare. You've been twitching away there. Can I get you anything?"

Adam rotated his head with care. Good. Better than earlier.

"How long have I been out?"

She checked her watch. "A couple of hours. Your body's been through a lot today. It's best to let it rest and mend. Are you hungry yet?"

"Hmm no. Well, maybe a little. But I'd give my good arm for a glass of water."

Bella had already refilled the cup. She brought it to his lips.

"You know I could hold that cup with my good hand, right?"

She smiled. "Let me be nurse?"

"Juliet would be proud." He took in the bloodstain on her blouse. "How did you not faint with all my blood and stuff?"

She sat down and blew a strand of hair from her face. "I have no idea. Adrenaline, I guess. You know what I'm like. Ordinarily, I'd be out cold at the sight of blood. I was worried about you."

"Sorry I made you worry."

"Don't be silly. It's not your fault you were shot. Talking of which, are you feeling up to chatting with Cam?"

"He's still waiting?"

"He's been here and back to the station, and then back here with a sandwich for me, and then he was called out to a case, but I think he's in the lounge out there again now. Want me to see?"

"Yeah. Now my head's in the game, I'd like to know what's going on, for sure." *My stuff.* "Do you know what happened to my phone and clothes?"

"It's all on the shelf under the window. Except your shirt—the paramedics had to throw it away, for obvious reasons."

"Of course." He should check his phone messages, but that sounded like too much work.

Adam pulled himself up a little, and Bella plumped his pillow.

"I'll go and fetch Cam, and see if the nurse can find you a snack to keep you going."

"And maybe some meds for the arm?" He winced.

"For sure. I'll be right back."

Bella padded from the room in bare feet. Adam smiled. She must have given up on the high heels. Why had this day ended so horrifically? It was supposed to be special and tender. Bella needed her truth and her answers. He glanced over at the table. The envelopes were piled one on top of the other, and he saw the top one was smeared with a little blood. Had she rifled through the contents yet?

"Adam." Cam strode into the room and stood by Adam's bed. "How are you holding up?"

Adam grinned. "Not bad for a guy who was shot, I guess. I've had better days. Have a seat."

"Thanks." Cam lowered himself onto the plastic chair and pulled out a notebook. Old school.

Bella joined them and placed a wrapped sandwich on the tray at the side of Adam's bed. "Sustenance. And the nurse will come in as soon as Cam's finished here."

"I won't keep you long." Cam shook his head. "I can't believe how today panned out. I didn't for one minute foresee such a terrible outcome. I'm sorry about this."

"Hey man, it's not your fault." Adam shrugged, and then grimaced with pain. "I need to know though, did you catch whoever did this?"

"That's the good news." Cam crossed his arms. "I know you hit the ground hard and I'm guessing you don't remember everything, but there were, in fact, several

244

witnesses at the entrance to the parking lot that time of the day. Three of them gave accurate descriptions of the car that bolted right after the gunshot rang out. One even managed to take a photo on his phone."

"Technology is awesome." Adam winked at Bella.

"It sure is," Cam continued. "We were able to put out a solid description with the license plate and the guy was pulled over within thirty minutes."

"The black Beemer, by any chance?" Adam raised a brow.

"You got it. The guy is a Michael Mack." Cam checked his notebook. "He's got some minor priors, but this was his first serious offense. Does the name sound familiar to either of you?"

Adam shook his head.

Bella shifted on the edge of the bed. "I've never heard the name before. But do we know yet if he's in any way connected with George and Susannah Robinson?"

He had to be. Adam tried to focus. "What other reason could he have to shoot me if he wasn't working for the Robinsons? He didn't rob me or steal my vehicle. Was he on drugs or something?"

"Nope. Clean as a whistle. Not the smartest tool in the shed, though—still had the gun in his possession when he was pulled over, so between solid evidence and the witnesses, there's no denying he was the shooter. I'm sure he'll cave and we can trace this back to the Robinsons." Cam turned to Bella. "I'll keep you informed. Officer Bingley is still outside if you have any questions and we'll keep security tight until we get to the bottom of it."

"Thanks, Cam. I want all this to be over." Tears glistened in Bella's eyes.

"I understand. My guys are looking into it here, and I know Max has a team running in Oregon. Adam, he's worried about you. In fact, he's driving up to take you home as soon as you get the green light. I suggested flying you back, but like he said, by the time you've waited at the airport, you might be just as comfortable reclined in the car."

Adam tried to concentrate but the conversation became foggy. What was the shooter's name? Mack something? And what about his jeep? He cleared his throat.

"Have you spoken with this Mack guy yet?"

"I'm heading there right now. He wouldn't talk at first, lawyered up, but now we think he's ready to spill."

Bella exhaled. "I hope so. I can't help feeling nervous, even with security outside the door. I don't trust George and Susannah for a minute. If this Mack is out of action, what's to stop them hiring someone else to get to us?"

Cam leaned forward and looked from Bella to Adam.

"I know today has been traumatic for both of you, but please, know you're safe here. If the Robinsons are in Seattle and Michael Mack can give us an address, we'll be hauling them in tonight."

"For real?" Bella's hands were trembling. Adam reached over and touched her arm. She was so close to finding the freedom she craved—they had to catch a break sooner or later.

"Yes." Cam flashed a rare smile. "If my guy at the station is right, this could all pan out rapidly. Even if the Robinsons are out of town, we can get an APB on them and they'll be found. They can't hide from us forever."

"Right." Adam squinted. "What do you think the chances are that they're here in the city?"

Cam closed his notebook. "I'm confident they're here. I think they would want to be close enough to grab whatever was in the safe deposit box and maybe then disappear. Start a life elsewhere."

"That's what I think, too." Adam looked up at Bella. "This could all be over soon, hon."

"I hope so."

Cam stood. "Bella, can I get someone to run you back to the place you were staying for a clean set of clothes or anything?"

"No, but thanks. I want to stay with Adam. Maybe I'll ask for some scrubs to borrow or something." She glanced down at the deep red stain. "It's gross. But I don't want to leave here tonight. The nurse said I can sleep in the chair."

Adam's heart swelled. "You can go back to Madison's for some rest. I'm sure Cam could give you security there, right?"

Cam nodded. "It's easier to keep you guys together, but I'd be happy to arrange that."

Bella shook her head. "No way. You won't get rid of me that easily. I got you into this situation, and there's no way I'm waltzing off for a comfortable night's sleep in a beautiful mansion when you're in pain in a hospital bed."

Cam chuckled. "Let me know if you change your mind. I'll call with any news, and come by tomorrow morning to check on you. Try and get some rest. Both of you."

"Thanks." Adam needed those pain meds and soon. "We appreciate your help."

"No problem. Take care."

Cam strode from the room and a middle-aged nurse bustled in to administer the drugs. Adam turned his head while she fiddled with his IV. When had he become so squeamish?

"There we go, young man. Should be feeling warm and fuzzy any minute. Press the buzzer if you need anything else tonight, you hear?"

"Thanks. I mean it more than you know."

Bella unwrapped the sandwich and handed it to Adam. "Pretend it's one of your fabulous concoctions. Not this dubious-looking ham and cheese medley."

Adam took it in his right hand and smiled. It was dubious. "In that case, this is shaved roast beef with homemade horseradish sauce." He bit into it. "Yummy."

Bella giggled. "I'm sorry. If it's any consolation, mine was no better. I can order something in if you'd like."

"No, this is fine. I have a feeling I'm going to be drifting off again any minute. Have you spoken to anyone at home?" He set the remnants of sandwich back onto the tray.

"Yes. They're all frantic with worry. Max went over to speak to your parents."

Adam wiped a hand down his face. "My mom."

"I know. Poor woman. I'm surprised she's not here already."

Madison and Luke. "We should let Madison know we won't be going to her place tonight."

"Juliet said she would give Madison a call and fill her in. I hope we haven't scared her—she opened her home up to us and everything. She could have been in danger, too."

"Madison will be fine. She has Luke with her and she knows we're safe in the hospital here. Let's call them in the morning to reassure them everything's good."

"No need."

Adam glanced to the open door and grinned when he saw Madison and presumably her new husband, Luke. Yes, he recognized him from the wedding photograph Juliet sent.

Bella let out a tiny cry and then rushed over and gave the Madison a hug, trying not to involve her blood-stained blouse. "What are you doing here?"

"Juliet called and told us what happened outside the bank." Madison wiped at her eyes when she looked over at Adam. "I can't believe it—Adam, you were *shot*?"

"Guilty as charged. It's not too bad though. Like I keep telling myself, it could have been a lot worse."

Bella hugged Luke. "I can't believe we're meeting you for the first time like this."

"Not quite the plan, was it?" Luke strode over to the bed and clasped Adam's good hand. "Hi, Adam. I'm sorry about what happened today, but I'm glad you're safe. How are you doing?" Compassion oozed from his being as he leaned over the bed. This guy was genuine, and Adam liked him already.

"Good to meet you. I'm okay. Tired and sore. But it looks like they caught the shooter."

"Well, that's a relief. We've been praying."

"And we brought you some provisions. Including a stash of chocolate." Madison smiled and held up Bella's overnight things and a plastic bag. *Chocolate? Hallelujah.* "I hope you don't mind that I went into your rooms. I didn't go through your stuff, I just grabbed your bags and then we picked up a few snacks on the way in."

"Thanks." Bella gave Madison another hug. "That's so thoughtful of you."

Luke held up Adam's duffel bag. "I'll set your things next to the bed here."

"Thank you, I'm going to need a clean shirt, for sure."

"You must let us know if we can help in any way." Luke held out his hand to Madison and she joined them at the bed. He slipped an arm around her waist and she leaned into his side.

A perfect fit. This couple was fresh from their honeymoon. What he wouldn't give to be in that place with Bella.

"Thanks, both of you."

"No problem at all. It's the least we could do. We should go and leave you to get some rest. I'm guessing you're sleeping here, Bella?"

Bella piled the bags in the corner of the room, and padded over to the bed where she ruffled Adam's hair. "How could I leave this one?"

"I get it." Madison smiled up at Luke. "I would be the same. But listen, you guys please feel free to text me or call. You have my number, Adam, so don't be afraid to use it. Whatever time it is. And we'll touch base with you tomorrow."

Adam shook Luke's hand again and accepted a gentle hug from Madison. Having new friends in the city was a blessing, for sure.

Bella saw Madison and Luke to the door and then walked over to the side table. "They are so sweet. But they must be confused. Here we were supposed to be going to a bank appointment... and you were shot? She shuddered. "I can't believe I put your life at risk for these envelopes. I'm so selfish. Can you ever forgive me?"

"Hey, come here."

Bella leaned against the side of the bed. She looked a mixture of little girl and grieving widow.

"You have to know I would do anything for you. Anything. What's important to you is important to me." He stroked the back of her hand with his thumb. "And now that you know about my past hurts, I hope you will trust me completely."

She nodded. "I do. I trust you one hundred percent." She bit her lip and looked up at the ceiling. "And it took that moment when I thought I might lose you for me to realize how much I love you and want you in my life. I believe God brought us together for a reason. He knows our deepest needs and He's healed our deepest hurts. We've both been through a lot, but we have so much to look forward to."

"Together?"

"Yes, together." She took both his hands in hers, careful not to shift his injured arm. "Will you make me the happiest girl in the world, Adam? Will you marry me?"

CHAPTER TWENTY-FOUR

BELLA'S NECK PROTESTED AS SHE adjusted her aching body in the vinyl armchair. She mustered up enough energy to open one eye. Light filtered in through the hospital blinds and a quick glance at the bed warmed her heart. Adam still slept, the rise and fall of his chest a sweet relief she would never take for granted again. Life could have looked differently this morning if that bullet had hit a few inches to the right.

She shuddered and pulled the scratchy blanket tighter around her shoulders.

"Morning. I'm Jessica." A new nurse stood at the doorway. She nodded at Adam's sleeping form and lowered her voice. "I'll come back to check on our patient after I've seen the others. I'm sure his body needs the rest. How about you, did you manage to get any sleep at all in this luxury suite?" Her eyes danced. Clearly a perky morning person.

"Not bad, thanks. I can sleep almost anywhere. Although, I may need some caffeine soon."

"I can get someone to bring you a cup of coffee if you'd like. I'm guessing you're being protected for a reason." The nurse pointed back at the hallway. "You have two hunks keeping watch for you out there."

"We do? I wonder if there's been any news."

"I'm afraid I have no idea what's going on, but I'm sure they'll keep you informed. In the meantime, you have your own personal bathroom and I can get you room service. I use that term lightly. Cream with your coffee?"

Bella grinned her thanks. "That would be perfect. I appreciate it."

"Consider it done. And the doctor will be coming by at around eleven to see if all's well for you to go home."

"Thank you." That would mean they could be home in Florence by nightfall. Would they get to see Madison and Luke again? Perhaps not. It looked like they had brought all of their belongings here last night.

She stretched the kinks out of her body and pulled her tangled hair back into a pony tail. She'd slept in her T-shirt and sweats, and the rumpled effect reflected how she felt right now. Juliet always gave her a hard time when she fell asleep on the couch after a night of frenzied writing. This was a whole other kind of frenzy. Why was life so unpredictable?

If Juliet could see me now, she'd be horrified. But she'd give my neck a decent massage.

Bella itched to phone Juliet and tell her about last night's proposal, but she had discussed it with Adam and they made the decision to tell everyone once they were back in Florence, where her engagement ring awaited them. She wriggled the fingers on her left hand. She was going to marry Adam one day in the not too distant future. Her heart skipped a beat.

"Hey."

Adam's croaky voice cut into Bella's musings and she hurried over to the bed.

"How are you feeling this morning?" She stroked his hair.

"Like I've been shot." He groaned and rubbed his eyes with his right hand. "Guess I look as rough as I feel."

Bella balanced herself on the edge of the bed. The dark stubble on his chin gave him a ruggedly handsome appeal, and though his eyes were a little drowsy, they glistened a vibrant green, reflecting the color of his hospital gown. "You look good to me. But maybe I'm biased." She kissed his forehead.

Adam chuckled and then stopped himself. It looked like he needed another dose of painkillers.

"The nurse will be here in a few minutes with your meds. She didn't want to disturb your sleep earlier."

"I went out like a light after—" Dimples appeared as he broke into a grin. "Please tell me I didn't dream our conversation and I wasn't hallucinating last night. We are engaged, right?"

That sounded good. "Yes, we are engaged. It may not have been as romantic a setting as the first one, but this proposal was a raving success."

He punched the air with the fist of his good arm. "Yes."

The next second, Bella's heart took a nosedive. "Do you think we're going to be safe? There are two officers outside our room, and although I'm over the moon about us, I'm petrified someone's going to try to hurt you again. I can't bear to lose you. You're going to be my family." Her breath caught in her throat. "Oh my goodness, I'm going to have a real family of my own."

Adam took Bella's hand and kissed it.

"You bet. And we won't live in fear and be on the run, I can assure you. That part of your life is over forever. Cam or Max will call as soon as they have news, and in the meantime, we're safe in this little antiseptic cocoon."

"How romantic. Our very own antiseptic cocoon. I love it. Can we stay here forever?"

"I'll see what I can do. Although, the ham and cheese sandwiches could get old in a hurry." He grimaced.

"True." Bella passed him a glass of water, which he downed in one go. She arched her back and rolled her shoulders. Coffee. She needed that coffee.

Adam cocked his head to one side. "Did you sleep on the chair all night?"

"Sure did. It wasn't so bad."

He squinted. "What about the envelopes? Did you take a look inside them yet?"

She bit her lip. How could she explain? She was furious with those envelopes. They had landed Adam in hospital.

"I'm not sure I want to." Her voice was a pathetic whisper.

He nodded.

"I know that's what we came here for, but if it weren't for those wretched envelopes, you wouldn't be laying in a hospital bed right now. You'd be running or body surfing."

"I'd be at the office." He looked down at his sling. "At least I'm right-handed."

"You know what I mean. This isn't just an inconvenience for today. It could take months until you're fully fit again, and it's because of my investigation into the safe deposit box. I'm sorry." Would she ever be able to forgive herself for putting his life in jeopardy?

"Come here." Adam pulled her against him on his uninjured side and held her. "This is not your fault. It's not the fault of the envelopes either. Some guy pulled the trigger of a gun and someone ordered him to do it. That's where the blame lies and that's where justice will be done. We came to Seattle for you to get to the truth, and who knows, perhaps me getting shot will even help in that."

"It should have been me."

"No. Please don't say that. It shouldn't have been anyone. But if this brings George and Susannah out of the shadows and we can get them put behind bars at last, then honestly, I'd do it again in a heartbeat. After all, I got a marriage proposal as a result."

Tears stung Bella's eyes. "You're impossible. And I love you for it."

"I know. But right now, there's a nurse with a cup of coffee staring at us from the doorway."

"Nurse Jessica with your room service."

Bella grabbed a tissue from Adam's bedside table and accepted the coffee from the nurse.

"You're a life saver, Jessica. Thank you." She retreated back to her chair and dug into the plastic bag Madison had brought last night. Inside, she found blueberry muffins, an array of fruit, and several chocolate bars. Perfect.

"No problem. One of the other nurses was grabbing some for herself anyway. Now how's our patient feeling this morning?" She checked Adam's blood pressure, wound dressing, and IV site in several smooth moves.

"I've felt better, but I think I'm doing okay considering."

"Hungry?"

"Starving. Do I get what she's having over there?"

Bella stopped mid-bite.

"You'll be excited to hear your special hospital breakfast is on its way. Only the best for you." The nurse grinned. "My work here is done. Everything looks in order, you'll be feeling more comfortable in a minute or two. We should be able to take that IV out later this morning and the doctor will let you know if you're all set to get out of here."

"Thanks. About the doctor, not the breakfast." Adam raised an eyebrow.

"You're welcome."

She disappeared from the room and Bella moved her chair closer to the bed.

"Are you going to eat that muffin in front of me?" Adam's attempt at "sad puppy dog eyes" was working.

"Oh, sorry. Would you like some?"

"No, I should wait for my own, I guess." He was a good patient.

"Then I'll wait until your feast arrives." She stuffed the rest of the muffin back in the bag and sipped on her coffee. The two brown envelopes were in her peripheral vision, sitting on the side table and waiting to be opened. She stared at them. Whatever could be so important that it was worth killing for?

"Go on."

"Hmm?" How long had she been daydreaming?

"They won't bite. You've been staring down those envelopes for ages."

Bella's shoulders sagged. "What if we're interrupted? Maybe I should wait until we get home."

"But what if there's something in there to help let us know who might have arranged the shooting or something?"

257

"I hadn't thought of that. I'm surprised Cam hasn't even asked me about the contents."

Adam shifted on his pillow. "He'll be here soon."

"Shall I?" Bella's palms were slick.

"Your call, but I've got nothing else to do at the moment."

"Right." Bella set down her coffee and leaned over to retrieve the envelopes. "Whoa. My heart's racing."

"That's because I'm in the room."

Bella looked up and smiled. Cheeky. "I'm sure that's the solitary reason. Here we go then."

She took a deep breath and picked up the first one and pulled back the flap. Paper. She slid the bundle out and turned it the right way up to read. It looked like several letters, each tied with a length of red ribbon.

She picked up the one on top. "This is the letter from Rose." Her hand trembled. "It's to me." Like earlier at the bank, tears sprang from nowhere, distorting the handwriting on the page.

"Want me to read it out to you?" Adam's voice was ragged. "Or we can do it later, whatever you prefer. I didn't mean to pressure you."

Bella wiped her eyes and passed the whole pile of letters over to him. "Please, go ahead and read. I've waited long enough."

Adam lifted the first letter and took a deep breath.

My darling daughter,

Where do I begin? Let me start by telling you that I love you. I know this may be hard for you to believe, but it's the absolute truth. I loved you the moment I discovered I was pregnant, and choosing to let you go was the hardest decision of my life. One I've bitterly regretted since.

I hope your adoptive parents are everything I want them to be: good, kind, honest, supportive, loving—all the things I longed to be, in an ideal world. I suppose I should try to explain myself...

Adam glanced up from the page. "Want me to go on?"

Bella had forgotten to breathe. She exhaled and nodded. "Don't stop now."

I've had a good life up until recently. Your grandparents are strict, but they just want the best for me. I'm an only child and they have showered me with all the material wealth a girl could dream of, but our family is somewhat lacking in the love department. I know they do love me, but have trouble showing it.

When I found out I was pregnant, I knew they would be furious. Daddy at least. He's had some mental health issues in recent years, and finds it hard to think rationally. (That's putting it mildly.)

I'm in the middle of college and want to go into interior design one day, but had to drop out when my morning sickness became unbearable. Actually, I had to drop out of more than college—I had to disappear.

I've made some poor choices, mostly as an act of rebellion against my perfectionist parents, but my decision to spend one night with a certain man was bittersweet. Sweet because it resulted in you, but bitter because he was trouble. Big trouble.

I have never told anyone his name, and he is not listed as your father—it's safer that way. Let's just say he was from a notorious family who took no prisoners, and if I had stayed with him it would have been hell for both you and I. I'm sorry I can't go into more detail, but trust me when I say running was our only option. I wanted you to have a chance in life. Not stifled and suffocated like mine, and not in constant danger with your biological father. I hope you have found it with your new family, dear one.

Adam blew out a long breath. "She had no idea about George and Susannah. Wow. She thought she was doing you a favor."

"I guess I'll never know who my father is." Bella's head ached with the onslaught of new information.

"Are you good with that?"

Bella nodded. "I think so. I trust Rose. Is there more?"

Adam found his place on the page.

I've always had a special fondness for lighthouses.

Bella's mouth dropped open. *Of course.*

Adam's head shot up. "Whoa. *That's* not weird at all. Sorry, let me keep going."

I had a lighthouse book as a young child and that's where my fascination began. After that, I would insist we go visit every lighthouse we could find as we travelled. There's something strong and safe about a lighthouse. It makes me feel grounded. Anyway, when I fled from my home in California, I knew where I wanted to hide. The Oregon Coast had been a favorite place to visit as a child. I hadn't been there in years, but I decided to hunker down in Florence, where I gave birth to you…

"Wait, I was *born* in Florence?" Bella stood and began pacing. "I don't want to sound creepy or anything, but do you think that's why I feel so comfortable there now? Of all the places I've lived, Florence is the only one where I feel like I've come home."

Adam shook his head. "It's wild, but it makes sense, doesn't it?"

"Will you carry on reading?"

"Sure."

I befriended a woman there, she was a little older than me with a young daughter of her own. We would sit up at the lighthouse and talk for hours. I could never give her exact details, but I shared my story with her and she agreed to help me when it was time to give birth to you. And that's why I left you at the lighthouse…

"Bella, no wonder you love lighthouses so much."

"She left me at the lighthouse?" A fresh wave of desertion washed over her. "I could have been killed or attacked by animals or frozen to death. What on earth?"

Adam ran a hand across the stubble on his chin. "I should read the whole thing. Maybe it's not as bad as it sounds."

"Seriously?" How could being abandoned as a newborn at a lighthouse not be *bad* in any universe?

"Listen up. Here we go."

Sweet girl—I never let you out of my sight for one minute.

Bella relaxed. She wasn't completely abandoned. She was cared for. Even from afar, perhaps as Rose had continued to do later on in her life with the white roses.

I knew I would have to move quickly once I gave birth, and I'd told my friend I would leave you up at the lighthouse one morning right before the lighthouse tour began, while it was still quiet. That way, when she arrived and found you there, there would be witnesses to see she was surprised and not involved in the whole thing.

You were never alone, I watched from the bushes until she came and found you, and then I followed at a distance while she took you home. She had a heart of gold. Deep down, I hoped she would keep you—that you would have a sister and a mother to love you from the start, but she had her own issues to deal with.

So I kept myself hidden away for the most part, peeking out from behind my curtain, cracking the door open to hear sounds of you. But when I saw in the local newspaper that you were being featured as the "Lighthouse Baby," I knew I had to disappear before anyone discovered who I really was.

"I was dubbed the 'Lighthouse Baby'?" Bella's hand flew to her necklace. Where was it? A quiver of panic shot through her mind.

"Hey, don't worry, I have your lighthouse necklace. I took it from you in the bank, remember? It should still be in my shirt pocket."

"The black shirt that you were shot in? The one that was thrown out?" She felt light-headed at the loss.

Adam closed his mouth.

"I don't want to sound pathetic, but I kind of need to see it. Do you suppose it might be with your other things?"

"Take a look on the shelf by the window. The necklace may have been put with my wallet or something."

Bella hurried to the window and tried to stop her hands shaking as she rifled through Adam's belongings.

"Oh, thank goodness. It's here." Relief flooded through her entire being. It had always been a cherished possession, but now this little pendant was infinitely more significant. *Thank You, Lord.* "Sorry to be dramatic, but it seems like a big deal now. You know?"

"Come and sit." She returned to his bedside where Adam took her hand and kissed it. "I understand. Want me to put it on you?"

"With your one hand? No, that's okay. I'll hold it while you read."

Adam found his place on the page.

I trusted my friend with my life. And yours, as it happens. She knew the adoption had to be secretive, so as not to inform my parents or your father of your whereabouts. It sounds clandestine, but it was all extremely private and quiet. The news died down right away.

My friend put word out to see if anyone was aware of a good family wanting a baby, just as we had discussed. A quick, private adoption. I left a package with a note, the bank details, and the key to this safe deposit box with you in your basket. My friend didn't know about the key, but I told her to pass the package on to the adoptive parents, promising a reward for when you turned eighteen.

It seems silly now, but I hoped they would take even greater care of you if they knew I was wealthy. I wasn't thinking clearly. After that, I don't know what happened. I watched from afar, trying to pick up bits and pieces, and I made one last phone call to my friend to make sure everything had gone as smoothly as possible.

She said all was well and that you were with your new parents. I suppose my greatest sorrow became their greatest joy.

Bella gasped. "They fooled her, didn't they? I wonder if she gave them any money up front. I still have difficulty wrapping my head around why they took on the role of parents for the sake of a pile of money eighteen years later. Who does that?"

Adam shifted on the bed in an attempt to get comfortable. "Perhaps they *did* want a baby at first. Is it possible they got jaded and weird as time went on?"

"I don't know." Bella sighed. "But things sure changed for the worse."

"I'm sorry, honey. I'm sorry for Rose, too. She thought she was doing the right thing."

Bella stared at the lighthouse pendant in her hand. "This is strange, hearing my mother answering the questions I've had floating in my head forever. I can't believe I'm hearing her voice in these words. It's beautiful, isn't it? Even though the content is heartbreaking. Poor Rose."

"It's special, that's for sure. There's a bit more yet."

One thing I promise you, dear daughter, is this: I will always be watching over you. Even though I can't contact you — that was the arrangement — I will find a way to make sure you are safe from your biological father and my family.

Please don't get me wrong, my mother would love you in a heartbeat, but my father has grown unbearable and I'm afraid of what he might do with you. I'm not sure if I shall ever return home.

When I left them, I took as much as I could with me in the way of money and jewelry, and set up the safe deposit box in Seattle. It was all mine, please don't think I would ever steal. In this box, I have stashed what is rightfully yours, although I'm afraid most of the money will have to be given to the Robinsons—again, it was part of our agreement. The cash is to go to them if they care for you until you reach the age of eighteen—the documents are all in place.

The jewelry is all yours, and you will find it is worth a great deal, enough to keep you comfortable for many years. Please feel free to sell any items if you need money. I'd understand.

If you are reading this letter and you're still a child, then I am so, so sorry. Something must have happened to the Robinsons—but I will find you, so please don't be afraid.

If you are reading this alongside your parents, then I hope you are all well and happy and can find a way to use the money wisely.

I can't quite imagine any other scenario, but if for any reason you are reading this for the first time as a grown woman (so hard for me to imagine after kissing your rosebud cheeks) then I wish you every joy in your life. I long to know you, talk with you, and tell you everything you want to know. Maybe we can find a way to connect one day. But if not, take these letters I have written to you for special times in your life, and I hope against hope you won't think too harshly of me.

Adam held up the bundle in his hand. "Wow. That's so cool."

Bella couldn't breathe.

I pray for you every single night and I will love you until my last breath.

Your mommy,

Rose

Bella's face crumpled along with her heart. Rose loved her. Like a mother should. And she would never get the chance to tell her she loved her back. Words stuck in her throat. What could she even say? The grief of losing Rose washed over her again and she ran to the en suite bathroom. Adam would understand. She just needed a minute.

She stared at her reflection in the rectangular mirror. Tears coursed down her heated cheeks and dripped into the porcelain sink. She was loved. Had always been loved, even when she felt alone and rejected. And she was strong now, stronger than she had ever been. Strong like Rose.

Did she look anything like her mother had in her early twenties? Did they share the same round, light-blue eyes and dark lashes, along with blonde, wavy hair? Had Rose worn hers long and unruly when she was young, too? Bella may never know. Unless she could find the friend who had helped Rose…

She turned on the faucet and splashed freezing cold water onto her face. The shock of it was pleasure and pain simultaneously. Grabbing the towel from the rack, she dabbed her cheeks and eyes. Less red and puffy. She took the toothbrush and toothpaste she had placed in here last night and set to work. Fresh breath always helped. She could do this.

By the time she slipped back into Adam's room, he had polished off a bowl of oatmeal.

"Hey, beautiful." He set his spoon into the tiny dish and held out his hand. "My breakfast arrived. Come here, you. I was worried, but I thought you might need a little space."

"And you're attached to that." Bella jerked her head toward the IV bag.

"Yeah. That, too. This is a lot to take in, right?"

Bella nodded and managed a smile of sorts as she sat on the bed. "I'm sad. Sad I never got to know her. I think we would have had a lot of good times together."

Adam's face fell. "I know you would."

"Although, now that I've had a minute, I'm kind of curious to see what else is in here."

Adam picked up his spoon. "You carry on, I'm going to finish this. It's not too horrific. Although, I might have room for one of those muffins afterwards."

"Okay." Bella picked up the other envelope and sat back in the chair. She dumped the stack of cash to one side and poured the rest of the contents onto her lap. "Whoa, these are heavy."

"Hmm. Five velvet pouches." Adam wiped his mouth with a paper napkin. "Interesting."

Bella's hands shook as she undid the first one. "Oh my."

A diamond bracelet sparkled in the fluorescent overhead lighting. She lifted it up to eye level. "It's breathtaking. Do you suppose it's real?"

"I'm no expert but, by what Rose said in her letter, I would guess so. What else do you have there?"

Bella opened all four of the other pouches and gasped. She glanced over her shoulder to make sure the door was shut—it could be awkward if someone walked into the room.

"Look at all this treasure. A perfect string of pearls, a ruby and diamond ring, a brooch with a humungous emerald, and a diamond necklace to match the bracelet. I don't know what to say."

Adam grinned. "These are gifts from your mother. They're your inheritance. We need to get them appraised and put away somewhere safe as soon as we can." He hit his forehead with an open palm. "I can't believe we had all that stuff sitting out here in the hospital room all night. What were we thinking?"

"To be honest, I was thinking how grateful I was that you're alive."

He nodded. "I guess neither of us were thinking clearly."

She picked the cash back up. "Look at all this." Bella held a wad of bank notes in her hand and a nervous laugh escaped from her throat. "They're hundreds. And there are piles of them. How much do you think is in here?"

Adam whistled. "Enough to shoot me for, I would say. It's all making me feel a bit skittish. Are those police officers still outside now?"

"Yes, I hope so at least. Do you think I should bundle it all back up and let them take it back to the bank or what?"

"Do you want to let it out of your sight so soon? I mean, it's up to you, but we do have our own personal bodyguards out there. Until we know who shot me, maybe we should keep it with us right here."

Bella slid the jewels and the cash back into the large envelope, and stuffed it into the bottom of her overnight bag. She rolled her shoulders. This was stressful.

"Did you want to see any more of these letters or would you rather wait until later?" Adam held the tied bundle up in the air.

Bella bit her lip. "I don't know how much more I can handle this morning. Let me skim the letters—it looks like she's put headings on the outside of each of them."

Adam passed the bundle over and Bella reverently handled each one. "This is sweet. She has one here for my first day in Kindergarten and one for my high school prom night. She couldn't have known I never experienced either of those. I guess she wanted me to look back and know she was thinking of me even then."

"They'll be special to read and keep."

"Yes. Yes, they will, won't they? There's another for my wedding day…"

"I can help you with that special occasion." Adam wiggled his eyebrows.

"Why, thank you. And there's one for when I have baby of my own." Bella's voice cracked. "How hard must it have been for her to sit down and write all these letters to me? I can't begin to imagine."

"She loved you."

"She sure did. There's another little letter at the end here. It doesn't have an occasion on the front—I wonder what that's for." Bella hesitated.

"Want me to take a peek?" Adam squeezed her hand.

Bella passed it back and held the rest to her chest. These words were worth more than all the cash and jewelry in the other package. Her mother was a writer, like her.

"Let's see what we have here." Adam opened up the folded sheet of paper.

This is a strange request, perhaps, but I feel I need to at least ask you this, darling daughter.

Should you ever find yourself in the Oregon Coast, would you look up my dear friend? Just to say thank you for everything she did when I was in such a desperate state. The one who helped me when I had nobody else to turn to—she saved us both, and I know she would be thrilled to meet you again. Once I left after having

269

you, I had to cut all ties with her, for her own safety. I have no idea if she will still be in Florence, but something tells me she will never leave that place now she has found it. She has her own demons she had to run from, and I think she's found her happy place. Thank you so much for trying—please don't worry if it doesn't work out...
she may be married by now, but her maiden name is Farr.

Pippa Farr.

CHAPTER TWENTY-FIVE

"WHAT DID YOU SAY?" BELLA'S heart stopped for a second.

Adam's jaw was slack and he didn't utter a word.

"Did you say Pippa Farr? Like *our* Pippa?"

He nodded and looked back at the page. "Maybe it's a coincidence..."

"For real? How many Pippa Farrs do you think there have been in Florence? And she had a daughter about my age, remember from the other letter?" Bella got up again and paced.

"Juliet? No. What?" He shook his head. "Could it even be possible you and Juliet met when you were babies? This is crazy. It's like some fiction novel."

"Except it's my memoir."

"Wow. Maybe one day in the future you'll be able to write about all this."

Her heart hammered in her chest. How amazing would that be? Painful, yes. But it could be cathartic and healing, too. Or maybe she would write it as fiction after all...

"This is *insane*. I don't understand how this all makes any sense. Do you think Pippa didn't clue in that I was the baby she helped?"

Adam rubbed his chin. "Maybe she didn't. Or, she might have been honoring the promise she made to Rose all those years ago."

"But how could Pippa have kept this a secret? She couldn't have spoken about it with Juliet. There's no way Juliet would have kept this from me."

"True. She would have said something by now, for sure. She didn't flinch when you mentioned Rose's name."

"But neither did Pippa."

He exhaled. "Oh, hon, I don't have any answers for you. Remember Rose wrote these letters over twenty years ago. Maybe Pippa didn't put two and two together this week. Or maybe she wanted to protect you. Or maybe Rose even asked her to never speak of it, even to you. Pippa strikes me as being a loyal friend."

Bella's head pounded. "I guess. Was there anything else in the letter or was that it?"

Adam retrieved the sheet of paper from his lap. "There's a bit more here."

Pippa won't know my real name. For the sake of staying hidden for as long as possible, I've gone by Rachel Smith during my time in Florence. Unoriginal, I know. Pip knows it's a fake name, but she's rolled with it and has never questioned me — that's just how she is. Please give her a hug from me. Thank you so much, sweetheart.

Sweetheart. Why did such a tender term of endearment hurt so deeply?

"Well, that makes a bit more sense, I suppose." Adam shrugged, and then winced.

"True. You poor guy. You're in pain, aren't you?"

"It's not too bad. I'm more concerned about you."

Bella leaned over and kissed his cheek. "You know, this is all so crazy, but maybe Pippa doesn't realize who I am. Why would she? She knows very little about this whole thing really. Juliet and I decided not to share any details with her and we kept things vague to avoid upsetting her... So, how could she possibly piece it together and know that *I* am the one? That I'm the Lighthouse Baby?"

"Right. Plus, she never knew the names of your adoptive parents. And it sounds like she didn't know there was a safe deposit key in the package Rose gave her to pass on to George and Susannah. So, that wouldn't have rung any bells either."

Tension crept up her neck. "I don't know about you, but I want to go home."

"Did I hear someone say *home*?"

Bella swiveled around to see Adam's nurse in the doorway grinning at them.

"You mean you want to leave us so soon? Well, I think that might be arranged. But in the meantime..." Jessica stepped to one side. "You'll want to see this gentleman right here."

Bella's breath caught in her throat. "Cam? Please, come on in. I hope you have good news."

Jessica left and Cam took three long strides to join them at the bed. He had a different collared shirt on from yesterday, but his red-rimmed eyes and disheveled hair hinted at a lack of restful sleep.

"Sorry I didn't call in earlier. How are you guys doing today?" He sat on the chair and leaned forward. "Sounds like the wound is in good shape. Not that any kind of gunshot injury is pleasant. I can vouch for that." He rubbed his thigh.

"We're both hanging in there, thanks." Adam fidgeted in the bed. "I'm hoping to get out of here today."

"As long as the doctor says it's alright." Bella tucked the letters back into the envelope.

Cam nodded and pulled a notebook from the breast pocket in his shirt. "I'm sure you're both anxious to go back home. And I do have some news for you."

"You do?" *Please, please let it be good news.*

"Our shooter eventually gave us George and Susannah Robinson. They hired him to steal the safe deposit box contents from you, whatever it took." He glanced at Adam. "He says he panicked when Bella wasn't with you and you weren't carrying any packages. Shot you hoping Bella would appear with the goods. Like I said, not the sharpest tool in the shed."

Bella gasped and sank into the plastic chair. "What? You have them in custody? George and Susannah? Have they been caught?"

Adam clasped her hand.

"Yes, ma'am. They were still living here in Seattle. They also had another place down in California, by all accounts. But we sent our boys to their home here in the city in the early hours this morning and brought them in for questioning."

"Are they talking?" Adam squeezed her hand. The rest of her body felt numb. In shock. "Is the word of the shooter going to be enough to hold them?"

"No. They're not talking right now, but that's not a surprise. The shooter, Michael Mack, has a record and is desperate to earn a little leniency when it comes to his sentencing. He's got no qualms with squealing. The Robinsons made a few enemies along the way by the sounds of it, and this is just one of their many business ventures."

That's all she had been to them, after all. A business venture. She had so many questions. What were they doing in California? What about the dead rat in the box? The motorcyclist? The red car and the black truck? The white roses...

"Cam, this may seem trivial, but has this Mack guy mentioned anything about the white roses yet? Was it him on the motorbike in Florence?" *How long have the Robinsons been leaving me roses?*

She bit her lip and waited for the reply. The thought of those comforting roses being left over the years by George and Susannah made her nauseous. *Please let it have been my birth mother watching over me. Caring about me. Being my sweet guardian angel...*

Cam consulted his notebook. "I'm not familiar with all the details yet, I'm afraid. But I know he's been talking."

Adam pulled Bella onto the side of the bed, his good arm around her trembling shoulders. Tears filled her eyes and she tried in vain to hold back the dam.

"I'm sorry. I wish I could tell you more." Cam shifted in his chair and pulled out his phone.

"Don't mind me, I'm an emotional wreck at the moment. The roses are just a silly little detail."

"Hey." Adam kissed the top of her head. "It's not a silly detail. Those roses were a connection with your birth mother for many years. Let's not allow the Robinsons to take that away from you."

Cam stood. "Excuse me for a moment. I'm going to call my officer who interviewed Mack and see what details we discovered regarding any white roses."

"I don't want to be a bother." As if the man didn't have enough to do.

"No problem. I can see it's important to you. I'll be right back."

Cam hurried from the room and Bella grabbed a stack of tissues from the side table.

"I feel ridiculous."

"Nonsense. You must have a thousand questions now that George and Susannah have been caught. And hopefully, they'll all be answered eventually. It might take some time and you may never comprehend why they did what they did, but the fact remains that you are safe now. You don't have to live your life watching over your shoulder, ready to run. That's awesome."

Safe. That sounded good. "You're right. It's going to take a while to sink in."

The small room seemed to close in on them as they sat in silence and waited for Cam to return. So much to process. So much to be thankful for. So much to—

"Bella, I have news." Cam breezed in and stood beside the bed.

"It seems that Mack was the guy on the motorbike. He wasn't sent to hurt you, just to scare you and leave the petals in his wake. He's been in their employ for the past two years, doing various odd jobs and such. One was to watch you from time to time during the past six months. He saw Rose Blake leave a white rose in the basket of your bike outside the bookstore one time and reported it back to the Robinsons."

Thank You, Lord. It was Rose. "She was in Florence. So they knew she was in contact with me. Well, kind of. I was merely on the receiving end of a rose a couple of times a year. Did they find her? Talk to her?"

"Mack was sketchy with details, but he claims he had nothing to do with the death of Rose Blake. He seems to think they handled that one themselves, so that's something we'll be looking into."

She swallowed hard. "Right." Were they capable of crashing into her and leaving her for dead?

"Bella?"

Adam was asking her something.

"Sorry, what did you say?"

"I said this means the Robinsons only sent that last rose to you. The one we found on Saturday. The rest were genuine. They were from your mom."

"From my mom. Yes. She was watching over me all that time." Should she laugh or cry?

Tremors ricocheted through Bella's body. A feeling of sweet relief ran through her veins like warm honey. George and Susannah could not take those precious memories away from her—the roses had been left to show her she was loved. They could not soil that sweetness. How long had she lived in fear of these people?

Adam squeezed her arm. "Are you alright?"

She shook her head from side to side and attempted to focus on the conversation. She cleared her throat and found her voice. "So, just to be clear, Cam, you're saying that the Robinsons can't hurt me, or anyone I love, ever again?" The truth seeped in.

Cam smiled. "Yes. Even without them talking, we already have enough to put them away for a long time. That's before taking Rose's accident into account, too. I know Max has people working on that further south." His mouth returned to a straight line. "I'm afraid it's not the end quite yet since there will be trials and interviews, which we will need you to attend."

Bella bit her lip. "I realize I'll have to testify." The thought of facing her adoptive parents after all this time made her sick to her stomach.

"You won't be alone." Adam lifted her chin and looked into her eyes. "I'm with you. We can do this. You can do this."

Cam nodded. "I have to say, I'm amazed at your resilience, Bella. From what Max has told me and the bits and pieces I've gleaned, you are one unbelievably strong young lady. The worst is behind you, and I think you can start looking toward a bright future." He tilted his head at Adam. "Including this guy, I guess."

Bella grinned. "He did take a bullet for me."

"Well, in that case, I'd say he's a keeper."

"He is." Bella stood and shook Cam's hand. "Thanks. You have no idea what this means for me."

"My pleasure. Now there's a doctor on his way through the ward, so I should give you all some space. You have my number if you have any questions at all."

Adam reached out his right hand. "Yes. Thank you. This is a huge relief. You have both our numbers if you need us. Assuming I get the green light to go home today, are you alright with Bella not being in town right now? We can fly up or drive in a few hours should you need her. We have some details to wrap up back in Florence. Not to mention getting these envelopes deposited down there."

Bella barely noticed the guys were talking. Exhaustion hit her full-on, as if she had been on high alert for years and now been given a reprieve. She watched Adam talking, and joy bubbled within. Could this really be happening? The truth had come out and freedom had followed on its coattails. Just like that Bible verse she clung to—John 8:32: "and you will know the truth, and the truth will set you free."

Bella blew out a long, slow breath. Free at last.

CHAPTER TWENTY-SIX

ADAM WALKED INTO HIS PARENTS' kitchen, where Bella leaned against the granite countertop. Mug in hand, she stared through the window at the spectacular ocean view. "Hey, beautiful, did you leave me any coffee?"

Bella swung around at the sound of his voice. She rewarded him with a smile. He could get used to that every morning. The sooner, the better.

"Hi. You're looking better today, more like your old self." She stood on tiptoe and kissed his lips. *Nice.*

"Less like a gunshot victim?" He grinned.

"Please don't joke about that." She took a swig of coffee. "There's nothing funny about getting shot."

"Just trying to keep things light, since it could get heavy later." *God, please give us wisdom and patience as we work through this.* "Do you want to head straight over to Pippa's place?"

A night at his parents' home had been luxurious after his brief stay in hospital, yet there loomed the awkward conversation Bella needed to have with Pippa. Her furrowed brow told him she wouldn't be able to relax until it was over, regardless of the outcome.

"I'm ready to go anytime, but you should eat something first. Pippa will be at the bookstore all morning. I checked with Juliet and she's not on shift at the hospital until this evening, so we should be able to speak to them both at the same time."

"Do you think Pippa will close the store for a while?" Adam helped himself to some black coffee from the pot.

Bella shrugged. "She does when she has to nip out and there's no one to cover her. I don't think I can wait until tonight to ask her about Rose." She bit her lip. "Am I being selfish?"

Adam put his good arm around her in an attempted hug. Her hair was still damp and smelled lemony. She must have used the toiletries from his parents' guestroom.

"I don't think you have a selfish bone in your body." His stomach rumbled its reminder. "Have you eaten yet?"

"I don't think I could. Your mom came down and made me a latte, though."

He opened the fridge. "Want to be my left hand for rustling up some omelets?"

Bella tilted her head. "For goodness sake. You know I can't resist your omelets. Yes, I'll help."

Adam chuckled. This would be interesting.

"Where did my mom go?" He scoured the fridge for ingredients. "I thought she'd be hovering here all day."

"She said she had errands to run, but would love us to be here for dinner tonight. I think she wants to give us a little space today." She set down her mug. "I thought she took all the news well. Your dad, too. It was kind of them to drive all the way to Seattle and back to collect us."

"I agree. I was wondering how I'd get my vehicle back here until Max showed up with Mom and Dad."

"Max is a good friend to you. He didn't have to take the time to help us out like that."

Adam passed a block of cheddar to her. "Yeah, he is a good guy. He went above and beyond for me. It gave us time to talk to my parents on the ride home, too—we needed that."

Bella found a bowl and a cheese grater in one of the cupboards. "They were so compassionate. I dreaded having to explain my past to them, but they only showed me love. I see where you get it from." She flashed a smile in his direction.

"They're awesome. I thought Mom's eyes would pop right out of their sockets when I told her you were the Lighthouse Baby. It's going to kill her to stay quiet until we've spoken with Pippa."

"Yeah, I could tell she remembered the scandal. I guess it was big news for the Florence area. Your mom is such a gracious woman. It was a huge amount of drama to absorb all at once but she took it all in stride."

Adam cracked eggs into a large bowl—that much he could do with one arm in a sling.

"Yeah. Dad, too. I thought he'd be mad that we'd kept him in the dark, but I think they're both simply relieved we're safe. And his offer to help with the name change and legal representation doesn't hurt, either."

Bella slid a chopping board onto the counter top and attempted to peel an onion. "I think it was smart to tell them about the engagement straight away. It'll give your mom something good to focus on."

"Something really good. She's ecstatic. Even though she's been sworn to secrecy for a while." Adam looked through the window at the whitecaps dotting the ocean as the sun lit up the entire vista before him. What had that old Englishman said on the beach, the night of the proposal? Something about storms always blowing over eventually, and the sun coming out again. *Thank You, Lord.*

He kissed the top of Bella's head. "This feels good, doesn't it? Cooking together and looking out over the Pacific."

Bella didn't answer. She was decimating that onion.

"You okay?"

She looked up at him with tears in her eyes.

"Oh, hon. It's not just the onions, is it?"

She wiped her eyes on her sleeve. "You have no idea how much I longed for normal. Me not crying would be a start. I've cried more in the past week than I have in my entire life."

"That's understandable, given the series of events. Don't be hard on yourself." He passed her a kitchen towel. "I think you'll feel better after we've had this conversation with Pippa, don't you?"

She nodded. "It's the final piece in my puzzle." She reached up and kissed him again. "And then we look forward."

"I'm not going to argue with that."

***

Adam clutched Bella's hand as they walked down Main Street toward The Book Nook. He stole a glance at her face. Her deep frown said it all.

"You texted, right?"

Bella nodded. "They're both here in the store. I feel like I shouldn't have eaten that omelet about now."

"You couldn't do this on an empty stomach. Besides, it was delicious." He gave her hand a squeeze.

"Yeah, it was divine. Bacon, avocado, and sour cream is my favorite." They stopped in front of the bookstore. "Here we go."

Adam pushed the door open and let Bella go through. Pippa looked up from her paperwork over at the front desk when she heard the tinkling of the bell.

"Bella, Adam, come here you two."

She sashayed past stacks of books and embraced Bella first, and then groaned when she saw Adam's sling. She kissed him on both cheeks instead. "Thank goodness you're back in one piece." She eyed Adam again. "Relatively speaking. Your poor arm. I can't believe you were shot." She grasped the glass beads around her neck and shook her head. "I can't even imagine what you kids have been through. Come on upstairs, Juliet's making tea."

She flipped the sign on the door to "CLOSED" and led the way up the staircase. That took care of the store issue.

Bella followed and at the top of the stairs, she turned to Adam. Her eyes were wide and her bottom lip quivered. He took her hand and kissed it, hoping to pass on some courage and love. The letters were stowed in her purse. Man, this was going to be one tough conversation.

"Bella." Juliet embraced her friend in a bear hug at the door. "What on earth? This turned into the craziest scenario. And Adam, you were *shot*? That's why I don't ever want to live in the city. I don't know how Madison can bear it." She led him into the living room and plumped a pillow on the couch for him to lean against. Juliet the Nurse was in action mode. The disturbed cat sat up and flicked her tail.

"Ebony, you can go find somewhere else to take a nap. Here, Bella, you sit next to our invalid."

The cat leaped from the couch with a shrill cry, unimpressed, and followed Pippa into the kitchen.

Adam smirked. "I'm fine, Juliet. I'm already feeling way better. You'd be proud of Bella's nursing skills."

"I've never seen so much blood." Bella's face paled as she spoke. "I don't know how I didn't faint. God held me up for sure."

Juliet sat cross-legged on the rug. "And He directed that bullet." She shook her head. "It could have hit any of your major organs or arteries."

"I'm glad everyone's home safely now." Pippa carried a tray with four steaming mugs into the room and set it on the coffee table. "Now, what's all this about having something to discuss?"

"Mom, let them at least have some tea." Juliet rolled her eyes. "Although, I am kind of curious about what was in the safe deposit box. You said there was a bunch of jewelry?"

Bella picked up a mug and nodded. "The most exquisite pieces of jewelry I've ever seen. When Madison and Luke popped back into the hospital before we left, I showed her, and she's convinced they're the real deal. And somehow I have a feeling she would know."

Adam gazed at Bella's beautiful profile, and his heart skipped a beat. *There's only one diamond I'm concerned about and I'm anxious to get it on your finger as soon as possible...*

"Wow. Yeah, I trust Madison's judgment with stuff like that." Juliet folded her arms. "So you're a rich girl now, Miss Bella."

"Juliet." Pippa shook her head. "If the jewelry is that valuable, you should get it tucked away somewhere, in case word gets out. This is a small town full of loose-lipped ladies."

Adam smiled. "Don't worry, we're all over it. My dad's best buddy is the bank manager here, so he deposited everything first thing this morning." Adam put an arm around Bella. "This young lady's set for life."

"In more ways than one." Bella took his hand and kissed it.

"What? Are you guys engaged for real now, too?" Juliet squealed.

"We sure are." Adam beamed. "I want to do the ring thing properly up at the lighthouse tomorrow, and make it official. But we wanted our favorite people to know first."

"Oh my. Congratulations, both of you." Pippa leaned over and planted a kiss on each of their foreheads. "That's fantastic news. You deserve your happily ever after."

Ebony took that moment to jump onto Adam's lap. Always the attention-seeking princess.

"Have you set a date or anything yet?" Juliet rubbed her hands together. "We could all do with a celebration."

"No, but it will be soon." Adam looked down at Bella's dainty hand in his. "This has been harrowing for us all, and I, for one, have learned to appreciate each and every day as a gift. I don't want to waste another moment of time."

"Here, here." Pippa raised her mug.

Bella looked into his eyes. "I'd love a spring wedding, up at the lighthouse."

"Perfect." Adam sealed the deal with a quick kiss on her lips. "I'd like to time it around the trial and everything, but that could stretch out for a while, so I think spring sounds awesome."

"Too bad you have to go through all that still." Juliet took a sip of tea. "Max says these kinds of trials can drag on."

"I know." Bella reached up and clasped the tiny lighthouse pendant. "But the thought of putting the whole nightmare behind me and starting fresh sounds wonderful. And I think I'd like to take you up on the offer to find a good counselor as soon as possible."

"That's smart." Juliet tapped the side of her nose. "I happen to know the best and you're going to love her. She'll help you get through all this, my friend, don't you worry."

"I know." Bella squeezed Adam's hand. "I have plenty of issues to navigate, but I want to focus on my future with this guy."

"I'm here for you every step of the way." Adam smiled down at his fiancée. Yes, his fiancée.

Pippa curled up in the armchair. "Well, I think there could be another wedding on the horizon in the not too distant future." She looked at her daughter and winked.

"Mom." Juliet's cheeks blazed to match the color of her hair. "For goodness sake, you can't go saying things like that. It'll scare Max away forever."

"I just know." Pippa shrugged. How did women know these things?

"I think your mom could be onto something." Bella grinned at her squirming friend.

"For goodness' sake. I'm not rushing into anything. Max is amazing, but it's still early days, you guys. Sheesh. Let's change the subject. What else did you find out from the box?"

Bella put her mug on the table. "I don't know where to start."

Pippa reached over and stroked Bella's arm. "Sweetie, Juliet explained your adoptive parents are being charged with a whole bunch of illegal stuff, but did you discover any more clues about your biological family? I know that's what you wanted more than anything."

Bella glanced up at Adam and he gave her a reassuring nod. She bent down and retrieved a letter from her purse.

"I did. This is the important thing I wanted you to know."

i

"You mean there's more than the engagement?" Juliet whistled. "I don't know how much more I can take in one day. Is that another letter from your mother there?"

"Yes, one of many. She had no idea how corrupt my adoptive parents were, and she did want the best for me. But the biggest surprise was that she had a friend right here in Florence."

"She did?" Juliet sat cross-legged on the rug. "How?"

"I was born here."

Adam held his breath. *God, help us out here?*

"What?" Juliet's eyes were twice their usual size.

Adam looked over at Pippa. She set down her mug with a shaky hand. A shadow flickered across her face as Bella continued.

"Rose hid out here while she was pregnant. She loved lighthouses, like me, and she didn't want her family or my biological father to know anything about me."

Bella stared down at her note, but Adam saw the moment Pippa put the pieces together. Her mouth went slack and her eyes filled with tears.

"Someone helped Rose to recover after my birth, and then later discovered me at the lighthouse and even found someone who would adopt me."

"No." Pippa gasped.

Juliet spun to see what was wrong. "Mom, what is it?"

Pippa shook her head and tears streamed down her face. "Rachel?" she whispered. "Your mother was Rachel? Rose was Rachel?" She peered at Bella. Was she searching for clues? Similarities? "I would never have guessed. It was so long ago…"

"I don't look anything like her then?" Bella looked up with the saddest smile Adam had ever seen. He detected the disappointment in her voice.

"She was beautiful, like you, sweetheart. Long, wavy hair like yours—only dark. Almost black. I can't get my head around this." She wiped at her tears. "Rachel was your mother?"

"Yes. She went by a different name for protection."

Pippa stood. "The adoptive parents—I wasn't allowed to know their names—but they came approved. They were a regular couple desperate for a baby to love. What on earth happened?" Her lip trembled.

Bella shook her head. "We may never know. They could even have been genuine in the beginning. But that's all in the past now anyway." She stood and took both of Pippa's hands in her own. "I was the baby you found at the lighthouse that day. The Lighthouse Baby." She half-laughed and half-cried. "And in this letter, my mother wanted me to give you a big hug and say thank you for everything." She enveloped Pippa's shaking frame.

Juliet searched Adam's face. What could he say? This was a shock for them all. There would be questions and confusion, but at least the truth was out.

"Mom knew Bella when she was a baby?" Juliet struggled to get each word out.

Adam nodded. "When she was *the lighthouse baby*. It's true. You would have been a one-year old, I guess. But you probably met her, too."

"What? I can't believe it. I was a tiny part of Bella's life way back then."

He shrugged. "Believe it. To think she started her life here—at the lighthouse. Really, it makes perfect sense."

Juliet buried her face in her hands while she absorbed the truth. Poor girl. It was a lot to take in for everyone.

Adam rhythmically stroked Ebony's soft fur, now at a complete loss for words. Nothing more needed to be said. He looked up at his fiancée and smiled.

In the midst of mess and mayhem, Bella and Pippa hugged and swayed and cried—just as they must have hugged and swayed and cried when Bella was the Lighthouse Baby, so many years ago.

CHAPTER TWENTY-SEVEN

"THIS IS PERFECT."

Bella closed her eyes and breathed in the intoxicating mix of salty sea air and wild lavender. Early autumn had ushered in the carpet of leaves and pine needles at her feet, but today the brilliant sun shone in defiance. She leaned back against Adam and sighed.

"You warm enough?" Adam's voice reverberated through her torso.

"Mmm. This is my favorite kind of day. It's like summer is trying to hang on by its fingertips and fall is nudging its way in. But you can keep your arms around me. I might get chilly at some point."

Adam chuckled and tucked her poncho snuggly around her body. He stood behind her, tall and strong, on the cliff's edge as they admired the whitecaps dancing across the deep. All was well.

How had everything culminated into this? Bella bit her lip. If a moment could be framed to treasure evermore, this would be that moment. Safe, solaced, satisfied.

"I could stay here forever. You, me, the lighthouse, and the ocean. I'm starting to feel like I belong here. Like I *truly* belong." She lifted her left hand and examined the perfect diamond. "I never dreamed I could be this happy."

"Me, neither. The whole Seattle chapter is behind you now. Behind us."

"Other than having to testify. I'm not looking forward to that. I can't bear the thought of having to face George and Susannah, but I will. If it means keeping others safe and seeing justice served, I'll do whatever it takes. I know God's been equipping me along the way. I'm stronger now than I've ever been, in spite of learning the truth about Rose's murder and the web of deceit surrounding my childhood. It sounds crazy to even speak about it now."

"I still can't get my head around Pippa being the one to help Rose all those years ago."

"It was no accident. It makes me think how God has had His hand on my life from the beginning. Even Pippa admits it's all too much to be a coincidence. I pray that one day soon she'll see Him as the Truth and find her own freedom."

"Me, too. Pippa's one special lady." He sighed.

"What a journey this has been. I'm ready for life to slow down and be normal, aren't you?"

Adam turned her around to face him, gently kissed her lips, and pulled back. Those ocean eyes just about caused her knees to buckle. Life with this man would never be dreary. They froze in place for several heartbeats before he reached down for the backpack.

"Wife-to-be, you know I brought you up here for a reason today, don't you?"

"Not only to make me happy? I have a book to read, we have your fabulous chicken salad and Pippa's chocolate-chip cookies. What more do we need?"

Adam looked like a little boy on Christmas morning. "I have a surprise for you, and yes, I know you don't love surprises, but I think you're going to like this one. So, please don't be mad or run away." A dimple deepened on each cheek.

Never again. "I've finished running, I promise."

"You have no idea how happy that makes me. This is kind of a big surprise, though, and here at your favorite lighthouse seems the right place to give it to you."

Bella tapped her chin. "Well, let's see, whatever can it be? A month ago you got down on one knee and proposed on this exact spot."

"Again."

"Yes, again. I love that we proposed to each other."

"Numerous times?"

Bella looked over her shoulder toward Cape Cove. "So much has happened since the first time, down there on the beach." She'd run so fast from the first proposal, her feet had been in shreds by the time she reached the lighthouse. Her haven. The truth that she had been left here as a baby held no shock value. The Lighthouse Baby. It made sense. She touched her pendant around her neck and smiled.

Adam cleared his throat. "I've been working on something for a while. If I'm going to be honest, I've been working on this for months."

"Is this the special project? The one I'm not allowed to see ever?"

"Yes. But now you're allowed to see it. Because it's for you. Well, for us."

Adam took her hand and led her to the bench in front of the lighthouse. She sat next to him as he pulled a roll of drawings from the backpack and handed them to her.

Bella's pulse raced. Was this the house they had dreamed about? A home for the two of them near the ocean? Dare she hope?

"What is it?" The breeze gained momentum along with her pulse. She pulled her hair over to one side, determined not to miss a single detail.

"Take a look. The first page will give you the general idea." Adam grinned like a Cheshire cat.

Bella took a deep breath and slid a red ribbon from the roll of drawings. A red ribbon just like the ones tying the precious letters from her mother. She unfurled the paper with care, and stared at the first page. A gasp escaped from her mouth and she turned to Adam.

"What-what is this? I mean is it… is it?"

"Yes." He laughed and put his arms around her. "These are the plans for a house I would like to build for you. For us, our family. The Lexingtons. If you like it."

Bella swiped at hot tears. Tears of pure joy. She wanted to see the plans clearly. It couldn't be. But it looked like—like a lighthouse.

He held the paper steady as Bella studied the beautiful drawing. The structure was hexagonal and wrapped in white siding, three levels with a crow's nest. Utter perfection. The sketch had it nestled among grasses and rocks on the oceanfront.

"Are you serious?"

"Painfully so, I'm afraid. I've been dreaming this up since I met you."

How could such a thing be possible? Living in a lighthouse, which wasn't an actual lighthouse?

"It's amazing. But where would we build it?"

"That's where the rest of our road trip will take us today. I've secured two possible lots a little further down the coast, south of Florence. But if you don't like either of them, I'll keep looking until we find our perfect place."

Bella laughed. "You *are* serious."

"You bet I am. In my business, I always go after interesting projects, the ones that are a little out of the box. Your love of lighthouses gave me the idea initially, and I've seen it done elsewhere. And then when we discovered you were the Lighthouse Baby, it was like confirmation."

"I can't believe it."

Adam's eyes clouded. "Wait—unless this is too painful. I didn't even think it might be inappropriate or be a reminder of your past..."

"No. I love the idea. I adore it. Like I adore you." She pecked his cheek. "This is the sweetest thing I could ever have imagined. It's going to be so much fun. Have you planned out the rooms?"

"I have, but they're all up for discussion. I want your fingerprints all over this." He turned to the next page. "I thought we could have your library on the top level, where you can read and write and look out over the ocean. And there's plenty of room for the children."

Bella raised an eyebrow. "For the children?" She set the plans on the bench and put her arms around Adam's neck. "So, we are going to have some little Lexingtons one day?"

"I'd love to raise a family in a home that feels safe like a lighthouse. What do you think?"

What did she think? "Yes. I say yes. Let's put the past behind us, embrace whatever happens to come our way, and let's have our very own lighthouse babies."

Was she really home at last?

A sprinkling of leaves lifted on the breeze and danced in the air before them like confetti. Bella kissed Adam on the lips, sealing the confirmation. She leaned her head on his shoulder and clutched the rolled-up plans on her lap. Life was fragile and there were some formidable mountains yet to climb, in the form of court trials and forgiveness and grief. But right now, with a solid lighthouse behind her and the wild ocean before her—the search for truth had enabled Bella to finally find freedom, and it had brought her full circle to a place of perfect peace.

Yes, she was home at last.

ABOUT THE AUTHOR

Laura is a published Christian author with a heart for inspiring and encouraging readers of all ages, with books for children, teens, and adults. Originally from the UK, she lives in British Columbia, Canada, as an empty-nester. Laura is a mom of three, married to her high school sweetheart, and is passionate about faith and family—and chocolate.
www.laurathomasauthor.com